BY MONICA MURPHY

One Week Girlfriend Series
One Week Girlfriend
Second Chance Boyfriend

SECOND CHANCE BOYFRIEND

SECOND
CHANCE
BOYFRIEND

A NOVEL

Monica Murphy 1970-

BANTAM BOOKS TRADE PAPERBACKS | NEW YORK

2013 Bantam Books Trade Paperback Edition

Copyright © 2013 by Monica Murphy
Excerpt from *Three Broken Promises* copyright © 2013 by Monica Murphy

Published in the United States by Bantam Books, an imprint of The Random House Publishing Group, a division of Random House LLC, a Penguin Random House Company, New York.

BANTAM BOOKS and the HOUSE colophon are registered trademarks of Random House LLC.

Originally self-published in the United States as an eBook by the author and subsequently released in the same format by Bantam Books, an imprint of the Random House Publishing Group, a division of Random House LLC, in 2013.

This book contains an excerpt from the forthcoming book *Three Broken Promises* by Monica Murphy. This excerpt has been set for this edition only and may not reflect the final content of the forthcoming edition.

Library of Congress Cataloging-in-Publication Data
Murphy, Monica.
Second chance boyfriend : a novel / Monica Murphy.—Bantam Books Trade Paperback edition.
pages cm
Summary: "The exhilarating conclusion to Drew and Fable's story—the star-crossed young romance that began in One Week Girlfriend"—Provided by publisher.
ISBN 978-0-8041-7679-8 (pbk.)—ISBN 978-0-9883694-5-0 (ebook)
1. Young women—Fiction. 2. College stories. 3. Love stories. gsafd I. Title.
PS3613.U7525S43 2013
813'.6—dc23   2013020476

Printed in the United States of America

www.bantamdell.com

9 8 7 6 5 4 3 2 1

To my family, who puts up with me sitting in front of my computer all the time—thank you for your love and support. You all mean the world to me.

"You can close your eyes to the things you don't want to see, but you can't close your heart to the things you don't want to feel."

—*Johnny Depp*

SECOND CHANCE BOYFRIEND

PROLOGUE

Have you ever done something so incredibly stupid, the guilt and regret hang over you like the darkest, heaviest cloud? Blurring your judgment, consuming your soul until it's the only thing you can see, hear, or think about?

I have. I've done a lot of things I regret, that fill me with guilt. But the absolute worst is the thing I did yesterday.

I left the girl I love alone, naked in her bed. Like some sort of macho asshole who uses a girl for sex and then leaves her—that's me. I've turned into *that* guy.

But I'm not really that guy. I love the girl I left alone naked in her bed. I just don't deserve her.

And I know it.

CHAPTER 1

Sometimes you have to stand alone, just to make sure you still can.
—Unknown

Fable

Two months. I haven't seen or heard from him in two freaking months. I mean, who does that to a person? Who spends the most intense week of his life with another human being and shares his most intimate thoughts, his craziest, darkest secrets, has sex with a person—and we're talking amazing, earth-shattering sex—leaves her a note that says I love you, and then bails? I'll tell you who.

Drew *I'm-going-to-kick-him-in-the-balls-next-time-I-see-him* Callahan.

I've moved on. Well, I tell myself that. But time doesn't stop just because my heart does, so I take care of my responsibilities. I've stretched the three thousand dollars I earned for my one week of pretending to be the jerkwad's girlfriend pretty well. I still have some money left in my savings account. I bought my brother, Owen, some cool Christmas gifts. I got my mom something for Christmas, too.

She didn't buy either of us anything. Not one thing. Owen

made me a shallow bowl he created in his ceramics class at school. He was so proud to give it to me. A little embarrassed, too, especially when I gushed over it. The kid wrapped it in bright Christmas paper and everything. I was blown away that he took the time to actually create something for me. I keep that bowl on my dresser and leave my earrings in it.

At least someone gives a crap about me, you know?

He didn't give Mom anything. Which—shallow witch that I am—pleased me to no end.

January is supposedly a time of healing. New year, new goals, resolutions, whatever you want to call them, when a person should be hopeful with all that unchartered territory spread out before her. I tried my best to be positive when the new year came, but I cried. That clock struck twelve and I was all by myself, tears running down my face as I watched the ball drop on TV. Pitiful, lonely girl sobbing into her sweatshirt, missing the boy she loves.

Most of the month is gone, and that's fine. But the realization hit me last night. Instead of dreading every single day that comes my way, I need to savor it. I need to figure out what I'm going to do with my life and then actually do it. I'd leave if I could, but I can't ditch Owen. Without me, I have no idea what would happen to him and I can't risk it.

So I stay. I vow to make the best of this life I have. I'm tired of living in misery.

I'm tired of feeling sorry for myself. I'm tired of wanting to shake my mom and make her see that she has children she should give two shits about. Oh, and that she also needs to find a job. Sleeping all day and partying all night with Larry the Loser isn't the way to deal.

And I'm tired of mourning the loss of a beautiful, fucked-up man who haunts my thoughts everywhere I go.

Yeah, I'm most sick of that.

Pushing all mopey thoughts out of my head, I go to the booth where a customer's waiting for me to take his order. He came in a few minutes ago, a blur of a tall man who moved quickly, dressed too nicely for a Thursday mid-afternoon jaunt to La Salle's. The bar is hopping at night, full of college kids drinking themselves into oblivion. But during the day? Mostly bum losers who have nowhere else to go and the occasional person coming in for lunch. The burgers are decent, so they're a draw.

"What can I get you?" I ask once I stop in front of the table, my head bent as I dig out my order pad.

"Your attention, maybe?"

His question—spoken in a velvety deep voice—makes me glance up from my notepad.

Into the bluest eyes I've ever seen. Bluer than Drew's, if that's possible.

"Um, sorry." I offer him a tentative smile. He instantly makes me nervous. He is *waaaay* too good-looking. Like beyond gorgeous, with dark blond hair that falls over his forehead and classic bone structure. Strong jaw, sharp cheekbones, straight nose—he could've walked right off a billboard. "Are you ready to order?"

He smiles, revealing even white teeth, and I clamp my lips shut to prevent them from falling open. I didn't know men could be this attractive. I mean, Drew is gorgeous—I can admit that even though I'm furious at him. But this guy . . . he puts all other men to shame. His face is too damn perfect.

"I'll take a Pale Ale." He flicks his chin at the tattered menu lying on the table in front of him. "Anything from the appetizer menu you can recommend?"

He must be joking. Beyond the burgers, I wouldn't recommend any food La Salle's serves to this ideal male specimen. Heaven forbid it might taint him. "What are you in the mood for?" I ask, my voice weak.

Lifting a brow, he picks up the menu and glances it over, his gaze meeting mine. "Nachos?"

I shake my head. "The beef is rarely cooked all the way." More like it comes out with a pink tinge. So gross.

"Potato skins?" He winces.

I wince back. "So nineties, don't you think?"

"How about the buffalo wings?"

"If you want to set your mouth on permanent fire. Listen." I glance around, making sure no one—as in my boss—is nearby. "If you want something to eat, I suggest the café down the street. They have great sandwiches."

He laughs and shakes his head. The rich, vibrant sound washes over me, warming my skin, followed quickly by a huge dose of wariness. I don't react like this to guys. The only other one who could earn this sort of reaction from me is Drew. And he's not around . . . so why am I still so hung up on him?

Maybe because you're still in love with him, like some sort of idiot?

I shove the nagging little voice that pops up at the most inopportune times into the back of my brain.

"I like your honesty," the man says, his cool blue gaze raking over me. "I'll just take the beer, then."

"Smart decision." I nod. "I'll be right back."

I head toward the back and slip behind the bar, grabbing a bottle of Pale Ale, glancing up to catch the guy staring at me. And he doesn't look away, either, which makes me feel uncomfortable. He's not watching me like a pervert; he's just very . . . observant.

It's unnerving.

A trickle of anger flickers through me. Do I wear an invisible sign around my neck? One that says *Hey, I'm Easy*? Because I'm not. Yeah, I made a few mistakes, looking for attention in the wrong places, but it's not like I dress with my tits or ass hanging out. I don't put any sort of purposeful swing to my hips, nor do I thrust my chest out the way I see plenty of girls do.

So why does every guy I encounter seem to blatantly check me out like I'm a piece of meat?

Deciding I've had enough of his crap, I stride toward his table and set the beer in front of him with a loud clunk. I'm about to walk away without saying a word—screw the tip—when he asks, "So what's your name?"

I glance over my shoulder. "What's it matter to you?" Oh, I'm such a bitch! I could really piss this guy off and get myself fired. I don't know what's wrong with me.

I'm almost as bad as my mom. She sabotaged her job with her drinking and awful attitude. At least I only have the bad attitude.

If I could kick my own ass, I would be doing so right now.

He smiles and shrugs, as if my smart-ass remark doesn't faze him. "I'm curious."

Turning fully, I face him, studying him as intently as he

studies me. The long fingers of his right hand are wrapped around the neck of the beer bottle, his other arm resting on the scarred and scratched table. His entire manner is relaxed, easy, and my defenses slowly lower.

"It's Fable," I admit, bracing for the reaction. I've heard endless jokes and rude remarks about my name since I can remember.

But he doesn't give me a hard time. His expression remains neutral. "Nice to meet you, Fable. I'm Colin."

I nod, not knowing what else to say. He both puts me at ease and shakes me up, which leaves me confused. And he definitely doesn't fit in at this bar. He's dressed too nice and has an air of authority about him that borders on entitlement, as if he's above it all—and he probably is. He reeks of class and money.

But he's not acting like an ass and he should, I've been so rude to him. He brings the beer bottle to his lips, taking a drink, and I watch unabashedly. He's handsome. He's arrogant. And he's trouble.

I don't want anything to do with him.

"So, Fable," he says once he's downed half his beer. "Can I ask you a question?"

Shuffling my feet, I glance around the bar. No one's paying us any attention. I could probably stand here and talk to Colin the mysterious customer for fifteen minutes and no one would protest. "Sure."

"Why is a woman like you working in a shit bar like this?"

"Why is a guy like you ordering a beer in a shit bar like this?" I retort, momentarily insulted. But then I realize . . .

he's complimenting me. And he referred to me as a woman. No one ever does that. *I* don't do that.

He tips his beer at me, as if offering a toast. "Touché. Would you be surprised if I said I came in here looking for you?"

Surprised? More like creeped out. "I don't even know you. How could you be looking for me?"

"I should rephrase that. I came here hoping I would find someone I could steal away." At my raised eyebrows, he laughs. "I own a new restaurant in town. The District. Have you heard of it?"

I had. Some fancy place that caters to the rich college kids, the ones with an endless supply of money they can use to eat, drink, and party. So not my scene. "Yeah."

"Have you been there?"

I slowly shake my head. "No."

Leaning back against the seat, he studies me, his lids heavy as he does a slow perusal of . . . me. Now he's totally checking me out and I can feel my cheeks burn with embarrassment. The guy is sort of a jackass.

I've always had a slight thing for jackasses.

"Come with me to the restaurant tonight. I'll show you around." His mouth curves into not quite a smile and I'm tempted.

But I've also sworn off men, so I know this is a bad idea. "Thanks, but I'm not interested."

"I'm not trying to ask you out on a date, Fable," he says, his voice low, his eyes glowing. I take a step back, glancing around. I need to get away from this guy. Fast. But then his words stop me in my tracks. "I'm trying to offer you a job."

Drew

"Let's talk about Fable."

I tense up but nod. I try my best to appear neutral, like our new topic of discussion doesn't bother me. "What do you want to know?"

My shrink watches me, her careful gaze steady. "It still bothers you to hear her name."

"It doesn't," I lie. I try my best to appear nonchalant, but my insides are churning. I both dread and savor hearing Fable's name. I want to see her. I *need* to see her.

Yet I can't make myself go to her. And she's clearly given up on me. I deserve her giving up. I gave up on her first, didn't I?

More like you gave up on yourself.

"You don't have to lie to me, Drew. It's okay if it's still difficult." Dr. Sheila Harris pauses, tapping her index finger against her chin. "Have you considered trying to see her?"

I shake my head. I consider it every day, every minute of my life, but my considerations are useless. "She hates me."

"You don't know that."

"I know *I'd* hate me for what I did if I were her. I shut down and shut her out, like I always do. She begged me again and again not to do it. Promised that she'd be there for me no matter what." Yet I left her. With only a stupid note that took me way too long to write, filled with a secret message that my smart, beautiful girl figured out right away.

But she's not my girl. I can't lay claim to her. I ignored her. And now . . .

I've lost her.

"So why did you shut her out? You've never told me, you know."

My psychologist loves to ask the tough questions, but that's her job. I still hate answering them. "It's the only way I know how to cope," I admit. The truth slaps me in the face on a daily basis. I always run.

It's so much easier.

I sought Dr. Harris out myself. No one else pushed me to do it. After we came back from Carmel, after I ditched Fable and left her that bullshit note, I withdrew into myself worse than ever. I fucked up my game play. I fucked up my grades. Winter break came and I ran away. I literally ran away to some crazy cabin in the middle of the woods I rented from some nice old couple in Lake Tahoe.

My plan? Hibernate like a bear. Turn off my phone, hole up by myself, and figure my shit out. I didn't anticipate how hard it would be, though, being alone with my thoughts. My memories, both the good and the bad, haunted me. I thought of the bombshell my stepmom, Adele, dropped on me. I thought about my dad and how much the truth—if it really *is* the truth—would affect him. I thought about my little sister, Vanessa, and how she died. How she might not be my little sister after all . . .

More than anything, I thought of Fable. How mad she'd been when I showed up on her doorstep, yet she let me in anyway. The way I touched her, how she touched me, the way she always seemed to break down my barriers and see the real me. I let her in. I *wanted* to let her in.

And then I left her. With a note that was rendered point-less because she tried her damnedest to rescue me and I wouldn't let her. She sent me exactly two texts. The second one surprised me, because I figured she was stubborn and thought she'd give up after I didn't answer the first one.

How could I answer it, though? She said all the right things. And I would've said all the wrong things. So it's better to say nothing at all.

She also left me one voice mail. I still have it. Sometimes, when I'm feeling really fucked up, I play it. Listen to her soft, tearful voice, those unbelievable words she says to me. By the time the message is finished, my heart literally hurts.

It's torture listening to it, yet I can't make myself delete that message, either. Just knowing it's there, that for one last minute she actually cared, is better than deleting those words and her voice and pretending she doesn't exist.

"I'm hoping to help you with that. Your coping mechanisms," Dr. Harris says, drawing me out of my thoughts. "I know how much she means to you, Fable. And I'm hoping that eventually, you'll go to her and tell her you're sorry."

"What if I'm not sorry?" I toss the words out, but they're meaningless. I'm so sorry I can't begin to explain how much of a screw-up I am.

"Then that's another issue we'll have to deal with," she says gently.

It goes on like this for another fifteen minutes and then I finally make my escape, walking out into the cold, clear winter afternoon. The sun is warm on my skin despite the temperature and I start down the sidewalk, heading for where I parked my truck. Dr. Harris's office is downtown, in a nondescript building, and I hope like hell I don't see anyone I know. The college campus is only a few blocks away and students hang out at the little stores, cafés, and coffee shops that line the street.

It's not like I have many friends, but hell. Everyone likes to think they know me. No one really does. With the exception of one person.

"Hey, Callahan, wait up!"

Pausing, I glance over my shoulder to see one of my teammates running toward me, a big grin on his goofy face. Jace Hendrix is a pain in the ass but generally a good guy. He's never done me wrong, not that any of them ever really have. "Hey." I offer him a wave and shove my hands into my jacket pockets, waiting until he stops just in front of me.

"Long time, no see," Jace says. "You sort of disappeared after that last failure of a game."

I wince. That last failure of a game had been all my fault. "I was feeling sort of fucked up over that," I confess.

Hell, I can't believe I just admitted to my failures, but Jace doesn't seem bothered. "Yeah, you and everyone else, man. Listen, what are you doing this weekend?"

The way Jace brushes off my statement—hell, the way he agrees with it—blows me away. "What's going on?"

"It's Logan's birthday. We're doing it up right at the new restaurant that just opened a few blocks over. Have you heard of it?" Jace looks excited, he's literally bouncing on his feet, and I wonder what the hell is up.

"Vaguely." I shrug. Like I care. The last thing I want is to be social.

But then Dr. Harris's words ring through my head. How she wants me to reach out. And act like a real person.

"Party's going to be there. Got a private room and everything. I haven't been there yet, but I hear all the waitresses are gorgeous, the drinks are great and loaded with alcohol, and Logan's parents arranged for a private room. Rumor has it strippers might've been hired out for this momentous event. Logan's turning twenty-one, so we want to get him all sorts of fucked up." Jace waggles his eyebrows.

"Sounds great," I lie. It sounds like torture. But I need to go. At the very least, make a quick appearance and then leave. I can report back to my shrink what I did. She can give me a gold star for making an effort.

"You'll go?" Jace looks shocked, and I know why. I rarely do anything with the guys and especially the last few months, since I've been like a ghost.

"I'll be there." I nod, unsure how I'm going to work up the energy to make an appearance, but I've got to do this.

"Yeah? Awesome! I can't wait to tell the guys. We've missed you. Haven't seen you for a while, and we all know those last few games were tough on you. They were tough on all of us." Jace's expression is solemn, and for a minute I wonder if he's playing my ass.

But then I realize he's sincere. Funny how I took full responsibility for those losses when I bet every single one of these guys on my team probably did the same thing.

"Tell the guys I can't wait to see them." The words fall easily from my lips because they're the truth. I need to stop wallowing in my own misery. I need to stop worrying about my past, worrying about my dad and my bitch of a stepmom and the little girl who died because I was too busy fighting with her mom and telling her to keep her goddamn hands to herself.

That's one of the biggest regrets I have, that I never fully explained to Fable what happened that day. I know she assumes I was off screwing around with Adele. I would think the same. But that was the day I told Adele never again. Whatever she was going to try, I wasn't interested. It was over. That was the day I became liberated.

And also the day I became a prisoner of my own guilt.

Forever.

"See ya around, Drew." Jace waves and turns, whistling as he walks away from me. I remain rooted to the spot, watching him leave until he's a speck of nothing in the distance, wishing like crazy I could be that carefree. That my biggest concerns were my grades, what girl I could get my hands on next, and how excited I was for the big party coming up in a few days.

Maybe, just maybe, I could lose myself in the mundane for a bit. Pretend that nothing else matters but friends and school and parties. Doc says I can't move forward until I face the past.

But what the fuck does she know?

CHAPTER 2

She's all broken inside but no one will ever notice.
—Unknown

Fable

"So." Owen slurps on the giant thirty-two-ounce soda I bought him at the gas station, where we stopped to fill up my mom's crap car on the way home. "Can I eat for free at this joint you're working at?"

I shake my head. "It's too classy. Kids aren't really welcome." The understatement of the year. The restaurant is definitely not kid friendly. In fact, I'm thinking it's not really Fable friendly either, but I'm willing to give it a chance. Colin claims I can make a ton of money in tips, though I'm not sure if I believe him.

My thoughts drift to Colin. He owns the restaurant because his rich daddy gave it to him to play with. That much I gleaned from him when he first brought me there. He's nice. He's attractive. He's charming.

Beyond chatting with him like he's my boss and I'm his employee, I'm avoiding him as much as possible. I took him up on his job offer, though it sounds almost too good to be true.

Funny thing is, I haven't quite given notice at La Salle's yet. Holding on to that job until I know for sure the new job is going to work out is the only way to keep the money consistently flowing in.

And as always, my inflow of money is the most important thing. Our mom isn't doing anything to ensure that's happening.

Owen puffs up his chest, his expression indignant. "Are you kidding me? I'm not a kid. I'm fucking fourteen!"

I slap his arm and he yelps. "Language," I warn because, oh my God, he needs to watch that mouth of his. And since when did the legal adult age get bumped back four years? In his dreams.

"Seriously, Fabes, you can't even sneak me in?" Owen shakes his head, his irritation clear. "I hear the chicks who hang out there are bangin'."

I don't need to hear my little brother talking about bangin' chicks and whatever else. Bad enough I found the baggy of weed in his jeans pocket when I did laundry a few days ago. I showed it to my mom and she shrugged, then demanded I hand the bag over.

She proceeded to open it and took a deep sniff, proclaiming the weed high-quality stuff. I know she took it with her over to Larry's house later and they probably got high as hell. I still can't believe it. How did I become so normal and stable when my mom is such a . . . child?

You had no choice.

Wasn't that the damn truth?

"Listen, the dinners they serve are like fifty bucks a plate. It's for couples and stuff. And there's a bar. After ten, the place is completely shut down to those under twenty-one," I explain. It's truly the most beautiful, elegant restaurant I've ever seen, let alone worked at. It's organized and efficient; everything and everyone has a place. The staff isn't very friendly, though. More like snobby. I'm sure they sneer at me behind my back, the white-trash townie who's come to work among their elitist ranks.

Whatever. All I care about is the tips. And the fact that Colin believes in me. It's been a long time since someone believed in me. I thought Drew did, but the longer he's absent from my life, the more it proves to me that was all fake. We just got a little too caught up in the fantasy.

"You can't even bring me any leftovers, huh?" Owen's question snaps me out of my thoughts and I glance at him, see the smirk on his face.

He's getting more and more good-looking as time passes. I have no idea if he has a girlfriend or not, but I really hope he puts that sort of thing off for a least a little while longer. Relationships are nothing but trouble.

"That's so gross." I roll my eyes. I used to bring him home burgers from La Salle's. Which goes to show I completely spoiled him.

"Well, Mom sure as hell isn't going to feed me. Sorry," he blurts when he catches my evil eye over his profanity. "And I feel like a jerk with how much I hang out at Wade's house. His mom has to be getting sick of me."

Guilt swamps me. I need this job. I need both of my jobs, and that means I can't be there for Owen. Making him dinners, keeping on top of his homework, forcing him to clean that dump of a room. The apartment has three bedrooms, a rarity but in demand in a college town, and the rent is getting more expensive. Considering my mom is never here and it's usually just Owen and me, I'm considering looking for another apartment. For just the two of us.

This little tidbit will piss my mom off when I tell her. It doesn't matter that she spends the majority of her time with Larry. It doesn't matter that she's hardly ever here and doesn't have a job and can't afford the rent. She'll still be angry and take it personally, like Owen and I are forcing her out.

I kind of am. I don't want her with us anymore. She's not a good influence. Owen's uncomfortable around her and so am I. I'm done.

But for whatever reason, I'm scared to confront her. I don't want to deal with a bunch of unnecessary drama. And that's what my mom is. Complete and total drama.

My cell beeps, indicating I have a text, and I check it, see that it's from my new boss. Unease slips down my spine as I read the message.

What are you doing?

I type in the good employee response.

Getting ready for work.

Hey, it's the truth.

I'm in the neighborhood. Let me pick you up and take you there.

I stare at his message for too long, ignoring Owen as he starts griping about what he's going to have to fix himself for dinner. What the hell could Colin want? Why would he be in my shit hole of a neighborhood? It makes no sense. Unless he purposely came looking for me . . .

I don't have to be at work for almost an hour, I reply.

I'll pay you for the extra time. Come on.

Sighing, I type in my answer: Give me five minutes.

"I gotta go," I tell Owen as I head for my bedroom. I haven't changed into my work uniform, if you can call it that. All the waitresses have to wear the most outrageous dresses I've ever seen. There are at least four different dresses and they're sexy as all get-out, with our boobs hanging out, or they fit us skintight. I get the sex appeal thing. We don't look slutty or anything, but if I bend over wrong, I'm giving everyone a flash of my ass. Boy-short undies are the name of the game for those dresses.

I'm grabbing my dress off the hanger when I catch Owen lurking in my doorway. "What's up?" I ask him.

He shrugs. "What do you think of me getting a tattoo?"

My head spins for a moment. Oh my God, where does he come up with this stuff? "First, you're only fourteen, so legally you can't get one. Second, you're only fourteen. What could you possibly want to have tattooed forever on your body?"

"I dunno." He shrugs again. "I thought it might be cool. I mean you just got one, so why can't I?"

"Maybe because I'm an adult and you're not?" A few weeks before Christmas, when I still believed Drew and I had a chance, I got one. The stupidest tattoo you could ever imagine. I thought by doing it, by having a piece of him, no matter how small, permanently etched into my skin, I could somehow call him back to me.

Didn't work. And now I'm stuck with it. Thank God it's small. I could probably have it filled in if I wanted to.

Right now, I don't want to.

"So you put some guy's initials on your body and it's cool,

but I can't get an artistic tat of a dragon on my back or what-ever? So unfair." He shakes his head, his dirty-blond hair get-ting in his eyes, and I want to smack him.

And I also want to draw him into my arms and ask where did the sweet, simple kid of not even a year ago go? Because he sure as hell isn't around here anymore.

"It's different." I turn away from him and yank the dress off the hanger, clutching it in my hand. "I need to change, so you need to go."

"Who's the guy, anyway? You never did tell me."

"He's no one." The words are heavy as they fall from my lips. He was definitely someone. He was my everything for the briefest, most intense moment of my life.

"He's not no one. He broke your heart." Venom fills Owen's voice. "I ever find out who he is, I'll kick his ass."

I smile because I can't help it. His defense of me is . . . awe-some. We're a team, Owen and I. We're all each other's got.

I slip outside of my apartment because I so don't want Colin knocking on my door and meeting Owen. Or worse, seeing the inside of our dingy apartment. Wherever Colin lives, I bet it's amazing. If his house is half as gorgeous as his restaurant, then it *has* to be amazing.

The second I step off the stairs, he's there in a sleek black Mercedes, the engine purring, the car so new it doesn't have plates yet. I take a step back when he opens the door and climbs out of the car, a blond god with a devastating smile and twinkling blue eyes.

He rounds the car, opening the passenger-side door for me with a flourish. "Your carriage awaits."

I hesitate. Is this a mistake, climbing into his car with him? I'm not afraid of Colin, yet I *am* afraid of the situation I might be putting myself in. He's a flirt, but I notice he flirts with pretty much everyone who works for him—and the customers. He never crosses a line, though; he's always polite and knows when to step back if need be.

But am I giving him mixed signals by allowing him to pick me up for work? He just happens to be near my apartment so he can swing by and get me? I don't believe it.

Not for a second.

"Did you come here specifically to pick me up?" I ask him the minute he climbs back into the car and slams the door.

He turns to look at me, our faces awfully close. The car is nice but small and the setting is rather intimate. He smells like expensive cologne and leather, and I wonder for a quick minute if I could actually feel something for this guy.

I realize just as quickly that I can't. My heart is still tied up in knots over someone else. Someone unreal.

"You're pretty straightforward, aren't you?" Colin asks, his eyes gleaming in the dim interior.

"It's better than doling out a bunch of lies, right?" I arch a brow.

Laughing, he shakes his head as he puts the car into gear. "Right. I really was in the neighborhood, Fable. And I remembered you lived around here, so that's why I texted you. I know you don't always have access to a car."

I've worked at his restaurant for three shifts and he already knows all this information about me. Is that a sign of a good boss or a creeper? "I had my mom's car today."

He pulls out of the parking lot and onto the road, his

hand draped casually over the steering wheel, his other arm resting on the center console. There's an easiness to him. No, make that effortlessness. He makes everything appear as if he could get whatever he wants out of life and he deserves every bit of it, too.

I envy him that. It's a confidence I could never hope for.

"Want me to take you back so you can drive it?" There's amusement lacing his deep voice. He must think I'm a joke.

"No." I sigh. This is stupid. What are we doing? "I won't have a ride home, though."

"I'll give you a ride."

I don't bother answering him.

I remain quiet, picking at my cuticles as he drives, both of us silent. My hands are dry, my cuticles bad, and I think of the other girls I work with who have perfect manicures and pedicures. I look like the still slightly ragged Cinderella who's finally been pulled out of the basement and set to work among the glittering, beautiful princesses. I might shine, but rub me a little bit and the tarnish comes through.

I feel . . . *less than* when I'm at my new job. And I don't like that.

"Nasty habit," Colin says, breaking the thickening silence. "You should go get your nails done."

Okay, that irritates the crap out of me. His assumptions are rude. "I can't afford it."

"I'll pay for it."

"Hell, no," I practically snarl. His offer irritates me more.

Colin ignores me. "And while you're at it, you should go see a hairstylist. I'll pay for that, too. There's too much bleach in your hair and it looks damaged."

The nerve! This guy is such an asshole. Why did I agree to work for him again? Oh yeah, the money. Greediness is going to get the best of me, I just know it. It's led to two really stupid decisions already. "Who are you? The fashion police?"

"No, but I'm your boss, and at The District we have certain criteria that we need to maintain."

"So why did you hire me? You knew what you were getting."

"I saw your potential," he said softly. "Do you, Fable? Do *you* see it?"

I couldn't answer him. Because the truth wasn't what he wanted to hear.

No.

Drew

I'm in class, though I don't want to be. I took a lighter load after my supreme screw-up of the fall semester. Why risk temptation to fail or drop classes again? I'll have to make it up over the summer break by taking a few extra courses, but I don't care. Where else would I go?

Not home, that's for damn sure.

At least while I'm on campus, I feel somewhat normal. I can forget about my dad and Adele and what she told me. I haven't spoken to her since the one time I called her and made her tell me everything. I've barely talked to my dad either. He knows something's wrong with me but doesn't push. I know something's wrong with him, too, and I don't push either. What's the point? Do I really want to find out what's wrong?

No.

I move through the day like a robot, checking in and checking out. The longer I'm alone, the more in my head I get. Remembering that I promised Jace I would go to Logan's birthday party this Saturday fills me with a sort of panic. Yet I have to do this. Dr. Harris said I need to make like a real person again, and she's right.

But it still scares the shit out of me.

I'm in my communications class, which is huge, and there's this girl who I sit close to every day. She's petite, her hair is long and blond, and she reminds me so much of Fable, it's almost painful.

But I'm a glutton for punishment. I like sitting by her. Pretending she's someone else, holding my breath when she turns her head in my direction, always ready to be surprised when I find out Fable really is sitting next to me.

Dealing with the disappointment when the truth is revealed. She isn't who I want her to be. No one ever will be.

The professor is droning on, but I'm not listening. I take out a sheet of paper and start writing. A letter I will never give a certain someone. But I need to pour my feelings out for her or I'm going to explode. Once my pen meets the paper, the words just flow, and I have no control over them.

Maybe it was a mistake leaving you.
And I don't know how to make it right.
Regret fills me every single day.
So much of it builds up I
Hate myself for
Missing you. Hurting you.
And I want you to know I . . .

Long for you
Love you
Others may come and go in our lives but . . .
We belong together

I stare at my stupid little poem that the girl I love will never read. I draw little squiggly lines around it. A cursive *F*, just like I was taught to write in elementary school. The first initial of her name. Fable. A story. A myth. A fairy tale. She's my story. I want to live and breathe and die for her, and she has no idea how much she consumes my thoughts. To the point I think of nothing else. I'd rather sit in class and write her love poems with secret messages in them than pay attention to what's really going on in my life.

What a fucking mess I am.

For a girl
As pretty as she deserves the
Best. No more
Lies. She is my
Everything.

But I'm not brave enough to tell her. I stare at this new bit I wrote for her and disgust fills me. I'm not good enough for her. I can't even tell Fable how I really feel about her to her face.

"Are you a writer?"

I glance up to find my pseudo-Fable smiling at me, and I frown. Her face is all wrong. She has brown eyes. And she's not as pretty, though she's definitely attractive. I don't know how I thought she looked like Fable. "What did you say?" I ask.

She nods toward the piece of paper filled with my scribbling. "You're not paying attention to the lecture. Are you writing a poem? It looks like one."

Sliding my hand over the paper to hide the words from her seeking eyes, I study her face, willing her to look more like Fable. But it doesn't happen. This girl is nothing like her. And I hate her for it. "I'm taking notes."

She smiles. "Don't worry. I won't tell if you're not."

"But I am," I insist defensively because these words are for no one else. They're for me and a girl who will never see them.

"No need to freak out," she whispers. Her gaze narrows, as if she can see into me, through me, and I'm tempted to run. "Or get so defensive."

I say nothing. How can I defend myself against that when she speaks the truth?

"Hey, aren't you Drew Callahan?" She cocks her head, her expression full of sudden interest. "Mister Big Shot Quarterback?"

Her voice is full of sarcasm. I let down the entire school at the end of the season in one spectacular failure after another. I fell apart and everyone knows it. I can see the contempt in her gaze, feel it radiating from her body, and I know she thinks I'm a joke.

Grabbing my backpack at my feet, I shove the piece of paper into it, along with my book. I get out of my chair and haul the strap over my shoulder. "He doesn't exist anymore," I mutter to her before I make my escape. Right in the middle of class.

But I don't give a shit. I just keep on going. Until I'm outside and breathing in the sharp cold air, the sun shining on me, people bumping past me as I push through the crowd. I hear someone call my name but I ignore it. All sorts of people seem to know me, but I don't know them.

That's my bullshit story, no matter how much I don't want it to be.

I feel my phone vibrating in my jeans pocket and I grab it, see that it's my dad. Normally I'd let it go straight to voice mail, but for whatever masochistic reason I'm in the mood to talk to him. So I answer.

"Drew." He sounds surprised.

"What's up?" My voice is deceptively casual. I should've been an actor. I'm so good at faking my life it's unbelievable.

"I was hoping I could come and see you." He clears his throat, and I can feel how uncomfortable he is even through the phone. "There are some . . . things I need to talk to you about."

My gut clenches and I feel like I'm going to throw up. He sounds serious. Scary serious. "Like what?"

"Well, I'd rather talk about it when I see you, but . . . I may as well tell you now." He takes a deep breath and so do I. "Adele and I are getting a divorce."

I feel like I've been smacked upside the head and little birds are tweeting in a circle above me, straight out of a cartoon. Glancing around, I catch sight of a bench and I sit heavily on the edge of it, my backpack knocking against me, making me wince. "What? Why?"

"I'd rather come there and tell you. Are you free this weekend?"

"Sure." I remember Logan's party. "Well, I have something to do Saturday night, but I can cancel it."

"I don't want to interfere with your plans." My dad usually doesn't give a shit about my plans, so his protesting is unnerving. He's not himself. Is he upset that he's getting a divorce? Does he view this as a good thing or a bad thing? Of course, I automatically blame Adele for everything.

"You won't be interfering, Dad. Trust me. It's just a stupid party." Dr. Harris is going to be pissed at me, but I don't care. I need to be here for my dad. Especially if he's finally going to end it with Adele.

I shouldn't be happy. I should feel sorry for him. But this is the right move. She's a sick bitch and I want her poison out of my life. Out of my dad's life, too. Plus—and this is completely selfish on my part—I don't want our secret revealed.

I don't even know if her secret is the truth. And that's what scares me the most. What's real, what's not? I'm not sure anymore.

"How about I'll come there Friday, stay the night with you, and go home Saturday? That way you can do what you need to do Saturday night," Dad suggests.

"You can stay the entire weekend if you want." I want him to. I miss him. We used to be close. Before I turned fifteen and my stepmom decided I looked far more interesting than my dad ever did.

You've grown up so much, Andrew. You're so handsome, so big and strong . . .

Closing my eyes, I shove her flirtatious voice firmly out of my brain.

"Let's play it by ear," my dad says.

That's all I can ask for, so I agree. And when we hang up, I feel a little lighter. My head's not as cloudy and for once, I'm hopeful.

I clutch that feeling close to me for the rest of the day.

CHAPTER 3

If there ever comes a day when we can't be together, keep
me in your heart, I'll stay there forever.
—Winnie the Pooh

Drew

My dad shows up Friday around noon and we go to lunch, at one of the popular cafés downtown that's full of college students and people on their lunch break from the nearby businesses. It's small and busy, and the tables are tiny and round. Our knees bump against each other because we're both tall, and it feels incredibly awkward. I'm not saying much beyond small talk, because he's the one with the major news.

Scratch that. I have major news, but I'm never going to drop that particular bomb on him now. It might scar him for life. Ruin our relationship forever.

I'm not taking that chance.

After the waitress brings us our lunch, he finally says something important.

"I filed divorce papers yesterday. Adele will be served sometime next week."

I lift my head to meet his gaze and find him studying me

pointedly. As if he's got everything all figured out. For a moment, I'm afraid he does. But then he digs his fork into the salad he ordered along with his sandwich and eats. Just as though what he said really didn't matter at all.

"Where is she?" I ask after I swallow. I can't bring myself to say her name.

Fable would like that. If she had a chance, I know she'd scratch that bitch's eyes out.

"She's still at the house. I asked her to leave and she refused." Dad wipes the corner of his mouth with his napkin. "Not quite sure what I'm going to do about that. I can't kick her out—yet. She really has nowhere to go. And she was the mother of my child."

Maybe. I swallow hard. "Where will you go?"

He shrugs. "I'm staying at a hotel for the moment. And she'll trip herself up. I have a plan."

My appetite leaves me. If this is going to be an ugly divorce and I'm somehow involved, I don't think I can take it. "What's your plan?"

His gaze is pointed again, directly aimed at me, and I want to squirm. "She's having an affair. I know it, I can feel it, but I don't have proof."

My stomach churns. If this has anything to do with her and me, I don't know what I'll do. God, that was so long ago! No way could their current problems have anything to do with me. "Who do you think she's messing around with?"

"That I'm not sure. It's only been going on for a few months, but I know she's involved with someone. And I don't think this is the first time she's done this sort of thing."

Shit. My dad's right. This isn't the first time. And I haven't been with her in years, so I'm sure I wasn't her only. More like the first in a long string of guys. She thrives on attention. Needs it like we need oxygen to breathe.

"I'm sorry, Dad." I am. I'm sorry that he has to go through this and deal with an evil, cheating, immoral bitch for a wife. He has no idea of the damage she's wrought to his family. My dad's oblivious. He definitely has his faults. I know he's not perfect—none of us are—but I wouldn't wish this on him.

He chose her, though. Now he has to deal with the fallout of their dissolving marriage.

"Don't be sorry." My dad waves his hand, dismissing my worry with a flick of his fingers. "She's a stupid bitch who finally ran out of options. Whoever she's fucking, I think he works at the country club."

She's slumming. Great. Dad must love this.

"And I think he's young," he continues. "She's dressing like she's twenty and listening to music that would only appeal to a silly teenage girl. I caught her working out in a Justin Bieber T-shirt a few weeks ago while listening to some boy band. She's too damn old to wear that sort of crap. What woman her age does that?"

I want to laugh, but I keep it to myself. I'm not laughing at my dad's irritation. More like at her desperation and the fact that she seems to like them young. I can either laugh or go into a complete rage. She's disgusting. "How do you know she's having an affair?"

"I'm not one hundred percent sure, but I hired a private investigator. He's tailing her now. Finding out all her juicy secrets. Bitch doesn't stand a chance."

Neither do I if he finds out the juicy secret I share with her. "I hope it doesn't blow up in your face."

"How could it? I'm not the one who's done wrong here. She is. I've been faithful to her our entire marriage."

My good friend guilt nestles in deep within me and I push my plate away. This is the last thing I want to hear. I'd almost prefer it if my dad admitted he'd cheated on Adele. "Really, Dad? You can be honest with me, you know. It's not like I'm going to tell."

"Really." His expression is hard; his eyes, as blue as mine, are cold. "I loved her. Deep down inside, I still do. But I have to wonder if she ever loved me. How long has she been unfaithful? Who else is involved? How deep do her lies go?" He shakes his head, his disgust clear. "She's wronged me. Made a fool of me in front of our friends. For all I know, she's been flaunting this boy toy of hers while I'm out of town working. I don't know."

"You talk like you want to get revenge on her." I don't know how to react. Don't know what to say. His words fill me with fear. He could push her to admit things I never want her to confess. I don't know if I've ever seen my dad like this.

"Maybe I do." He laughs, but it's an angry sound, as if torn from his throat. "Maybe I want to make her suffer. Make her look like a stupid slut. I gave her everything. When we first met, she was perfect. Beautiful, fun, thoughtful, and amazing in bed."

I grimace. Last thing I want to hear. "Didn't need to know that."

"Come on, Drew. You're an adult. That sort of comment shouldn't bother you." He studies me. "Now that I think of it, you haven't mentioned your little girlfriend. Are you two still together?"

My entire body stiffens at the reminder of Fable. "We broke up." Not really, but technically we were never together, so what else can I say?

"That's a shame." His words are completely insincere. "Not that I thought she was the sort of girl for you."

"What the hell is that supposed to mean?" I growl, flexing my hands into fists.

"You know exactly what I mean. She's the sort of girl you screw on the side, not the one you keep forever."

I stand so fast I knock my chair into the person sitting behind me. My blood boiling, I glare at my father, but all I can see is red. "You have no idea what you're talking about. Fable is one of the best people I've ever known. She's loyal, kind, sweet . . ."

Dad's gaze meets mine, his eyes full of contempt. I'm making a scene and he doesn't like it. I really couldn't give a shit. "If she's so great, why aren't you with her?"

The truth falls from my lips with ease. "Because I'm not good enough for her."

I leave the restaurant without another word.

Fable

"You look different."

I smooth my hand over my newly colored hair, my freshly painted nails catching my eye. They're red, as bright as the color coating my lips, and I feel like a different person. But I want to show indifference. As if this sort of thing is common for me. That handsome men who just so happen to be my boss whisk me to a popular and expensive hair salon in the late afternoon without an appointment and pay for my complete makeover. All the while he's standing by with a satisfied grin on his face, as if he's solely responsible for my transformation.

Which he sort of is.

I should be insulted. Colin taking me to the salon is basically saying I don't look good enough to work for him. That I need to change—at least physically.

But secretly, it's also flattering, his attention. No one pays attention to me. They all just . . . count on me to get stuff done. My mom, my brother, my old boss at La Salle's—yep, I gave notice this morning, finally. Drew paid attention for a little while, but he's too wrapped up in his own problems to worry about mine.

I miss him. I hate that I miss him, but I do. Funny how someone can come into your life for such a brief time yet leave such a lasting impression. He permanently imprinted himself on my heart, and I permanently imprinted his name on my skin.

It's silly, longing for a man who doesn't long for me.

"Your hair—the blond is darker." Jennifer smiles at me, nodding with approval. "I like it. Suits you better."

Colin is a great boss, but he employs a bunch of bitches at his restaurant. And I'm starting to realize why they're so bitchy—we're all in direct competition with one another, not only for being the most wanted waitress at The District, thus getting the most in tip money at the end of the evening, but also to be the most wanted waitress in Colin's eyes. Which is all sorts of fucked up if I think about it too long.

So I banish the realization from my brain, something I'm so good at.

Jennifer so far has been the nicest to me, but she was the new girl on the block until I showed up, so she's probably thankful there's a fresh target here for them to hate. She's pretty in an exotic, almost mysterious way, which I find amusing considering her standard, every-girl name. She has long straight-as-paper black hair, large dark brown eyes, and olive-colored skin, and she's so incredibly tall, I get a crick in my neck if I stare up at her for too long.

She's everything I'm not. We're complete opposites in every way.

"Did Colin take you to get your hair done?" she asks as we set the tables for the evening. I'm doling out the silverware, she's setting out the freshly polished glasses, and I'm so startled by her question, I stand there with my mouth hanging open for a second. Long enough that she speaks again.

"It's okay to admit it. He took me for a haircut and mini makeover when I first started." She smiles, her cheeks tinged red. "Colin likes to take in strays and fix them up. 'Bring us to our full potential,' is how he phrased it to me."

Her words make me feel the tiniest bit less special, and I want to smack myself. "Don't you think that's sort of . . ."

"Weird?" she finishes for me with a rueful smile.

"Yeah." I finish setting the silverware on the table and watch her as she carefully adjusts the last water glass, placing it sit just so. The table linens are a perfect, creaseless white, with an equally perfect silver bowl sitting in the middle, full of freshly cut flowers the colors of spring. All vibrant pinks and lavenders and whites, they add a touch of sophisticated glamour to an otherwise plain palette.

The entire restaurant is like this. Sexy yet restrained elegance. No wonder all the beautiful people love to come here.

"Colin likes to think of himself as a knight in shining armor to all of us. Like he swooped in and rescued us from our horrible lives and gave us new ones," Jennifer explains.

I frown. I don't need someone in my life with a hero complex. With Drew, I was the one with the hero complex, and that got me absolutely nowhere.

And why the hell does everything still have to come back to him? I need to let him go, once and for all. "That's ridiculous," I say.

Jennifer shrugs. "It's the truth, isn't it? Where were you working before? I was at some crappy bar on the outskirts of town, where the customers couldn't keep their hands off me. I hated it. Colin came in there one night over a month ago, all clean and golden and shiny. He practically begged me to come work for him, but I didn't trust him." Her eyes darken even more, shading secrets from me, I'm sure. "It was just before Christmas, and I was pretty much broke and alone. He took me in and I haven't looked back since."

"Took you in—what do you mean?"

"I'm staying at his house." Her gaze skitters away from mine. "I'm not the first. I won't be the last."

Wow. He's like the Pied Piper, and we all follow after him like a bunch of hypnotized mice. I feel like a fool for thinking the attention he gave me was special. Unusual. I was just another in a long list of girls who work here he's taken under his wing.

I'm such a skeptic, I still can't help but wonder if he has an ulterior motive.

"There's a private party coming in at nine." Tenerria walks into the dining area, her demeanor all business. She's the shift manager, having worked with Colin at his previous restaurants. He brought her with him to help open The District and I'm not sure if she's a permanent fixture or eventually moving on. I respect the hell out of T, which everyone calls her, but she also scares the crap out of me. "Fifteen confirmed college football players celebrating a twenty-first birthday, so be prepared. That confirmed number will probably fly out the window."

My heart drops to my toes. *Football players.* Could Drew be one of the people coming tonight? He's not one to be social, and last I heard—because the rumor mill is rampant in this small town—Drew had left. Not that I ever pay too much attention to rumors. They're usually all lies.

"I'm throwing you to the wolves tonight, Fable," T continues, a smile curling her bright red lips. We're all wearing the new "uniform" Colin gave us earlier: black shorts, white lace tops with a black bra underneath. I added the black heels that I teeter precariously on. He even gave us the same lipstick, so that we'd all match. "You and Jen both are working the private party. We have an extra bartender on staff as well, so you should be set."

Nerves eat at my stomach. "Okay," I say weakly. Being around football players will make me think of Drew. Plus, they'll probably give me shit because yep, I'm ashamed to say, I've been with a few. Nothing major, mostly make-out/grope sessions, but still. It was back when my self-esteem was in tatters and I thought their attention was the only kind I deserved. So embarrassing! I hope they don't say anything rude.

More than anything, I hope Drew's not there.

Okay, I lie. A teeny-tiny part of me hopes Drew shows up. Not that I know what I'd say to him.

Fuck you for stomping all over my heart!

Hmm, yeah. That would go over real well.

"What do you think of the new duds?" T asks.

I glance down at myself. The shorts are extra short but at least I'm not in a dress, where I'm always afraid my ass is hanging out. And the lace tops are most definitely see-through, but I don't feel like my goods are on blatant display. I'm always afraid I'll get cold, but there's too much running around throughout the evening for that to happen. "I like them."

"I do, too," Jen pipes up, moving so she stands beside me. "I prefer the shorts to the dresses. Feels like I can move better in them."

"Same." I nod in agreement. "Why did he pick out new clothes for us? And even gave us all matching lipstick?" Saying the question out loud makes me realize just how odd the situation is.

I mean, who does this sort of thing?

"He likes all of us to look the same yet different. Bring some of our own personality to the outfit, you know?" T runs her gaze over Jen and me. "I know you were just given the outfits but the next time you work, make sure you add something to give yourself a little more pizazz. Individuality."

"What if I can't afford it?" I had to ask. I'm mostly a broke joke. The biggest extravagance I've given myself is the damn tattoo with the initials of a man who ditched me. The expensive shoes I wear? A gift from Drew. The same ones I wore the night of that crazy country club dinner, when he kissed me for the first time.

Just the memory of his lips grazing mine sends a shiver stealing over me.

"Fable, you can go to one of those cheap stores in the mall and pick up a three-dollar necklace. There's Target and Walmart, too." Shaking her head, T starts to walk away. "Get those tables set up. Doors open in fifteen!"

Jen and I busily finish setting up the tables, polishing glass, lighting candles, and sweeping the bare wood floors. Colin comes in, offering murmured words to Jen I can't quite catch before he locks his gaze with mine and heads toward me.

"Much improved," he says, stopping directly in front of me, crossing his arms in front of his chest. He's wearing a black T-shirt that stretches across his wide shoulders and chest and black pants. The dark clothing only seems to emphasize the golden hair, the golden skin, and the pale blue eyes.

Ugh! I hate that I'm noticing this. And I hate how proprietary he seems. Yet that approving light in his gaze secretly pleases me. Makes me want to stand tall and preen like a good little girl who's done right.

Sick and twisted, I know.

"You were there for the transformation yesterday." It had taken hours. We finally left the salon after nine. Luckily enough, I wasn't scheduled last night and considering he was the boss, he could show up at the restaurant whenever he felt like it. He'd even driven me home. Now he's acting as if he hadn't seen the end results last night.

Weird.

"You're right. I was. But it's different, seeing you here tonight. In your element." He flicks his chin in my direction. "Like the new uniforms?"

They were proving to be the hottest topic of conversation around here. "Kind of see-through, but yeah, I like them."

"I'm glad." Reaching out, he squeezes my arm as he passes. "Nice shoes," he tosses out over his shoulder.

A little smile curls my lips and I glance up, catching Jennifer watching me with a narrowed gaze. She turns and leaves before I can say anything and I watch her retreating back, wondering what that was all about.

Wondering what sort of weird little love triangle I might've let myself walk into.

CHAPTER 4

I hate the idea of anyone else having you.
—Drew Callahan

Drew

They scream and shout my name the second I slip inside the private room at The District, the new restaurant where Logan's party is being held. Every one of my teammates is already shitfaced and it's only ten. I can see it in their blurry eyes and red cheeks, hear it in their too-loud voices.

But hey, at least they're happy to see me. I figured I'd become the enemy. The asshole who lost their chance at a bowl game. We'd been close, so close every one of us had started to taste that faint glimmer of victory.

Then I met a girl, we went home together, and I let everything that happened there fuck my head all up. *Stupid.*

Logan approaches and gives me a shoulder-slapping hug. He reeks of alcohol and I push away from him, startled when Jace appears by my side, placing a beer in my hand and telling me to drink up.

I dutifully do as I'm told, ready to lose myself for at least a few hours. The visit with my dad had turned tense the mo-

ment he insulted Fable. Crazy, considering we weren't together anymore, but I wasn't going to stand by and let him
say rude crap about her. Truthfully, she was above all of us
and I refuse to let him drag her through the mud, even if it
was only to me.

After that fiasco of a lunch, he dealt constantly with Adele
calling him, texting him, calling him again. I didn't need that
reminder, so I stayed away. Which meant we were apart for
much of his visit, until he finally told me this morning he
needed to go back home and attend to "business."

Bullshit. Business was code for Adele. I didn't call him on
it, merely nodded and let him go. Promising him we'd get together again soon.

Yeah, right. I don't see that happy reunion happening anytime soon.

"You've been in hiding," Logan says as he sits next to me,
a drink clutched in his hand. His head lolls, as if he can't quite
keep it upright, and I shake my head, chuckling as I sip from
my beer. Sierra Nevada, the beer of choice in this town—it's
about the only kind I can drink. The rest tastes like swill.

"I've been around," I say with a shrug. "Lying low. Taking fewer classes this semester. I needed a break."

"I get it, man. I get it. And hey, don't let Coach mess with
your head. It wasn't your fault, our spectacular losses at the
end of the season." Logan's expression goes serious. As serious as it can go, considering how drunk he is. "We all sorta
fucked up, you know?"

I take another, bigger swig of beer. I need it, since the topic
of conversation has veered in a serious direction. "You think
so?" I wonder if he's just feeding me a line.

"Definitely." He nods eagerly, his head still bobbing. "I'm

glad you're here, man. You never go out with us. I feel like I'm special or something, you showing up for my birthday and shit. Not every day a jackass like me turns twenty-one."

We both laugh. "You're right. You're a total jackass." Not really. Logan's a decent guy. And besides, I couldn't sit at home with my thoughts any longer. I was driving myself crazy.

Logan grins. "You need to hang out with us more. Wait until you see the waitresses who are ours for the night. They're fucking hot. One of them everyone knows, some blond groupie with an amazing ass. The other one is tall and dark. Looks like a damn model."

An uneasy sensation slides through me at the description of the blonde, but I push it aside. What are the odds? And there are plenty of blond team groupies out there. "Cute, huh?" I feign interest.

"Cute doesn't begin to describe either of them. They're complete opposites and completely hot." Logan tilts his head back so it bumps the back of the chair. "I need to get laid," he says at the ceiling. "I haven't had sex as a twenty-one-year-old yet. I think tonight calls for a celebration of the get-laid kind."

"I'm surprised there's no girls here." My teammates are known for having crazy parties with half-naked girls in attendance. Half the reason why I would never go—half-naked females coming at me used to scare the shit out of me.

They still make me uncomfortable because they always, always want something I can't give them. Like my attention, my time. Forget that shit. There's only one half-naked female I would welcome with open arms if she came at me right now.

And she hates me.

"Oh, the girls are coming later." Logan smiles and closes his eyes. "Actually, we're going to go and see them. Promise me you'll come with us."

"Uh . . ." Sounds like a nightmare.

Logan cracks open his eyes. "Promise me. I'll start shouting and making a scene if you don't promise."

"Fine, fine, I'll go." I have no idea what I just agreed to but it can't be good, judging by the sight of the wide smile Logan's wearing. Besides, he'll probably shout and make a scene no matter what I say.

A tall, dark-haired girl enters the private room, a smile curving her full red lips as she starts passing out drinks from the heavy tray she carries. She comes to me after she empties her tray, her dark brown gaze connecting with mine. "Ah, a fresh face. I see you have a beer already, but do you need anything else? Something to eat, another drink?"

"Get him a shot," Logan says, his voice already slurred. "Tequila. Patrón."

She looks at me expectantly but she's talking to Logan. "Only one shot, birthday boy?"

"Get us a round of eight."

What the hell? "I'm not doing a bunch of shots with you. I don't care if it's your birthday or not."

"Don't be such a downer." Logan waves a hand. "Eight shots of Patrón, pretty lady. Hey, what are you doing later? Wanna come with us when we take the party to our next stop?"

She laughs and shakes her head. "Sorry, I work until one. I appreciate the offer, though." Her gaze meets mine once more. "Another beer, maybe?"

"Sure." I shrug. I'll do one shot and the second beer and then I'm done. Being drunk means being out of control, and I don't like that.

Turning on her heel, she threads her way through the crowded room, earning more than a few appreciative glances and low whistles. The minute she's gone, they all start talking about her. Her ass, her tits, her pretty face.

"She has a mouth made for cock sucking," Jace says with all the authority in the world.

I nod in agreement, feeling like an ass for doing even that. Put a bunch of guys together, fill them with alcohol, and we turn into complete assholes.

"Wait till you see the other one," Logan pipes up. "Talk about a mouth made for cock sucking. And from what I hear, she's done that and more with a few lucky bastards that are here tonight."

Laughter rings throughout the room. Logan says it loud enough and I know. I know without a doubt they're talking about Fable. She admitted it to me when we were together. How she messed around with a few of my teammates, though she said she never took it too far.

Had she lied? Just trying to save face so she wouldn't look like a slut? I don't think she's a slut.

You thought she was a slut when you hired her to be your fake girlfriend. That's the reason you chose her.

I shove the irritating-as-shit voice out of my head and finish off my beer. The alcohol is already working its magic, sliding through my veins, buzzing through my head. Miss Tall, Dark, and Pretty shows back up relatively quick, handing a fresh beer over to me with a smile before she lines up the eight shots of Patrón in front of Logan with a little flourish.

He immediately takes a near overflowing shot glass and raises it toward me. "Come on, Callahan."

I grab one, a few other guys grab one as well, and we're all clinking glasses, saluting Logan before we down them simultaneously. The tequila burns down my throat and I grimace, laughing when Logan shoves another shot glass into my hand, and I toss that one back, too.

Within minutes I'm feeling no pain. Fuck my problems, I'm good. I've polished off three shots and two beers and nothing can hurt me. Nothing.

Until the girl I love more than anyone else in the world strides into the room looking like my every fantasy come to life.

Fable

I told myself again and again no way would Drew be here. And then I enter the private room where the party's being held to relieve Jen so she can take a break, and there he is.

Breathtakingly gorgeous, looking as shocked as I feel . . . and drunk.

I see it in his eyes, his expression, in the wobbly way he jumps to his feet as if he's going to come for me. But then it's as if he remembers himself, remembers where he's at. He settles back into his chair, laughing at whatever the guy sitting next to him is saying, but his gaze never, ever leaves me.

I want to run to him. I want to run away from him. Holy shit, this is *so* not how I saw it going down when I finally came face-to-face with him again!

"You're looking good, Fable." One of the senior football players—I think his name is Tad? Ty?—eyes me, his mouth curved in a knowing smirk.

Knowing because yes, he's a shameful moment from my past. Barely out of high school and so eager to please, I used to watch the team practice, sitting on the sidelines in the heat of the summer in my too-short shorts and my skimpy tank top. Tad, Ty, whatever his name is asked me out, and I accepted and ended up giving him a blow job while in his car on our first and only date.

Not one of my proudest moments. But at the time, I cherished the attention he gave me. I was so needy, so foolish.

Of course, the jerk never called. Not that I would've gone out with him again. One awkward blow job was more than enough between us, thank you very much.

"Thanks." I smile, pretending I don't know him. "Would you like to order something else?"

"Yeah." He moves in close. He's tall and broad, all muscle, with dark hair buzzed short and a nasty gleam in his eyes. I step back and he grabs my arm, holding me close to him. Dipping his head, his mouth is next to my ear as he asks, "How about another blow job later tonight?"

I pull out of his grip, anger blazing through me so strong my body's shaking. "Fuck off," I mutter and turn away from him, his gritty laughter following me as I push through the throng of well-muscled athletes that crowd the room.

All the while I'm trying my best to avoid Drew. I can feel his eyes on me. I know he sees me, is watching me, and I don't want to approach him. What would I say? What would I do? I both want to throw myself into his arms and throw a right hook into his perfect square jaw.

He asks me to rescue him and then he ditches me. Tells me he loves me in a note and never replies to my calls or texts. He's a jerk.

He's an asshole.

I'm in love with a jerky asshole and damn, that's painful to admit.

Gathering my bearings, I take orders, clear empty bottles and glasses, and lollygag enough in the hope that I won't make it to the back left corner. I finally flee the stifling room minutes later, leaning against the wall for a few seconds, desperate to catch my breath.

I didn't expect this, yet part of me did. I thought I could handle seeing him, but I can't.

This situation I'm in is hopeless. I hate that he didn't approach me and I'm so thankful he didn't. I probably would've done something really stupid. Like beg him to tell me why.

That's all that keeps running through my head as I stand at the bar minutes later, waiting for my orders to be filled. Why did he leave me? Why didn't he ever call me back? Why didn't he text me? That was the absolute least he could have done. Text me back a simple *we're done.* I would've let him go. I would've been hurt, angry, and sad, but I could've handled it.

It would have been better than how he actually did treat me. The asshole.

Why, asshole? That might be a fun way to confront him. But knowing Drew, he'd run.

He's real good at that. Running.

I take my full tray of drinks back into the party room, the anxious nerves running through me making my knees shake.

The guys are even rowdier than when I left them only minutes before, giving me an endless bunch of grief, talking dirty, talking loud. They're keeping a running tab; Logan's parents arranged the party since they're bazillionaires who live in Marin County, and I bet they're going to end up spending about two months of my wages tonight in a matter of hours.

Crazy.

"So, Fable." It's Ty again. I heard someone call him that, not Tad. Nice that he made such an impression I can't even remember his name. "I promised Logan you would give him a special birthday present."

I roll my eyes, offering a sweet smile to the birthday boy. I'm not about to insult him. His parents are spending the big bucks so he can celebrate like a drunken frat jock. "Don't make promises you can't keep, Ty."

Logan laughs, his gaze never leaving me. He's wobbling on his feet, his eyes are bloodshot, and I know he's good and drunk. No surprise, though, since he just turned twenty-one. This sort of drunken evening celebrating a twenty-first birthday is a ritual in these parts.

"I told him I'm sure I could arrange a blow job just for him." Ty smiles, though it never reaches his eyes. "From you."

My smile fades, replaced by a scowl. I want to sock this asshole in his smug face, but I restrain myself. I've worked here only a week. I can't screw this up. The money is too good. And this place is way classier than La Salle's.

But still full of drunk jerks. I can't escape them no matter how hard I try.

"Very funny," I say, trying to keep it light. I turn away

from them, ready to gather more discarded glasses and bottles, but Ty reaches out and grabs my arm. Again. Stopping me in my tracks.

I glare at him over my shoulder and tug. "Let go of me."

"Say you'll do it." His voice is firm, his gaze like ice. "Say you'll give Logan a blow job. It's his birthday. A hummer is the least you can give him."

"No." I try to escape his grip but it's like a vise. "Get your hands off me."

"Not until you swear you'll give him a BJ. Come on. Not like you haven't given it up practically to the entire team." His voice is firm as he steps closer to me. "Say it, Fable. Say you'll do it."

My knee twitches. I want to slam him in the balls with it. I can't believe he's talking to me like this. Looking at me like he wants to tear me apart. What a pervert.

"Ty, let her go," Logan says, his voice timid.

"Shut up." Ty never looks away from me and he pulls me even closer, though my feet drag, making me stumble. I so don't want to be close to this guy. He gives me the creeps. "Stop pretending you're a good little girl, Fable. You know all about getting on your knees and sucking cock, am I right?"

His words offend the hell out of me and I part my lips, ready to read him the riot act, when all of a sudden, all the hairs on my body are standing on end. I'm hyperaware someone is behind me. I can feel his warmth, his strength. Smell him. Clean and fresh and so deliciously . . . Drew.

"Let her go, Ty, before I break every fucking bone in your body." His voice is low, menacing. I wouldn't fuck with him if he sounded like that to me. Anger makes his deep voice vibrate and a shiver slithers down my spine. "Show the lady some respect."

Ty releases me with a little shove. Shaking his head, he laughs, though he doesn't sound amused. Pissed is more like it. "Like this whore is a lady. And since when the hell do you care about chicks, Callahan? I always wondered if you preferred dick."

"Don't be an asshole," Logan starts, and Ty glares at him.

I inhale on a sharp breath, my entire body tingling when Drew settles his hand low on my back so he can guide me out of his way.

And lunges straight toward Ty.

"Drew, no!" I shout as I leap back from the fray. One second everyone is having a good time, the next there's a damn riot.

All the guys run toward Drew and Ty, who are both struggling to get that first punch in. I grab hold of a belt loop on Drew's jeans and tug, screaming at him to stop, and finally he glances up, his beautiful—and wild—blue eyes meeting mine.

"Stop!" I repeat, desperate to keep my voice calm. "Please. Before you get in trouble."

He pushes Ty away from him and stands, wiping the corner of his mouth with the back of his hand. His gaze locks on me, anger radiating from him in tangible waves, and I swallow hard, trying my best to keep my composure.

But damn, Drew Callahan is hot when he's mad.

"He called you a whore," he mutters, the fury in his eyes igniting to full-on flame. I don't think I've ever seen him this angry.

"Lots of guys call me a whore," I say, my cheeks heating

MONICA MURPHY

with embarrassment. It's true and I hate it, but I've made my own whorish bed and on occasion, I have to lie in it.

"I won't fucking stand for it, Fable." Hearing him say my name sends pleasure washing through me, leaving me weak-kneed. I've missed him so much and to have him here, standing in front of me, despite the crappy circumstances, fills me with so much happiness tears threaten to spring.

I blink them back, feeling infinitely stupid.

"I don't need a knight in shining armor." Funny, that's the second reference tonight to noble knights. And I'm lying. I do need someone to come and rescue me. And I still want it to be him.

Drew.

"Right. Of course you don't. You're stronger than the rest of us, right? Sure as hell stronger than me." He turns away and leaves me without another word. I stare, gaping at his retreating back, wondering what the hell provoked that comment. What did I do to deserve his anger? Isn't *he* the one who ditched *me*?

I refuse to feel guilty. I refuse to chase after him and ask him why. Ask him if he's okay. Ask him if he's still talking to that horrendous bitch who fucked up his head so thoroughly.

Furious, I grab my empty tray and gather beer bottles, stacking them until they're rolling back and forth, clanking against one another. Jen finally enters the room, oblivious to the ruckus that just played out only minutes earlier, and I smile in relief when she approaches.

"Why is it so quiet in here?" she asks.

"A couple of them almost got into a fight." I decided not to mention that the fight was about me.

Jen rolls her eyes and starts to help me clear the tables. "Figures. Get a bunch of testosterone-laden men in close proximity and watch them beat their chests until they prove who's the mightiest of them all."

I don't answer. I continue to clean up and then stalk out of the room toward the bar, where I dump everything in the trash, the bottles again clanking together with an immensely satisfying sound. Irritation makes me want growl at anyone who so much as looks in my direction.

Shit! I'm dying for a smoke.

"What's your problem?" T appears out of nowhere, startling me.

"Uh . . ." I don't know what to say. Don't want to bitch for fear of looking like I can't handle my job. Don't want to tell her what happened, either, since she might ask me why they were fighting and how I became involved.

So instead, I shrug. "Men suck."

Well. That's close enough to the truth.

Her expression changes to pure sympathy. "Yeah, they do. Listen. Go cool off for a few. You look ready to blow a gasket."

"But I just took a break—"

"I'll cover for you. You've got five minutes." T smiles, pats my arm, and heads for the private party room.

And I dart outside for that much needed smoke.

CHAPTER 5

None of your scars can make me love you less.
—Unknown

Drew

She's gone. One minute she's in the same fucking room as me, breathing the same air, and then Ty Webster has to act like a disgusting pig and insult her. The girl I love. The girl who I haven't been with in so long, just seeing her steals my breath and hurts my heart.

So I did what any guy would've done to defend his girl. I went after Ty. Was ready to beat the shit out of him, too, until all my teammates came at us to break us up. And Fable. Staring at me, grabbing me and trying to pull me off of him. I let her. I looked her right in the eyes and listened to her soft pleas. I left Ty alone all for her.

I would've also kicked his ass for her. Even though she's not really my girl anymore.

And whose fault is that?

"Dude, you need to go apologize to Ty." Logan is in my face, looking a little more sober. I think the argument sobered up a lot of us. "I can't have my friends fighting on my birthday."

"Tell him to apologize to Fable and then we'll talk." I shake my head, my earlier buzz gone, gone, gone. Which sucks, because it helped me forget, even for a little while.

But then she had to walk into the room. Beautiful and sexy, and everything I've ever wanted. Something was a little off about her appearance, though. She looked like my Fable, yet . . . she didn't.

"Who the hell is Fable?" Logan frowns.

"The waitress he called a whore." I can barely get the word out I'm so pissed.

Logan sighs. "You know how he is. Chicks don't mean shit to him."

"Yeah, well, he needs to learn some respect." Before I'm tempted to go back and finish what I started with Ty, I leave the room and head down the narrow hall, where I spot a door that leads outside to the back of the restaurant. I need to cool off. Get my head back together. Maybe just flat-out bail.

I'm sure no one wants me around anymore. I tried to start a fight with one of my teammates over a girl they all consider a whore, and that kills me. Bros before hos, and all that other bullshit.

No matter that we're not really together anymore, Fable will always come first.

I push open the door and find myself in a narrow alley. The unmistakable scent of cigarette smoke lingers in the air and I glance to my right to find her. Fable. Sitting on the edge of an overturned giant plastic crate, puffing away on a cancer stick like it's her last salvation.

"Smoking kills, you know." I said that to her the night of the country club dinner. The night I first kissed her, first learned her taste, how she felt beneath my hands, the breathy little sounds she makes when she's becoming aroused.

She sends me a withering stare, accompanied by an exhale of smoke in my direction. "Then leave so you don't have to breathe my cancerous air."

I'm rooted to the spot. Afraid to approach her for fear she'll tell me to fuck off, which I deserve. "I'm glad I found you. I wanted to talk to you."

"Really?" She arches a brow, her cigarette dangling from her fingers. "What more could you have to say? I mean, I got your message pretty loud and clear after I didn't hear from you."

"You're right. It was a dick move. I totally deserve your anger." I take a deep breath. "Listen, I know what I did was wrong. I shouldn't have walked away from you."

"You didn't just walk away. You stayed away for over two months. Probably would've been longer, too, if you hadn't seen me tonight, right? Were you just going to avoid me forever?" She bends over and stubs the cigarette out in the tray that's sitting at her feet.

I stare at Fable, overcome with having her in front of me after not being near her for so long. She's beautiful, pissed at me, and so . . . *God*. I don't even know what to think. Seeing her again is like having a million electric shocks jolting through my veins, both paralyzing me and goading me into action. I'm . . . overcome.

All I know is I need her. Now more than ever. "I don't know what I was going to do," I finally say.

"Typical. I feel like a doll. Like a stupid, pretty doll no one cares about, forgotten on a shelf. Every once in a while, you

SECOND CHANCE BOYFRIEND

or whoever else wants to take me down from the shelf and play with me for a bit. Just enough to get my hopes up and make me believe someone really cares about me. Then I'm forgotten again. Like I don't even exist." She tosses her head back and gazes up at the dark sky. "My mom was pretty dead on when she named me Fable, wasn't she? I don't feel real to anyone."

"You're real to me," I whisper. So damn real, it hurts not to touch her.

I want her in my arms so bad it's killing me.

She stands and crosses her arms in front of her chest, plumping up her breasts in the sexy-as-hell black bra that I can see through the thin white lace shirt she has on. The outfit kills me. I want to both tear it off of her and throw a coat over her shoulders so no other guy can see her like this. "I can't do this, Drew. I can't pretend like seeing you after so long is no big deal when really my heart is cracking in two." A laugh escapes her, though it lacks humor. "I think it's best if we stay away from each other. Having you in front of me hurts too much."

My heart bottoms out. Completely. I can't believe she's saying this. Fighting the panic that threatens to sweep me under, I step closer to her. "Fable . . ."

She steps back, looking scared, as if she has nowhere to go, and that makes me feel like shit. "You should go."

I take another step toward her, and she takes another one back, bumping against the wall behind her. She's trapped, she knows it, and all I can think is thank God she can't run away from me. "You don't want me to leave."

"Yes, I do." She nods, her expression firm, but her voice is weak.

61

I move in so close I invade her personal space. Her warmth, her scent wraps around me, intoxicating me, and I brace my hands on the wall above her head, my arms bracketing her. I've got her completely caged in, and as I gaze down at her pretty, angry upturned face, all I can think is how much I want to kiss her and smudge that bright red lipstick all to hell. "How late do you work?" I ask, my voice low, my thoughts . . . dirty. I want to get her home. Naked. In my bed. Impossible considering how I've ruined this fragile thing between us, but I have hopes I can turn everything around.

The trembling in her body is a clue she's not over me. The way she's looking at me with all that pent-up longing in her gaze tells me I still have a chance.

"Too late to meet with you after." Reaching out, she pushes at my chest, her slender hands resting on my front, and I hiss in a breath as if she's burned me.

But *shit*! It feels like she has. Having her hands on me again after so long, it's as if she's branding me. Making her claim with just a touch.

She has no idea I've belonged to only her for months.

Without thought I lean in, my lips going for hers, but she turns her head at the last second and I end up kissing her cheek instead. She's quivering, little shuddering breaths escape from her parted lips, and I close my eyes, desperate to calm the pounding of my heart as I nuzzle the side of her face. "I really fucked up, didn't I?" I whisper against her skin.

Fable nods, draws in a deep breath as her hands drop away from my chest. "You did."

"Tell me what I can do to make it up to you." I need to know. I can't let her think this is over between us.

She still keeps her face averted, as if she's afraid to look me in the eyes. "It's too late. There's nothing you can do. It's o-over between us."

I remove my hand from the wall to cup her cheek, forcing her to look at me. Those big, scared eyes meet mine and for a moment I'm lost. It's as if we're back in time and at my parents' guesthouse when we were about to embark on something big. Something serious. I had this girl in the palm of my hand and she had me. But I was such a chickenshit, I let her slip right out of my grip, and now look at her.

She's . . . different. Her entire life has changed in a matter of weeks. And I had nothing to do with it. She's moved on, while I'm still stuck.

The realization is staggering.

"I need to get back to work," she whispers. "You should go back to your friends."

I stroke her face, let my fingers trace the delicate line of her jaw. She closes her eyes. I notice the subtle movement of her throat as she swallows and I dip my head, this time making that connection I so desperately want. My mouth on hers, breathing her breath, tasting her lips, the sweet, mysterious depths within. She parts her lips immediately and I take advantage, slipping my tongue inside, tangling it with hers.

A groan escapes me and she breaks the kiss first, our eyes opening at the same time, and we stare at each other without saying a word, her gaze dropping to my mouth again. I know what she wants.

I want it, too.

We can't resist each other. This one moment is proof. I

need to do something, say something to continue this connection.

I need her. And she needs me. I know it.

"Fable. Everything okay?"

We both turn our heads to see some guy standing a few feet away, big and intimidating, dressed all in black, his gaze sharp as it lingers on me. He looks like he wants to kick my ass.

Great. After his interruption, the feeling's mutual.

"I'm fine. Just getting back to work." She shoves at me and I step back, letting her escape. Just like that.

Fable doesn't look at me as she heads into the restaurant. Doesn't say a word to me or the guy and we're left outside alone, glaring at each other, sizing each other up. He's older, at least in his late twenties, and big.

But I'm taller. And broader. I could take him if I had to.

That I'm thinking like this is totally ridiculous.

"Who the hell are you?" he asks, his voice quiet but edged with steel.

"I could ask you the same question," I toss back.

He crosses his arms in front of him. "I'm her boss."

Shit! I don't want to screw up anything at her job. This place is nice, way nicer than La Salle's, and I bet she likes working here a lot more. Bet she makes more money, too. "I'm her boyfriend."

He lifts his brows, a little chuckle escaping him. "Really? Funny, she didn't mention you when we were together last night."

I'm so fucking shocked by what the asshole says that by the time I find my voice, he's gone.

Fable

I hurry back to the private party room, thankful Drew doesn't follow me. Even more thankful Colin doesn't follow me either. I wish I could sneak off to the bathroom to gather my thoughts, take a deep breath, something, *anything,* but I need to get back and help Jen. It's not fair, leaving T in there helping out when she should be supervising the restaurant.

But I can't stop shaking. Breathing deep, I can smell him. Drew's familiar clean scent clings to my skin and my clothes. I press my lips together, run my tongue over them.

God, I can still taste him. He's all over me and I don't know if I can stand it. The words he said, how my body reacted when he touched me, when he kissed me . . .

I want him. But I don't. He's put me through hell and back and with one glimpse of him and a few whispered words, I'm lost.

Drew Callahan is my absolute weakness. Like a drug I can't get enough of. He's my addiction and if I'm being honest with myself, I'm not looking to kick that particular habit anytime soon.

Slipping inside the room, I see Jen standing in the corner closest to the door by herself. T must've left, and I immediately feel like crap.

"Are you okay?" she asks me as I approach.

Jen's low-spoken question pulls me out of my Drew-addled head and I offer her a reassuring smile. "I'm fine. Just . . . tired."

"The guys are leaving." She studies me, her dark gaze careful. "I heard about what they said. They're assholes, Fable. Don't let them bother you."

Great. So they were still talking about how much of a slut I am. In front of my new co-worker and potential friend. "Maybe what they said is true." I square my shoulders and stiffen my spine. Trying for defiant and probably failing miserably.

"I don't care." Jen shrugs. "Who am I to judge?"

I think I could like this girl. Could possibly consider her a friend, and I don't remember the last time I had a close female friend.

We watch as the guys stroll out of the room, the majority of them offering us leering stares as they pass. The birthday boy is the only one who shoots us a semi-apologetic look when he approaches, then slaps a one-hundred-dollar bill into my palm and another one in Jen's simultaneously.

Well. That made the insufferable evening a little more worth it. Just barely.

"We're continuing the party elsewhere. This place has turned into a drag." Ty stops directly in front of me, blowing his beer breath in my face. I wrinkle my nose in disgust. "Wanna come with us? Bring your friend? We'll show you both a good time, I promise."

"Screw off, jackass," Jen mutters, startling Ty.

And me.

Grinning, I tilt my head toward her. "You heard the lady. See ya later."

He glares at us for a long, quiet moment, his nostrils flaring before he flees the room, leaving us completely alone.

"What a jerk!" Jen says, shaking her head. "I can't believe he's so . . ."

"Blatant? Rude?"

"All that, wrapped up in disgusting slimeball. What a waste."

"What do you mean?" I start cleaning up the room, as does Jen.

"He's not bad-looking. A complete waste of a handsome face." She shrugs. "The bigger assholes are usually the really good-looking ones, I've noticed."

She has a valid point.

Colin strides into the room, his gaze alighting on me as if he's been searching for me for days. "Who's the guy you were talking to?"

I'm taken aback by his question, the tone of his voice. "What does it matter?" I ask warily.

Jen's watching us; I can see her out of the corner of my eye. I really don't want to be having this conversation with her as a witness.

"Jen, could you give us a few minutes of privacy? Why don't you help out in the bar for a bit?" Colin suggests, his gaze never leaving mine.

She leaves without a word, and we're alone. The noise from the restaurant diminishes and I shift on my feet, waiting for the axe to fall. He's going to fire me. And on the very day I finally felt comfortable enough to give notice at La Salle's.

I bet I could beg for my old job back if I had to.

"I don't like having boyfriends sniffing around my restaurant staff in a proprietary manner," Colin says.

His words startle the crap out of me. "Boyfriends? Who are you talking about?"

"The guy I caught you with outside. He told me he's your boyfriend."

My lips part but nothing comes out. I'm still so disgusted by what Ty said to me and Jen, I thought at first Colin was talking about *him*. But he was referring to finding Drew and me together outside. Drew's arms around me, holding me close, kissing me. "Not anymore," I finally say because as far as I'm concerned, we're not together. We never really were.

But Drew said he was my boyfriend? This . . . baffles me.

"Well, maybe you should explain that to him. Last I saw, he was still hanging around outside. Almost like he's waiting for you." The disgust on Colin's face is clear. He doesn't want to deal with my personal problems lingering around his business. Not that I can blame him.

I feel like an absolute screw-up.

"I'm sorry. Do you mind if I go see if he's still around? I can tell him to leave." Such a weak excuse. I just want to catch a glimpse of him again.

"By all means, get rid of him." Colin waves a hand toward the door.

I start to go but he stops me, grabbing hold of my arm before I exit the room. "If this becomes a problem, *you* become a problem. You do realize this, right?"

I nod, embarrassment making me want to run. But I face him head-on, my gaze meeting his. I want him to know I'm not about to risk my job over a guy. They're so not worth it. "I understand. I'm sorry. It won't happen again."

"Better not." His voice gentles, as does his touch, and he slowly releases his hold on my arm. "I like you, Fable. I don't want to have to lose you because of your personal problems."

Ouch. His honesty hurts, but I need to face up to the fact that I caused some trouble tonight. The fight happened because of me. Yeah, the guys had been drunk, but the arguing all stemmed from me. My slutty—and not-so-slutty—past is catching up to me and messing with my future.

I hurry down the narrow hall that leads to the back door and push it open, coming out into the alley to find myself alone.

Drew is gone.

Glancing toward the parking lot, I see him with the rest of the jerks. For whatever stupid reason, I feel betrayed. He doesn't really like those guys. Never felt as if he fit in—he admitted that to me during our one week together.

So what's he doing? Why is he with them? I watch in disbelief as he climbs into the car of one of the other guys, leaving his truck in the parking lot. He's actually . . . going with them. I'm stunned.

Irritated.

Without thought I stalk back into the restaurant, seeking out Colin. I find him in the front, at the hostess station, and I go to him, tapping him on the shoulder so he turns around to face me.

"The problem's been taken care of," I say with more finality than I actually feel. I'm lying to Colin since I didn't talk to Drew, but I'm not too far off base. No way is Drew coming back here to bug me.

I won't let him.

"You talked to him." He raises a skeptical brow.

I nod. "Sure did. Told him not to bother coming back. That we don't want any trouble."

Colin is contemplating me. Looking at me like I'm completely full of shit. Which I am. "He comes back here, I'm going to be mad. At you and him."

"I know." I swallow hard.

"I don't like trouble at my restaurant. I don't like my employees dating each other, and I don't like jealous boyfriends and girlfriends lingering around, waiting to catch their significant others in a bad position. I'm sick of that crap. You need to walk the straight and narrow, Fable, if you're going to work here. I know I can't tell you what to do on your personal time, but your business time? My time? I expect you to adhere to my rules."

What a drill sergeant. His words and his attitude surprise me. He usually seems so laid back. "I get it. I'm sorry. It won't happen again."

Colin nods and without another word, leaves me where I'm standing. I can almost guarantee it's never going to happen again because I'm so pissed at Drew, I don't want to see him ever again.

He left with those guys. He's off fucking around and doing whatever crazy, stupid thing a bunch of oversexed, drunken jocks do on a Saturday night. Probably going to drink and flirt and mess around just like all the rest of them.

Tears sting my eyes and I blink them away. I don't own him. I rejected him outright only moments before. Gave him a free pass to do whatever the hell he wants.

So why am I so upset? Why do I feel like he somehow still belongs to me?

CHAPTER 6

Don't give up just because things are hard.
—Fable Maguire

Drew

They brought me to a strip club that's on the outskirts of town, the building nondescript and small, the sign flashy and bright in the otherwise dark, cold night. Gold Diggers is what the place is called. I've heard of it before but have never been there.

Usually I'd protest, bail on them, whatever. But when Jace asked if I wanted to ride with him here, I readily agreed. Didn't help that I was still blown away by what Fable's fucking boss said to me.

Her boss. She's messing around with her boss. I can't believe it. The devastation that still lingers within me is strong. Like bring-me-to-my-knees powerful. I don't know what to think. I *can't* think. It hurts too damn much.

So I left. Running away from my problems as per my usual mode. Funny thing is, this time I've surrounded myself with other people. Guys I know and would like to consider my friends. I wonder if my shrink would be proud of me for at least this part of my denial.

I'm definitely a little drunker than I was when we first arrived, and I'm still angry—at Ty for insulting Fable. At Fable for pushing me away. I can't win. Avoiding her led me straight to her. It was inevitable that we'd see each other again. But how could I have prepared myself for the shock of seeing her there, looking so beautiful? It made me so angry, believing she's still mine when she's already moved on.

Pain lances through me and I let it, soaking the near physical emotion the same way my body is soaking up the alcohol. I hate letting my emotions control me so completely. I'm usually numb to this sort of thing. Enduring what I went through in my past made it easy for me to throw up barriers and pretend everything was fine—or more like nothing mattered.

She matters, though. Or at least, she did.

So I'm sulking like a baby as I watch half-naked women gyrate on a stage, their bodies on blatant display, their expressions bored, looking like they've done this sort of thing a million times and they hate it, which they probably do. The club is packed, we're probably the youngest guys there, and the beer is flowing.

Straight down my throat, as fast as I can drink it.

"Having fun?" Logan nudges me, the leer on his face wobbly. He's drunker than I am—fitting, since he's the one we're celebrating. May as well get shitfaced like him, right? I've got nothing to lose and nothing but sorrows to drown.

Woe is me. I've turned into the worst sort of broken record.

I shrug. "The beer's good."

Logan laughs. "The beer is shit. The women are fine. They all have great racks." He tips his head toward a dark-skinned girl dancing not twenty feet away from where we sit. "Ty's arranging a lap dance for me with her."

I scowl. Hearing Ty's name irritates me. We've sat on opposite ends of the group the entire time, no interaction between us whatsoever. Probably best, considering if he comes near me again, I might hit him.

And keep on hitting him until he's bloody and broken. Only then would I feel an ounce of satisfaction. Though why I keep wanting to defend Fable when she's out fucking around with another guy while I mourn the loss of her, I don't know.

Fuck.

"I'm sure he could arrange a lap dance for you, too," Logan continues.

"Hell, no. I don't want one." I shake my head and down the rest of my beer in one swallow. I feel hot. My head is spinning. I'm definitely losing control and for once, I don't really care.

"That you say you don't want one only makes me want to get you one even more."

I turn to see Ty standing there, beer in hand, smirk in place. I want to slap that shitty look off his face but I remain calm. Nonchalant. "Why would you want to waste your money on a lap dance for me? Get one for yourself."

Ty laughs. "I want to see you squirm, Callahan. I know this isn't your scene. Hell, I'm surprised you're here with us. I'm even more surprised at how you tried to kick my ass over a stupid girl."

I say nothing. I'm surprised, too, but I'm not going to let on that I am.

"You know Fable? Been with her or something?" Ty

shakes his head. "I took her out once, a long time ago. It was mostly forgettable."

If he so much as goes into detail about their supposedly forgettable date, I'll bash his face in.

"I don't know her that well," I bite out, every word sharp because I'm a complete liar. "But you don't disrespect women, Ty. It's an asshole thing to do."

"I've never said I was anything *but* an asshole." The smirk on Ty's face slowly disappears. "That's why I already got you that lap dance, buddy. With a pretty little blonde who reminded me of our mutual friend." He flicks his head and I turn around.

"Hi." She smiles at me, all bright and fake, and I'm momentarily taken aback. She does eerily resemble Fable at first glance, much like my fake classmate Fable, but then I realize she's nothing like the girl I'm in love with.

This fake Fable is taller and skinnier, with shorter hair and bad skin. Her nails are long and painted neon pink. She tosses her hair behind her shoulder and thrusts her chest out, her hard nipples poking against the thin fabric of her neon-pink bikini top.

Ty plants his hand in the middle of my back and shoves me toward her. "Aren't you going to greet your present? You need to respect women and all that other shit you talk about, right?"

Asshole. "You don't have to do this," I tell her, ignoring Ty's snicker. I glance around, looking for Logan, but he's long gone. Probably off getting his own dance.

The girl frowns. "He paid me to do it. It's my job."

"Just keep the money," I tell her, reaching out to grab her

arm so I can take her somewhere else. Somewhere we can pretend this is happening instead of putting on a show for everyone.

She shakes her head, touching my chest with her free hand. "Don't you like me?"

I study her, my vision blurry. If I squint, she could almost pass for Fable. She strokes my forearm, her light touch sending a shiver through me. "Come on," she murmurs, her voice low.

Seductive.

No way should I do this, but I let her lead me over to a chair and she pushes my chest so I have no choice but to sit. I fall into the chair heavily, my head spinning, and the music starts as the woman on the stage begins to move.

Just like the woman in front of me.

For a moment, I let my imagination run away from me. Instead of a stranger, it's Fable in front of me. Dancing for me, so beautiful as she moves, her lips curved in a seductive smile, her eyes glowing as she watches me. I stare back, my mouth going dry, my skin tight and hot . . .

I hear Ty's unmistakable laugh, snapping me back to reality.

The girl smiles at me, her hands on my shoulders, her barely covered breasts in my face as she twists and turns to the beat of the music. Her hips roll and thrust toward me as she reaches behind her back, deftly undoing both straps on her bikini top so it falls from her chest and lands on the floor.

She has small breasts and big nipples, nothing like Fable's. Of course she's nothing like her. I need to stop comparing all women to her. It's a mistake. Hell, it's a sickness. One I need

75

to cure myself of and quickly, since she already has someone else.

The realization makes me almost sick to my stomach.

"Put your tits in his face!" Ty yells and she tosses her hair and laughs, thrusting her chest directly in my face as Ty commanded, her skin brushing against mine. I smell sweat, cheap perfume, and alcohol emanating from her pores and I wrinkle my nose.

This girl is nothing like mine. She's nothing like any sort of girl I'd ever be interested in.

"You're hot," the dancer whispers and I tilt my head back, our gazes locking. "Want to hook up after I get off work? My shift ends in an hour."

I slowly shake my head. "I don't think so." That she solicits me so easily makes me think this isn't her first time doing this sort of thing.

She pouts. "I bet you have a girlfriend, right? All the quiet, good-looking ones do."

"Yeah, I have a girlfriend." A fake one, one I lost claim to months ago. But it's easier to agree than to explain myself.

Her pout turns into a deep frown. "I'm sure your friend who bought you the dance is available, huh? I'm sure most girls wouldn't tolerate his crap for long."

The girl is perceptive. She's danced for me for three minutes tops and has both of us all figured out. "He's definitely available."

She grimaces. "Of course he is."

The song ends, as does my dance, and she steps away from me, a little smile curving her lips. I never noticed until now that her lipstick color matches the neon pink of her bikini and fingernails. She glows in the black lights, giving her a weird and unnatural effect. "You're quite the gentleman." She bends over and snatches her bikini top from the floor. "Take that as a compliment."

"Thanks," I say weakly, immobile in my chair. My head is still spinning. I drank way too much and I'm almost afraid to stand. I might collapse like an idiot. "For the dance and the compliment."

Flashing me a smile, she wiggles her fingers at me, then heads over to Ty. He immediately grabs her like she's his piece of property. His hands are sprawled across her back and butt as he hauls her close into him. She hasn't even put her top back on yet and he's got his hands all over her, his mouth at her ear. She shoves at his chest and I'm tempted to go and tell her to get away from him, but then I hear her giggle and I know she likes it.

Likes him.

Disgusted with myself, I stand and glance around the room, waiting for the spinning to ease. It's so dark and there are so many guys in the place, I can't make out who's who. No way could I find my friends in this crowd. I need to get the hell out of here. I need to get home, but I'm far from my apartment complex, which is clear on the other side of town. My truck is at the restaurant where Fable works.

I'm freaking stranded.

Frowning, I pull my cell out of my pocket and study the dark screen. I could do it. I practically dare myself to type in the one word that might send her to me.

Or that word might make her run away. It should. I don't deserve her help.

Deciding to go for it before my balls shrivel up and retreat into my body forever, I tap out eleven letters, spelling a word that both makes me happy and haunts my thoughts.

Fable

My phone buzzes in my pocket just as I'm getting ready to clock out. It's late, the restaurant was packed till the last possible minute, and my feet are killing me.

I check my messages and audibly gasp at the one word that seems to fill the screen, daring me to ignore it.

Marshmallow

Anger surges within me. How dare he use that word? What the hell does he want? Does he need me to rescue him yet again? I can't believe his audacity.

But then the worry kicks in, and the anger subsides. What if he's in trouble? He's with those jerk assholes he doesn't really like and probably shouldn't trust. What if they did something to him and he's lying in a heap on the side of the road, bleeding to death?

God, my drama-filled brain is on overdrive tonight.

Furious at my concern, I hurriedly type in a response to him and hit send before I can second-guess myself.

Where the hell are you?

He answers within seconds.

Gold Diggers.

Ugh! He's asking me to rescue him from a strip club? I want to kill him.

Like I'm driving all the way out there. I don't even have a car.

Seconds later, he responds again.

I left my truck at the restaurant.

Frowning, I study the words he just sent me. I can't do this. I shouldn't. Rescuing him gives me hope, and I should feel hopeless when it comes to Drew. He's not worth all the heartache and drama.

Is he?

No key though, I finally type, feeling sorta cheery. How can I drive his truck with no key?

"You need a ride?"

I glance up to find Colin standing in front of me, his handsome face filled with concern. My phone beeps and I read Drew's message, a detailed description of the exact location where the spare key is hidden on his truck.

Tempting me more and more to go rescue him, no matter how stupid I know the idea is.

"Fable?"

"Yeah, um, thanks for the ride, but I don't need one." I smile, realizing I need Colin to leave before I do if I don't want him to see me drive off in Drew's truck.

Not that he'd know it was Drew's truck, but Colin is a smart guy. He can put two and two together real easy.

"Are you sure?" He reaches out and touches me, his fingers drifting across my arm, and I don't react. I might've yesterday. Hell, I might've about four hours ago, before Drew walked back into my life so easily, but now there's nothing.

Absolutely nothing.

Nodding, I offer him a bigger smile. "Really. I have a ride. But I appreciate the offer."

"All right. Jen's catching a ride home with me, so we'll both see you tomorrow?"

My first Sunday working at the restaurant. My shift starts

79

in the mid-afternoon and I'll get off at a decent time, too, since I'm only scheduled for four hours. I'm sort of excited about it. Owen and I already have plans. Either breakfast, if I can get his lazy ass out of bed, or a late dinner after I get off work. Maybe even a movie if we're feeling ambitious.

I feel like treating my brother to something special. He deserves it. I haven't been around much and neither has Mom. He's drifting, and I need to reconnect with him. No fourteen-year-old should drift, especially my own brother.

"See you tomorrow," I say as I watch Colin leave with Jen by his side. I wonder if they're a couple. And if they are, why he would flirt with me. Why would he flirt with anyone? I don't understand the dynamics there.

I don't understand the dynamics between Drew and me either, so who am I to judge?

I pull into the parking lot of Gold Diggers fifteen minutes later, driving around to the side of the building, where I find Drew leaning against the wall. His upper body is slouched forward, his hands nestled deep in his jeans pockets, and his head is bent. It looks like he didn't even hear the truck pull up.

Rolling down the passenger-side window, I whistle low and he glances up, his gaze meeting mine.

"Need a ride?" I ask, trying my best to keep my voice even, but I hear the slight waver. Did he?

I hope not.

Pushing away from the building, he saunters over to the truck and leans in through the open window, his arms propped on the ledge. "So you found the key."

"I told you I did." I'd texted him when I left work that I was on my way. Did he already forget or what?

Sniffing the air, I catch the distinct scent of beer. He's been drinking. And he's always more of a handful when he's been drinking. Not necessarily in a bad way, though. Not like the guys my mom always ends up dating. Those types are mean and sometimes use their hands to get their point across.

"Thanks for coming to get me." He pushes away from the truck and pulls on the handle, opening the door so he can climb inside. Settling into the passenger seat, he rolls up the window, pulls the seat belt on and clicks it into place, then leans back against the seat, his eyes closing. "I appreciate it."

That's it? That's all I get? No *oh my God, you're my hero, Fable* or professions of undying love? Not that I expected the last one, but holy hell, we go from not talking to or seeing each other for over two months to all sorts of conflicting interaction with each other in the span of a few hours.

I don't know if I can take this, especially when he's acting like our reunion is no big deal.

"Need directions to my place?" he asks when I pull out of the parking lot.

"Um, I thought I could go straight to my house." I don't want to take him to his place. Then how would I get home?

"I can't drive. I'm all sorts of fucked up."

In more ways than one, I want to tell him, but I keep my lips shut. "So what? If I take you home, who's going to take *me* home?"

"Call your boyfriend." He shrugs, but the venom in his words is clear.

"My boyfriend?" I stop at a red light and turn to look at

him. His eyes are open and he's watching me, his expression wary. "Who are you talking about?"

"The guy who interrupted us earlier. Your fucking boss, Fable. Or should I say the boss you're fucking?"

Oh. My. God. Where the hell did he get that idea? "I should pull over right now and dump you on the side of the road."

"Go for it. I'll call the cops and say you stole my truck."

Who is this guy? I give him my best, meanest stare, the one that scares the crap out of Owen every time I use it on him. "You wouldn't dare."

He glares at me right back. "Try me."

The light turns green and I gun the engine, my foot pressing the gas pedal so hard we both lurch forward in our seat. The truck takes off quickly, the tires squealing against the asphalt, making me wince. Drew is muttering curses under his breath, but I don't care. I ignore him, let the power of the truck's engine propel me down the road, erasing my thoughts until all I feel is the speed.

But I can't control my mind, no matter how much I want to. It's awhirl with questions. Why did he think Colin and I were together? Why would Drew text me to come get him if he thought that was the case? Why was he at the strip club? Did he have his hands all over a stripper? I swear I can smell cheap perfume lingering on his clothes. The idea that he was with another girl, had his hands on some stupid stripper even momentarily, fills me with so much rage, my foot presses on the gas pedal even harder.

"Are you trying to get us into a wreck?"

His quiet voice pierces my thoughts, reminding me I'm

driving like a reckless jackass, and I ease up on the gas, evening out to a more moderate speed. "Sorry," I murmur, embarrassed that I'm acting the fool.

My usual mode of operation when I'm in Drew's presence.

We're silent the rest of the drive, with the exception of Drew telling me where to turn to get to his apartment. The neighborhoods gets nicer and nicer the farther and farther I drive. I'm filled with envy as I take in the trees that line the street, the perfectly manicured lawns with bright bursts of colorful flowers, even in the middle of winter. Landscapers maintain all of the lawns on this side of town and they are utter perfection.

Unlike the grass and yards in my neighborhood, which are uneven and brown in spots. No pretty flowers in sight where I live. We mostly have overgrown shrubs at my apartment complex. They hide all the flaws well.

"Nice place," I say once I pull into the parking spot he directs me to. It's covered, of course. And the complex is gated, keeping the riffraff out. Like me. I'm considered riffraff, I'm sure.

"Do you need to call your boyfriend to pick you up?" he asks, his voice low. Downright menacing.

I shut off the engine and turn to him, hoping my expression is as incredulous as I feel. "I don't have a boyfriend."

He raises his brows. "So the guy who basically told me to take a hike isn't your boyfriend."

"He's not. He's my boss. That's it." I slowly shake my head, pissed that I even have to explain myself.

"Why would he say he was with you last night, then?"

I'm gaping. I can't believe what Drew just said. *"What?"*

"That's what he told me. He asked who I was and I told him I was your . . . boyfriend. Then he laughed and said something like, where the hell was I since he was with *you* last night." Drew's mouth tightens into a flat, thin line. "Were you with him?"

God, I was. It sounds so bad, too. I don't want to admit the truth, but I can't lie to Drew. There shouldn't be any more lies between us. Honesty needs to be our only policy. "Yes," I admit, my voice small. I don't want to tell him Colin took me to a salon and paid for my makeover, a makeover Drew doesn't even seem to notice.

He looks away from me, blowing out a harsh breath. His jaw is tight, I see a slight tic in it, and I know he's beyond pissed. "Just admit it, Fable. You've moved on. I can't blame you. I fucked this all up by not responding to you. I asked for this."

"Asked for what? I'm not with my boss, not in the way you think. We're definitely not together."

He looks at me again. "You're not?"

"No," I say, slowly shaking my head. "We're not. He's my *boss*. I wouldn't screw around with my boss."

Drew says nothing, but his silence fills up the truck's cab just the same as an endless stream of words would.

"Listen, you left me, remember? I'm finally getting on with my life, moving on from you, and then you go and text me that stupid, *stupid* code word. You have a lot of nerve, you know. I don't know why I bothered coming out here to rescue you. Accusing me of being with someone else like a complete jealous jerk." I need to call him out on his shit so I can get to the truth. I need the truth. I've been in limbo waiting for him and hating him, loving him, wanting to kill him, wanting to save him, for way too long.

I'm done. He either needs to come clean with me and we can get to the bottom of this or we'll continue swimming in an endless circle that will both drive me crazy and exhilarate me, all at once.

"I didn't know what to think," he finally says. "What he said put thoughts in my head and fucked around with . . . everything."

"You have no right to accuse me of this crap." I take a deep breath. Drew may have jumped to conclusions, but I'm starting to think Colin didn't help matters by implying that something's going on between us. Which it's so not. "Who are you going to believe? Some guy you don't know or me?"

He lifts his lids, his gaze meeting mine. His eyes are bright, even in the dim light of the truck, and I wish I could lean into him. Touch him. Kiss him.

"You," he whispers. "I'm going to believe you."

CHAPTER 7

Do magic. Enter her heart without touching her.
—Unknown

Fable

I'm taken aback by Drew's admission, and all I can do is sit here and stare at him. I don't know what to say, how to react, anything. I think I'm still in shock that we're sitting in his truck, together. Alone. As if the past two months haven't happened and we're right back where we started.

But I know all of his secrets. Well, most of them. And they're horrible. He knows a few of mine, not that I have many. I was an open book for him from the start. My few remaining secrets aren't as life-altering as his. My mom is a drunken, jobless loser. My dad has never made contact with me my entire life. Drew already knows those facts about me.

Oh, and my brother is skipping class and smoking pot and there's not much I can do about it. Drew doesn't know much about Owen. Or about my own insecurities and fears, how they keep me trapped here in this going-nowhere life. How I feel like I have to take care of my little brother all the time because our mom sure as hell isn't doing it.

The only thing I can completely control is me and my re-action to my life. At this very moment, I can control only my reaction to Drew. So I sit here and wait. Wait for him to say something first, because I'm not speaking until he does. It's his turn to make the next move.

Despite the warning bells clanging in my head, I want him to make that first move.

"Fable, I . . ." He pauses and swallows hard. "I'm not sober enough to drive you home."

Disappointment courses through me. There went the first move. "I'll call a cab." Like I can afford it, but what the hell else am I supposed to do?

"No." He shakes his head. "I want you to stay with me. Tonight."

Everything inside me screams to run far, far away. There's also a tiny part of me that says I should stay. Crash out on his couch and wake up the next morning refreshed after spending the night in the same house with the one I love. We won't do anything. Maybe we'll talk. Maybe I'll get him to confess why he asked me to rescue him with that beautiful, tragic note, then refused to answer my texts or voice mails.

Yes, I still want an answer in regard to that particular fi-asco.

"I shouldn't," I whisper.

"Please." He clears his throat. "Nothing will happen. I promise."

I close my eyes, my thoughts and my wants conflicted. I'm at war with myself and I hate it. Maybe I want something to happen. Maybe I want to have outrageous, dirty, mind-blowing sex with Drew Callahan. But his words and his gentlemanly ways might overrule him. The guy is downright chivalrous.

I really don't want chivalry tonight. I want comfort. Passion. I crave what Drew can give me. Delicious hot kisses, unbelievable pleasure . . .

"We can talk." He reaches out and settles his hand on my arm. His palm is warm, his fingers slightly rough as they stroke my skin, and instantly my body reacts. I'm all tingly and my heart rate has kicked up. I think of how Colin touched me earlier and nothing happened.

I think of how Drew merely looks at me and I immediately want to shed my clothes and bare my very soul to him.

"Talk about what?"

"I need to tell you what's . . . what's going on." He squeezes my arm and I squeeze my eyes shut, overwhelmed with sensation. God, his touch feels so good. "I need to apologize for the shitty way I treated you."

An apology is a start in the positive direction. I might be fooling myself, but I want to hear what he has to say. I need an explanation. "Okay. I'd love to hear an apology from you."

"Are you going to make me say it now?"

"For the first one, yes." I nod.

"There's going to be more than one?"

I glance in his direction to see he's teasing me. And it's sort of cute, the way he's looking at me, the smile on his face. "Definitely," I say with another nod. "I want the first one now. Before we leave the truck."

He schools his expression, looking incredibly solemn and serious. "Fable, I'm sorry." He lifts my hand and brushes a kiss across my knuckles.

His mouth on my skin leaves me weak-kneed and I'm not even standing. The playful way he's acting doesn't help matters, either. I need to remember he's drunk. He's not in the right state of mind.

"Now, come inside with me. I won't try anything, I promise." He makes an X at the center of his chest with his index finger. "Scout's honor."

"Were you really a scout?"

"No." He smiles. "But you can trust me."

I know I can. I both want him to give me space so I can absorb everything that's happened tonight and want him all over me. I'm confused.

This is what he does to me every time we're together.

We get out of the truck and I follow him across the parking lot without protest. Let him guide me to his front door without a word, though I can feel his presence behind me. I inhale sharply when he sets his hand low on my back to steer me in the right direction.

He doesn't remove his hand until we get to the front door. It's as if he needs that connection.

I need it, too.

When he unlocks the door, he indicates for me to walk in first and I enter his quiet, dark apartment. He flicks on a light, revealing a room devoid of anything beyond a couch, a matching chair, and a flat-screen TV. There are no pictures, no knickknacks, no mess. Nothing beyond the basic essentials.

The room lacks warmth. It's as though no one real lives here. It reminds me of the Drew I first met. That version felt nothing, acted like nothing affected him. He'd been an emotionless shell of a human being.

I like to think that I changed him in a matter of days. That I taught him to feel. To open up and deal with his emotions, his wants, and his needs. That my influence taught him it might be okay to be human again.

Turning to face him, I study his expression. His eyes are bleary, his hair is mussed, and his cheeks are pale. He looks tired and a little loopy. Yet again, I want to touch him. Touch his bristly cheek, trace his expressive mouth with my finger . . .

"Do you want to talk?"

His question startles me. He doesn't look like he wants to talk. More like he probably wants to collapse in bed. "Do you?"

"There are things I should say to you, yeah. But I'm drunk and I'll probably mess it up somehow." His voice is soft and he runs his palm across his cheek, doing the very thing I wanted to do only moments before.

My hands literally itch to reach out and touch him.

"Maybe we should sleep on it first." I can't face everything yet. My mind is working on overtime and I need to quiet it. Plus, I'm scared about what he might say. What if I don't want to hear his explanations? What if he's only being kind tonight and wants to let me down gently?

But then I remember his jealousy over Colin. The way he looked at me. How he kissed me, how his arms felt around me.

Drew still wants me. I know it. And I still want him. Being with him tonight would most likely be a mistake. Am I strong enough to resist him?

Is he strong enough to resist me? The pull between us is there, like an invisible thread that draws us closer and closer when we're in the same room together.

"Can I sleep on your couch?" I wave my hand in the couch's direction. It's big and looks comfortable enough.

He shakes his head with a grimace. "No way. I'll take the couch. You can have my bed."

Oh, God. I can't take his bed. It'll smell like him. My imagination will run wild the moment I touch the mattress, the second my head hits his pillow. It's been too long since we've been together and having him so close, I want to launch myself at him and never, ever let go.

"I'd rather have the couch." My voice is shaky and I breathe deep, trying to control my emotions, but I'm ragged. Completely undone. A tear sneaks down my cheek and I sniff. I hate crying. I rarely do it.

"Fable." His deep voice is so low, it rumbles through me and I bend my head. I don't want him to see my useless tears. "Look at me."

I shake my head. "No."

He slips his fingers beneath my chin and tilts my face up so I have no choice but to look at him. His gaze is dark as he wipes away a tear from my cheek with his thumb. "You're crying."

I blink hard. "No, I'm not."

He strokes his thumb across my chin, his nail grazing the edge of my lower lip. "I hate that I've made you cry."

I close my eyes, the still-falling tears getting tangled up in my eyelashes. "I'm just . . . I don't know how to handle this anymore. You. Us."

"I'm sorry." He steps closer. I can feel his body heat burning into me. And then his mouth is at my forehead, his lips brushing my skin in a tentative kiss. "So sorry." Another kiss at my temple. "I didn't know what to say to you after I left. I

91

was ashamed of everything that happened, everything you witnessed. You deserve better." He kisses the tip of my nose.

Without thought I sling my arms around him, anchoring myself. He's big and warm and solid, and my heart eases at having him so close again. "I deserve *you*," I whisper. "When will you realize that?"

We're quiet for long, agonizing minutes. My forehead is pressed against his chin, my arms loose around his waist. He slips his arm around me so his hand settles at my hip. His other hand is in my hair, smoothing it back, tangling his fingers in the long strands, and I sigh at his gentle touch.

I never want this moment to end. I want to forget all our troubles and just focus on the two of us together.

"I don't deserve you," he finally says. "You accept me so easily, no matter how hard I push you away. You need to know I don't do it on purpose. It's just . . . the only way I know how to deal is to run."

His honesty breaks my heart.

"I'm learning, though, that running away doesn't solve my problems." He takes a deep breath. "I'm seeing someone. A psychologist. She's helping me a lot."

I chance looking up at him and our gazes clash. He's worried that somehow his admission might drive me away, I can tell. "That's good. Did someone arrange that for you?" Had he told his father anything? Or was he still keeping all his secrets?

"No, I sought her out myself. We've talked a lot about what happened. And about you."

"About me?" I'm shocked. After he left so easily, I figured he'd forgotten all about me.

"Definitely about you." He trails his fingers down my cheek and I release a shuddering breath. "You have no idea how important you are to me, do you?"

I slowly shake my head. "When you left, I figured we were finished. I thought you were over me."

"I could never be over you." Drew clamps his lips shut. I wonder if he wants to say something else.

I know I do. But I can't. I'm not going to be as quick to reveal my emotions to him again. Not after everything we've been through. I'm too scared.

So I go with an easy admission. One not too far from what he offered me. "I'm not over you either," I whisper.

Before I can say anything else, he yanks me closer and presses his mouth to mine. His lips are soft, damp, and very, very persistent. I open for him easily, our tongues sliding against each other, his low moan fueling me on. Fueling us both on.

Just like that, I'm lost.

Drew

Finally. I'm kissing her again, tasting her, holding her in my arms. It feels so good, so fucking right, having Fable with me. In my apartment, back in my life. I don't know what I did to deserve this gift, but I refuse to screw it up again.

I'm not letting her go. Ever. I need her too much. I love her too damn much.

I wanted to tell her that, too. I wrote the words in that final letter I left for her the last time we were together. Now, with her standing in front of me, my courage has evaporated.

I'm scared she might reject me. At the very least, reject the words and the emotion behind them.

Instead, I kiss her. I'd rather show her how I feel than tell her.

"Take me to your room," she whispers against my lips after she breaks the kiss. "Take me to your bed, Drew."

Grabbing her ass, I lift her up and she wraps her legs around my waist, her arms around my neck. She weighs nothing; her soft, curvy body fits against mine perfectly as I carry her toward my bedroom, all the while she's kissing and licking my neck. Making me so hard I don't know how I'm going to stand the torture of not being inside her another second.

Damn it, I want to make this last. I want to take my time with her and go slow. Being with her again is like my every dream come true and I want to savor it.

But she's squirming against me, her hot breath against my neck making me shiver, and I know this is going to happen way too fast.

We fall onto the bed together and I'm careful not to land on her since she's so little. And perfect. Amazingly perfect as I pull away and study her from head to toe. Her long hair spills across my pillow, her chest rising and falling quickly. The lace top does little to hide the black satin bra she's wearing and I can see the creamy skin of her flat stomach.

I desperately want to kiss and lick her there.

The little black shorts she's wearing only emphasize the dip of her waist, the curve of her hips, the length of her legs. I lift up on my knees so I can see her more fully. She opens her eyes, the smile curving her lush lips a full-on seduction. It's working. Fable can seduce me with one glance, one word, one touch.

"What are you waiting for?" She reaches toward me, hooks her finger around the belt loop of my jeans, and tugs, but I resist.

"I'm looking at you first."

Her cheeks turn the faintest shade of pink. "You can look all you want later. I need you, Drew. Please."

"What you're wearing . . ." I shake my head. "It's killing me."

She laughs. "You should see the other outfits I have to wear as my uniform for work. You'll hate them all if you don't like this one."

Jealousy flares within me and I tamp it down. "As long as the customers don't touch you, I don't have a problem."

Her laughter dies. "Are you jealous?"

"When it comes to you? Always." I slip my hand beneath the lace top, trace my fingers along her stomach. She sucks in a breath, her skin quivering beneath my touch, and I slide my hand up, until I'm playing with the clasp at the front of her bra. "You're mine. You know that, right?"

She nods slowly, her gaze never leaving mine. "I—I wasn't sure. After what happened between us. I always wanted to be yours but you left me."

I close my eyes for the briefest moment, angry for making this beautiful, perfect girl doubt herself for even a second. "I've hurt you and I hate that. I'm going to make it up to you, Fable. I swear it."

The snap on her bra springs open with ease and I'm eager to get everything off of her. I want to see her naked, see if she's as beautiful as I remember, and she laughs again when I tug impatiently on her clothes, trying my best to help her but really just making a mess of it. She slaps my hands away and slowly takes everything off, until I'm left with my mouth dry and my body hard when she's completely naked.

Fuck me, she's even more gorgeous than I remember. It's dark, I can hardly see a thing, so I lean over to the window above my bed and yank on the cord that cracks the blinds open. The fog is thin outside, letting the moon's light shine inside, casting Fable in a silvery glow, though the room is still mostly shrouded in darkness. My gaze sweeps over her, lingering on all the important, pretty bits.

"Like what you see?" She spreads her legs like a temptress intent on driving me crazy, and I swallow hard.

"Yeah," I croak.

Fable sits up in front of me, her breasts swaying with the movement, her dusky pink nipples hard and earning my undivided attention. She settles her hands on my cheeks and draws me close, her lips brushing against mine in the softest kiss. Again and again, she kisses me like this and I reach for her, cupping her breasts in my palms, stroking her nipples with my thumbs.

She arches into my touch, our kisses growing more frantic, hungrier, and then I'm consuming her, my hand slipping lower, settling between her legs. She's wet, so fucking wet for me, and I groan against her mouth.

I need to be inside her now.

Leaping from the bed, I shed my clothes, aware that Fable is watching my every move. I open the drawer of my bedside table and pull out a condom. Condoms purchased in anticipation of Fable and me being together again someday. Hell, at least I was always hopeful.

I tear open the wrapper and roll the condom on, not about

to waste another second. I want inside her so bad, I feel like I'm going to burst.

A wistful sigh escapes her and I turn to find her blatantly checking me out. "What's wrong?"

Fable jerks her gaze up to meet mine, her expression slightly embarrassed. "You have the most beautiful body ever. You know that, right?"

No, but she makes me feel like I do with just a look. A few casually spoken words. "Are you trying to embarrass me?"

She shakes her head with a smile. "That you're embarrassed makes you even cuter. And sexier. You're built like some sort of god, Drew Callahan. If we weren't in such a rush, I'd spend hours exploring your perfect body."

"Really?" I climb back onto the bed and over her. We're face-to-face, our bodies perfectly aligned. "That sounds promising."

"Oh, yeah." She nods, settling her hand at the center of my chest, her fingers drifting down. Gooseflesh rises with her touch. "You'd love every second of it."

"I would?" I thrust my hips against her, nice and slow. Probably a huge mistake considering how close I am to coming already.

"Mmm-hmmm." She arches beneath me like a cat, brushing against the very tip of me, and I swear, if she does that one more time, I'm done for. "I'd use my hands and my fingers and my mouth and my tongue. Until you'd finally beg me to stop and put you out of your misery."

I groan at her words. "I'm already in a world of agony."

"Then let me help you with that." She reaches for me, her fingers curling around my cock and guiding me toward her. I slowly sink inside her, her wet heat bathing me until I'm nestled deep, and I hold myself there as steady as I can, savoring the sensation of her body accepting mine so easily. So beautifully.

"I've missed you," I whisper against her lips before I kiss her. "So damn much."

"I've missed you, too." Her voice is shaky, her entire body is trembling, and I slowly withdraw from her, pulling almost all the way out before I sink back inside.

We both groan at the sensation and continue the torturous slow movements for long, deliciously agonizing minutes. Over and over, I thrust in, then pull almost all the way out before I sink back inside again. Being with her again feels amazing. Already the tingling at the base of my spine is starting. I'm going to come and it's going to be a big one, but I need to make sure Fable's along with me for the ride.

"Fable." I whisper her name in her ear, my thrusts growing harder. It's as if I have no control over my body whatsoever. I'm consumed with the need to come. And to make her come, too. "Are you close?" I reach between us and touch her between her legs, her little whimper telling me I hit the right spot. "Please tell me you're close."

"So, so close. Oh my God, Drew. Please . . ."

Holy hell, she is so hot like this. All needy and desperate. She's literally clawing at me and I rear up on my knees, grasping her by her waist so I can push deep inside her. She's getting louder, sexy little murmurings I can barely understand, and when I hit a spot within her that's particularly deep, she comes completely apart beneath me. Her body is racked with shudders, her head thrown back as she convulses all around me.

Sending me straight into my own spectacular orgasm that

nearly leaves me blind. I collapse on top of her, my body still shaking, the aftereffects of my orgasm lingering for long, miraculous minutes, and she wraps her arms around me, holding me close, running her hands up and down my back. Soothing me, arousing me all over again.

"You're crushing me," she finally says, her voice muffled against my chest, and I move off of her with a quick apology, getting up so I can toss the condom in the trash before I slide back beneath the covers and pull her back into my arms.

Now that I have her back in my life, it's going to be near impossible to let her out of my sight again. Which is ridiculous and unrealistic, but hell. I lost sight of her—and myself— already. And almost lost her.

I can't risk it again.

"I know we should talk but I'm too tired," she says with a yawn. "Can we talk tomorrow?"

"Yeah." I keep my arm around her slender shoulders and press a kiss to her forehead. I'm tired, too. Sated. Satisfied. Sex makes me nervous, it always has. My past haunts me and renders the act forbidden. Shameful. Usually, I'd rather avoid it. Avoid women in general, since they always want something from me that I can't give.

Not with Fable, though. Never with Fable. Being with her so intimately feels right. Perfect. I like getting naked with her, both physically and emotionally. Laying myself bare, showing her everything I have, everything I am. I'm not afraid when I'm with her.

It's liberating. Freeing.

Like a little miracle.

CHAPTER 8

I'd do anything to be your everything.
—Drew . . . or Fable?

Fable

I think I have finally stepped into that fairy tale I always wanted to live in, ever since I was a little girl. I'm living it, right at this very moment, getting dressed and ready for a lazy Sunday morning with Drew.

He gently wakes me up by kissing me all over my face. Soft little kisses that make me giggle since his lips tickle my skin. When he slips his hands between us and starts tickling my stomach I laugh harder, our legs tangling up together, our naked bodies brushing against each other. Which in turn leads to us having slow, delicious morning sex.

But before the slow, delicious morning sex, I searched his body as promised. Mapping it with my lips and my tongue and my hands and my fingers. Imagine my surprise when I discovered a tattoo on his rib cage, written in elegant script. It's a paragraph, more like a string of words in a poem. I trace each word with my finger, trying to decipher their meaning.

For a passion that's
Able to shine like ours
Blessed are we to
Love
Each other

I'm in shock that clean-cut All-American Boy Drew Callahan has a tattoo. And that he got it after we were together.

"What does it mean?" I ask him, slowing skimming the words, each individual letter, with my index finger.

He seems surprised by my question. "Read it again," he says quietly. "Slowly."

I do so, realizing that the first letter of every sentence spells my name. Reminding me of the marshmallow note he left for me. I'm shocked. Overwhelmed. Touched so deeply, tears form in my eyes, and he kisses them away as they fall onto my cheeks. "I wrote those words for you," he murmurs against my mouth before he kisses my lips. "You've turned me into a poet, Fable."

God, he's so sweetly romantic I want to lose myself in him forever.

We take a shower together and that eventually leads to more delicious sex, leaving me so spent afterward, my legs are like wobbly noodles when we finally climb out of the tub. He towel dries me, his fingers sliding between my still-wet legs, and he brings me to another earth-shattering orgasm.

Together, we're absolutely ridiculous. We can't keep our hands off of each other. And I love it.

I love him.

I put back on my shorts from last night but it's too cold to wear the stupid lacy top, so Drew lets me borrow an old sweatshirt. I pull it on, laughing when it stops just above my knees. I know I look ridiculous but he says I look cute, and then he sweeps me up into his arms and kisses me. Again. Thoroughly.

So thoroughly I finally have to smack his chest and tell him I need to get home so I can check on my brother before we get carried away again.

The disappointment on his face is clear, but he respects my wishes and we take off to my crappy apartment. The closer we get, the more nervous I become. What if my mom is home? No way do I want her to meet Drew. Not yet, anyway, because if this is going to continue between us, then eventually they'll have to meet. It's just a reality I'm not ready to face.

My mom is so incredibly embarrassing, with her drunken, trashy ways, how she flat-out doesn't care about anything or anyone but herself. Drew thinks his family's all fucked up—well, they are, let's not fake ourselves out here—but my mom is no prize either.

What's scary is that I'm constantly afraid I could turn into her. It would be so easy. We're a lot alike, as much as I hate to admit it.

When we pull into my apartment complex parking lot, I notice my mom's car isn't there, thank goodness. The relief that floods me is palpable and I immediately feel lighter. Drew comes with me to my apartment, even though I tell him he can go ahead and leave since I have to work this afternoon. But he insists on walking me to my door like a gentleman.

I think he's afraid to let me go, truthfully. And I feel the same way.

Pulling my key ring out of my purse, I go to unlock the door, when it swings open, startling me so much I drop my keys. Owen is standing there, clad in sweatpants and an old T-shirt, his hair an absolute mess. He throws himself at me, his arms so tight around my middle, I can hardly breathe.

"Where have you been?" he asks, giving me a shake when he withdraws from me. "I've been worried sick!"

"I thought you were at your friend's house." His outburst surprises me. Talk about a role reversal. I can't remember the last time I've seen him so worked up.

"I've been home *alone* all night. Mom's over at Larry's house. She thought you were coming home. So did I. I tried to text you and call you but you never answered."

Crap. "My phone must've died." I bend to grab my keys. The excuse sounds weak, but it's the truth.

Owen glances over my shoulder, his gaze alighting on Drew. "Who the hell is this?"

Jeez, why does he sound so hostile? The look he's sending Drew could kill, it's so intense.

"Um . . ." I don't know how to answer. This is awkward. I didn't expect my brother to actually greet us.

"Wait a minute." Owen steps around me so he can stand directly in front of Drew, who towers over him. "You're Drew Callahan, aren't you?"

Oh, shit. I didn't expect my brother to recognize him, but Drew is one of the star players on the college team. They have some minor celebrity status here in town.

"I am." Drew's smile is easygoing and full of warmth. "You must be Owen."

"Yep. And you're the asshole who broke my sister's

heart." Without warning, Owen rears back his arm and punches Drew right in the chin.

And sends him sprawling to the ground.

"Oh my God!" I grab at Drew's shoulders but he's already picking himself back up, his expression full of disbelief. Thank God, he doesn't appear angry. More like stunned.

I'm stunned, too.

"What the hell was that for?" I ask Owen, who's rubbing his knuckles as if they hurt.

Little shit. They probably do. He deserves the pain for pulling a stunt like that.

"He's the reason you've been so miserable these last few months. I can't freaking believe it. You went out with *Drew Callahan*?" Owen points a finger at Drew. "When the hell did this happen?"

"Watch your language!" It's the only thing I can think of to say. I don't know how to answer him. I certainly don't want to confess exactly how Drew and I came together in the first place. It sounds so sleazy.

"If you snuck around to see him, I don't know why. He's a big deal, Fable. Huge." Owen shakes his head. "I'm so stupid. I can't believe I didn't put it together, what with his initials on your foot."

"What does he mean, my initials on your foot?" Drew's gaze drops to my feet. I'm wearing my black heels from last night, and the tattoo is obvious in the daylight. Hell, it was obvious last night and earlier this morning, but I don't think he was paying much attention to me below my thighs.

The simple little outline of a heart sits high on the top of my left foot, the letters *D* and *C* stacked on top of each other in the middle. My homage to Drew and the week we spent together. The love I have for him. I got the tattoo in a fit of irrationality. I wanted to prove to him that I loved him enough to have him permanently etched into my skin.

And he never showed back up. A foolish wish for my foolish heart, I guess.

This was so not the way I wanted him to find out about the tattoo. Besides, compared to the beautiful poem he wrote for me, my tattoo seems sort of trite. Meaningless.

"She got it right after Thanksgiving," Owen explains, glaring daggers at Drew. "She wouldn't explain what the *DC* stood for, either. Claimed it was for her favorite city, but I knew she was full of absolute shit. I mean, come on. She's never even left California. Sorry, Fabes," he adds when he notices I'm ready to chew him out for the curse.

"You got a tattoo. With my initials on your foot." Drew shakes his head, his expression incredulous. "Why didn't you tell me? Show me?"

I shrug, not willing to have this conversation in front of my brother. "It's silly."

"It's definitely not silly." He rushes toward me and takes my hands, his gaze dropping to my feet. I notice his jaw is red, it looks a little swollen, and I can't believe my brother hit him so hard. The element of surprise had definitely been in Owen's favor. "I love it."

"Your tattoo has so much more meaning," I whisper as he draws me into his arms right in front of my brother. I can feel Owen's glare boring into our backs, but I ignore it. "You wrote a *poem* for me, Drew."

"And you put my initials forever on your foot, Fable. I think we're both on the same wavelength here or something."

I hug him close and laugh, because I don't know how else

to react. Owen clears his throat, reminding me he's why I'm here in the first place, and I pull away from Drew, offering him a reassuring smile. "Maybe we should talk later tonight? After I get off work?"

"Yeah." Drew smiles, his blue eyes glowing. "That sounds good. Want me to pick you up?"

"Yes, that sounds perfect." He leans in and kisses me again as if he can't help it. "I'm off at eight."

"You have a ride to work?"

"I can figure something out." I smile and he walks away, glancing at me over his shoulder one last time before he heads down the stairs and toward his truck.

"What in the hell was that?" Owen asks when I drag him into our apartment and shut the door.

"What are you talking about?" I stick my hands in the front pocket of the sweatshirt and breathe deep, inhaling Drew's scent. God, he smells good. I might never want to give this sweatshirt back. Might never want to wash it, either.

Gross but true.

"You're seeing Drew Callahan? He's your boyfriend?" Owen's eyes are wide. "This is crazy shit, Fabes. He's a total superstar. Like, a college legend. And you're *with* him?"

I shrug. "I'm not quite sure how to define what's going on between us, but yeah. I'm with him. I guess."

"Holy hell." Owen starts to laugh. "I need to tell my friends. Wade is going to shit a brick! Does Mom know?"

"No, no one knows. I don't want anyone to know yet." I want to hold Drew close and keep him my little secret for a few more days. Once people start to figure out we're actually a couple, things might get a little weird.

"Why the hell not? He's awesome!" Owen scowls, as if

remembering my misery. "Well, not really, considering how he must've hurt you pretty bad to make you so mopey. I've never seen you like that. What happened between you two?"

"It's too hard to explain." I wave a hand, dismissing my past with Drew. Like I'm going to tell my brother any details. "Besides, let's talk about the fact that you punched him. What the hell where you thinking?"

"That was amazing. My hand still fucking hurts. Sorry." I smack him on the head before he ducks out of my reach. "I can't believe I actually threw a punch at Drew freaking Callahan and he didn't knock me out for it."

"I think he was too startled by the fact that a little kid tried to kick his ass," I said wryly.

Owen shakes his head. "I'm not a little kid anymore, Fabes. When are you going to realize that?"

I roll my eyes but refrain from making a remark. Let him think fourteen is all grown up. He'll know the truth someday. "I'm starved. Still want to go to breakfast?"

"Yeah, sure. But how are we going to get there? We don't have wheels. Should've kept your boyfriend around and made him drive us there."

"We can walk to that little diner down the street. It's not too far," I suggest. I need to talk to my brother alone, not with Drew as a witness. I'm eager to have him back in my life, but I need to ease him into the chaos that is my immediate family.

Drew

Ever been on a complete and total high, only to have it come crashing down within a matter of minutes?

Yeah. Me, too.

All morning I felt amazing. Like I was walking ten feet off the ground. Even getting punched by Fable's brother didn't faze me, though my jaw still ached. The kid is packing some strength, I'll give him that.

I headed back to my apartment and crashed, my face buried in the pillow Fable used last night. I could smell her; her scent filled my head and I wanted her. Bad.

She has a life, though. A job she needs to go to, a brother she needs to take care of. I understand, I get it. I'm just damn thankful she's allowed me back into her life and is giving me the opportunity to make up for all the stupid shit I did to hurt her.

I drifted off to sleep with her scent surrounding me, her face in my thoughts. Now, I wake up to my cell phone ringing and I'm hopeful it's her, but it's not.

It's my dad.

Great.

"What's up?" I try to infuse some cheeriness into my voice but I'm afraid it sounds false. I saw him only yesterday morning. What happened that he needs to call me within twenty-four hours of leaving me?

"I had a long talk with Adele last night," he says, his voice grim.

My stomach lurches. Just hearing her name makes me sick. "Yeah?" God, what could she have said? What did she tell him?

"I'm reconsidering the divorce proceedings."

Damn. Just when I thought we could have her out of our lives for good. "Why?"

"She swears she's never been unfaithful to me. That it's all a bunch of vicious rumors spread by some women at the country club who hate her." Dad pauses, takes a deep breath. "Should I believe her?"

"That's not for me to tell you," I automatically say because hell no. I'm not playing any part in his decision.

Besides, I know she hasn't been faithful to him—from personal experience.

God, I feel like I'm going to throw up.

"She's messing with my head. She called me when I was driving back from seeing you and when I told her where I'd been, she freaked out. Demanded that I come and see her right away. So I went home and she . . . attacked me."

I close my eyes, wishing he would shut up.

"She was crazed. Like she couldn't get enough of me. I know you don't want to hear it, but it was the best sex we've had in . . . years. I don't get it. I don't get *her*."

"She's using sex to keep you with her, Dad." My voice is tight and I feel completely strung out. I hate hearing all of these details. Worse? I hate hearing that she attacked him after she knew he'd spent time with me.

What did that mean? I can only assume that maybe she thought of me when . . .

Fuck. I can't finish the thought.

"She probably is," Dad readily agrees. "But if she keeps it up, I might not be ready to let her go yet."

He's an idiot. I want to tell him that, but I keep my mouth shut. Their problems are none of my business. "I guess that's up to you," is all I say in response.

"Listen. We talked a lot last night, Adele and I. She wants

you to come home for the summer. She says she misses you and wishes you were around more. And I agree. Could you consider it? For us?"

That would be a mighty hell no, but I'm not going to be a dick to my dad now. He's still too fragile over this whole should-I-divorce-or-not deal with Adele. And look at her, trying to worm her way back into my life. Trying to get me to go back there. Does she think I'm an idiot? "I gotta go, Dad. Call me if you need to talk again."

"Tell me you'll at least consider it, son. Adele misses you and loves you so much. Ever since we lost Vanessa, she hasn't been the same. You know this. You could bring some happiness back into her life."

"See ya, Dad." I hang up before he can say anything else. I don't think I could stand it.

My appetite gone, my nerves shot, I pace around my apartment, completely on edge. I throw on some shoes and head out for a run, trying to clear my head, but all I can think about is my dad staying with Adele. Of her trying to convince me to go back home and spend the summer with them. I can't go back there. Thanksgiving had been bad enough. I still haven't fully accepted what she told me. It's hard for me to wrap my brain around her revelation.

Could my little sister really have been my . . . daughter?

Panic fills me and I stop running, glancing around as I stand in the middle of the sidewalk. Wishing like hell I had someone to talk to. Anyone.

Fable.

But she's at work. It's late afternoon and her shift started at three or four. Hell, I can't remember. I can't waltz back into her life and lay the heavy shit on her anyway. I wish it wasn't a Sunday or I'd call Dr. Harris . . .

Deciding to hell with it, I yank my phone out of the pocket of my sweats and dial her number. She answers on the third ring.

"I'm surprised to hear from you on a Sunday," is how she greets me. "Are you all right?"

"Not really," I admit, thankful she doesn't berate me for contacting her on her day off. "My dad called."

"Hmm. That doesn't sound good. Lucky you, I'm in the mood for a coffee. Want to meet for one in, say, twenty minutes?"

Relief floods me. How did I get so lucky to find Dr. Harris in the first place? Maybe this isn't commonplace, her meeting a patient for coffee on a Sunday afternoon, but I need to get all this bullshit off my chest. Not just the bad stuff that happened with my dad, but also my night and morning with Fable. "I'll be there," I tell her after she rattles off the address of a nearby Starbucks.

"So how do you feel about what your dad said?"

I take a drink of my iced coffee. "I'd rather he divorce her. I want her out of my life for good."

"I thought Adele was already out of your life." Doc looks at me in that certain way she has. The one that reminds me I'm an adult and I'm the one in charge of what happens to me.

"She is. But I want her out of my dad's life, too. As long as she's still married to him, she's a barrier between us. One I don't want to cross," I say with a finality I desperately want to believe in.

"That's your decision to make and one you're allowed to have. You know it will hurt your father if you cut him off completely without an explanation." She sips from her straw, her expression one of utter contentment, but I know what she's trying to do.

"No way am I telling him what happened between Adele and me. He'll hate me for it." I shake my head.

"He shouldn't. You're his son. You were a child when it started. You were still a child when you put a stop to it. She was in the wrong. Don't you think he'll see that?" she asks, her voice soft.

I have no idea. I'm too scared to take that chance. "He'll see what he wants to see. He'll believe what he wants."

"Do you really have that little faith in your dad?"

Ouch. I never thought of it like that before. "It's not that I don't have faith in him. It's just . . . she knows how to twist everything up. She's a master manipulator and she's been playing the two of us for years."

"You give her too much power. She knows it and she revels in it," Dr. Harris points out.

I shrug. "Maybe I do. It's easier to avoid her rather than face the truth."

"You know how I feel about you constantly running away from your problems. It's not healthy. And they always catch up to you sooner or later." She takes another sip of her drink and then pushes the cup aside so she can rest her arms on the edge of the table. "Enough focusing on the bad. Let's talk about the good. Let's talk about Fable."

Just like that, I'm smiling as I study my cup, running my finger through the condensation that's formed there. "I already told you I was with her last night."

"Have you two talked much?"

"I said I was sorry."

"For what?"

"Ditching her." I meet Doc's gaze from across the tiny table. The Starbucks is emptying out; it's already near six. Most people are home fixing dinner or whatever. "We need to talk more."

"That sounds like a good idea. Are you going to explain to her why you ran away? It seems that she's good for you," Dr. Harris says with a slight smile. "I don't think I've ever seen you look so happy."

My smile grows. "She *is* good for me. I'm in love with her." Saying the words out loud makes them that much more real. And scary.

"Have you told her that?"

"Not yet."

"Why?"

"What if she doesn't love me back?" My absolute biggest fear is that I lay it all out on the line for Fable and she doesn't feel the same. Or worse, she laughs at me.

Though I know deep down inside she would never do that. I also know deep down inside that she probably feels the same way about me that I feel about her.

It's easy to write the words *I love you,* to compose poems about her, declaring my undying love for her with a bunch of flowery sentences. It's another thing entirely making that declaration to her face. Scary enough just saying the words out loud to my shrink.

"Loving someone is taking a constant risk with your emotions. When you find the right person, the one you know you want to be with, that person becomes worth the risk." Dr.

Harris pauses, studying me carefully. "Do you believe Fable is worth the risk to you?"

"Yes," I say without hesitation.

She smiles. "If that's what you believe, then she'll want to hear those words, Drew. I bet she thinks you're worth the risk as well."

CHAPTER 9

We are afraid to care too much, for fear that the other person does not care at all.
—Eleanor Roosevelt

Fable

The restaurant is relatively quiet, which is the norm for a Sunday night, according to Jen. My shift drags, the four hours feeling like twelve, especially because I'm not keeping constantly busy, which usually helps pass the time.

I check the clock and see that it's seven thirty. Finally. Thirty minutes until I see Drew, and I can't wait.

Sucks that Colin is here, though. I don't want him to see Drew pick me up. I promised him there wouldn't be any drama and that I would keep Drew far away from here.

How was I supposed to know we'd literally kiss—and plenty of other things—and make up? I seriously thought we were through. Done. Finished.

Plus, I'd been so freaking angry with him. Mad that Drew came back into my life like he'd never left and tried his best to screw with my head. Kissing me, saying he missed me. All the things I wanted to hear, but not like that. A confrontation at my work is not the way to go in reconciling a romance.

Funny, how things change completely in a few hours. I feel as though my life has been flipped completely upside down.

In a good way.

"You're antsy," Jen says as she passes by me.

I'm bouncing on my heels. Sort of hard to do, considering the shoes I'm wearing. We're in the black dresses tonight. They skim our bodies and end mid-thigh, though the skirt always rides up. The one I make sure and wear boy-short-cut panties under for fear I'll show everything I have with one wrong move.

I wonder what Drew will think of my dress. I like the way it makes my boobs look, and I'm wearing a special bra just for him.

"Full of nervous energy," I explain, which sounds plain stupid but hey, I'm not lying.

"Why?" She raises a brow, crossing her arms in front of her. We're hanging out at the waitress station near the bar, out of sight of the few customers who still linger in the dining area. "Does it have anything to do with the guy last night?"

Well, shit. There are no secrets in this place, are there? "Maybe."

Jen smiles and shakes her head. "Colin is going to kill you."

"Oh, give me a break." I wave a dismissive hand, but my stomach starts turning. What if Colin gets mad about me being with Drew? Not that he can control my personal life, but I did promise him there would be no boyfriend trouble.

"He's worried about you. He thinks the guy who was hanging around here last night could become a problem. Who is he, anyway? I thought he looked sort of familiar."

I'm not telling her. Bad enough Owen is still flipping out over the fact that I'm dating Drew. If that's what I can call it.

"He's no one that you would know," I lie, because practically everyone in this small town has heard his name mentioned at least once or twice.

"Huh. Well, if I were you, I'd keep him a secret," Jen warns.

Okay, now I'm getting irritated. "What's up with Colin being so nosy about our personal lives, anyway? It's sort of weird, don't you think? I mean, he's our boss. Isn't he afraid of crossing a line?"

"Trust me, he always stays far enough over the line to never do anything improper," Jen says, rushing to his defense, which is no surprise. She lives with the guy, after all. Talk about improper, but who am I to judge? "He doesn't want any trouble at work. There's been drama at his restaurants in the past, especially with the people who've worked for him. He has a strict no-dating policy for his employees."

Oh, I bet he does. So why does Jen live with him?

"And I'm sure you're wondering what's going on between us, but it's nothing. Absolutely nothing," Jen says as if she can read my mind. "He's merely kind enough to offer me a place to stay while I get my crap together again."

"That's very nice of him," I say, and she rolls her eyes.

"I'm sure you think we're having some sort of secret love affair."

"If you say you don't, then you don't." I shrug.

"Just . . . be careful, Fable. I like you. You're the nicest person in this place because as I'm sure you realize, we work with a bunch of bitches." We both laugh over this. The other

117

girls virtually ignore us. Luckily enough, it's only T who's working with us tonight and she's too professional to be catty. "But Colin considers you on probation, so one wrong move and he might fire you."

"I won't make any wrong moves," I reassure her. No way can I afford to. I need this job.

"Good." Jen smiles and pats me on the arm. "I need to go check on my table."

I watch her leave, wondering if she harbors some sort of secret crush on Colin. If she does, I can't really blame her. I may have feelings for Drew and think he's the most gorgeous man on the planet, but there's no denying how attractive Colin is. He's charming, too. I can see why girls might fall all over themselves just for a chance to get with him.

For a brief, shining moment, I almost wanted to get with him myself. He has a powerful allure that's hard to deny. But I'm too wrapped up in Drew to want any other guy.

For once, I feel relatively secure over my feelings and relationship with Drew, too. "Relatively" being the key word, since I don't quite know what to call what's happening between us.

I need a definition. Tonight, we're going to talk, Drew and I. I'm going to get to the bottom of this and figure out what's happening between us. If he so much as tries to bolt the minute I confront him with this, I just might kick his ass.

The last thirty minutes go by quickly and I'm thankful Drew doesn't come into the restaurant to pick me up, as shallow and silly as that sounds. But Colin is lingering around the hostess desk, his gaze questioning when I tell him good night as I head toward the door. I'm prepared when he asks if I need a ride home, and I offer him a breezy no-thanks as I push open the door and head out in the dark, briskly cold night.

I spot Drew's truck in the lot and I hurry to it, excitement coursing through me when I see him open the driver's-side door and climb out. He's wearing jeans and a hooded sweatshirt and he looks amazing.

"Hi," he says when I approach, offering me a crooked smile. "Nice coat."

It's the same stupid puffy coat I wore the night he asked me to be his pretend girlfriend. The one I hate with a mad passion, but it's the warmest coat I own and it's an extra-cold night. I decided to forget being vain and went with the warmth factor when I slipped it on before I left for work.

"Thanks. I hate it," I say with a laugh, making him laugh, too. "It's so puffy. It makes me look like a little round ball."

"It definitely doesn't make you look like a ball," he says, his gaze doing a slow perusal of me. "Actually, you look like you have nothing on underneath it, which I know can't be the case. Unless I'm dreaming and you happen to reveal that you really are naked under there."

I shiver. Not only from the cold, but from his words, and from the heat in his gaze. "Keep dreaming. I'm afraid I'm going to have to disappoint you."

"Damn." Chuckling, he grabs my hand and draws me toward him, giving me a quick, warm kiss. "You ready to go?"

I nod slowly. I could so get used to this, my boyfriend coming to pick me up from work, offering me sweet kisses and sexy words. Then we can go back to his place and get naked together.

Yeah, that sounds like a dream come true.

I climb into the truck and we head to his apartment, though he does ask me if I'd rather go home so I can be with Owen. I find the offer sweet but reassure him Owen is at his friend's house for the night. They're working on a project together that's due tomorrow, and Wade's mom promised me she would supervise.

I really love that lady. She's so good to Owen—and to me, too. I think she knows our mom sucks and is rarely around, so she tries her best to help us out. I gave her a Christmas gift to show my appreciation, and she practically cried when I handed it to her.

"Are you hungry?" Drew glances at me out of the corner of his eye, saving his concentration for the road. "I'm starving."

"I could eat, I guess," I say with a shrug. I don't care about eating. I could live on the high I get just being in Drew's presence. It's exhilarating, having him so close, knowing he's all mine.

"Do you want to go somewhere? Or we could order something in." He looks at me when he hits a stoplight, his gaze smoldering.

Um, like I want to draw this out any longer? "Let's order something in," I suggest. "Maybe pizza?"

"Pizza it is." He reaches for me, linking our hands together. "There's some stuff I want to talk to you about."

Worry gnaws at my gut and I know it's written all over my face. He squeezes my hand reassuringly when I don't answer. "Nothing bad about us. It's about my dad. And . . . you know. I had to have an emergency meeting with my shrink earlier."

"I didn't know shrinks offered emergency meetings." It must be bad, what he wants to tell me.

"Mine is extra cool. You'd like her. She likes *you*," he says, releasing his grip on my hand.

I miss his touch, as lame as that sounds. "She does?"

"Oh, yeah. I've told her a lot about you. She's glad you're back in my life." He doesn't seem too upset, which is promising. I'm glad he has someone to talk to about his personal stuff objectively. If he mentioned that bitch of a stepmother's name to me, I'd just want to go and kick her ass.

I really, *really* hate her.

We talk about mindless stuff the rest of the drive to his apartment. I tell him how dead the restaurant was, how long I've worked there, how I've made a friend. I also tell him about my breakfast with Owen and how bad he felt about punching Drew.

Okay, the last part is a lie. My brother is still thrilled he clocked Drew in the jaw, but I can't tell him that. How rude is this kid, getting all hopped up over the fact that he punched my new boyfriend in the face for making my life miserable?

I secretly sort of love how quickly my brother defended me, though. It's sweet. And it shows that I *have* reached him. No matter how frustrated I get or how often I think he's not listening to me, he is listening. He loves me and wants to make sure I'm okay. Just as much as I love him and always want to make sure he's okay, too.

Well, I'm probably the more protective of the two of us, but I'm the older one. The responsible one. I have to watch out for him.

"You're a good sister," Drew says as he pulls into the

parking lot of his complex. "I hope your brother appreciates everything you do for him."

"I think he does."

"How about your mom?"

I'm immediately defensive. "What about her?"

He parks the truck and shuts off the engine. "Does she appreciate everything you do?"

"Half the time, I don't think she realizes we even exist." My voice is bitter but I can't help it. I think of her and I'm filled with instant bitterness. It's like instant coffee, only worse. "She's never around. She lost her job before Thanksgiving and now she's always hanging out with her loser boyfriend instead of taking care of Owen or, you know, working."

"She hasn't found another job?" He sounds incredulous.

"It's not that easy when you don't have a large skill set."

"So who's paying the rent at your place?"

"You're looking at her." I jab my thumb at my chest.

"And all the bills? The groceries and whatever else needs to be paid for?"

"That would be me."

He slowly shakes his head, the respect in his gaze clear. "Why are you so fucking amazing?"

His words send a rush of warmth through me but I bat the sensation down. "I'm just doing what I need to do. Don't make me out as some sort of hero."

"Anyone your age would bail. Seriously."

"I don't think so," I start, but he cuts me off.

"I do. You're only twenty, Fable. And you carry the weight of the world on your shoulders. You take care of your brother and you pay all the bills. You're always working and trying your best to keep your head above water." He shakes his head slowly. "I admire you so much. You're so strong, no matter what life throws at you."

"I don't have a choice," I say with a shrug. "I do what I have to do to get by."

"I could take lessons from you, you know that?" He leans over the center console and cups my cheek, pulling me in for a lingering kiss. "We always have a choice. And you choose to stay. Don't ever downplay that. Most people would run like hell from all that responsibility. *I* would."

I gaze into his eyes, see all the admiration and passion and . . . something else in their beautiful blue depths. "You underestimate yourself, Drew. As usual."

"Fine. I've always run away in the past. But you, Fable. You make me want to stay."

Drew

The minute she walks into my apartment, Fable unzips the puffy coat she hates and tosses it on the chair that sits closest to the door. Revealing a short black dress that fits her so tight, I swear I almost swallow my tongue when I first see her in it. Her body is amazing. Her legs, even though she's short, look endless, and I'm tempted to slowly peel the dress off her body and do every wicked thing I've imagined doing to her since I left her with her brother this morning.

Instead, I ask her what toppings she prefers on her pizza and call in the order.

After I hang up, she tells me she wants to get out of the dress and wear something more comfortable, so I offer up a

T-shirt of mine. She follows me back to my bedroom, her sweet scent surrounding me as she stands by my side, and we go through my dresser drawers together. When I pull the shirt out for her, I watch in disbelief as she casually yanks the dress off over her head, letting it fall to the floor.

Standing in front of me in only a black lace bra and black panties that look more like shorts but are still somehow incredibly sexy, she holds her hand out and wiggles her fingers at me, indicating she wants the shirt. I hand it over, my mouth too dry to speak, and she tugs the T-shirt over her head. It's old, a pale blue with a Hawaiian design on the front. I picked it up when I went on one of those shitty family vacations to the big island, and I rarely wear it since it reminds me of a time—and a person—I'd rather forget.

But I love seeing the shirt on Fable. How it swallows her up—the hem hits her at about mid-thigh. I know exactly what she has going on under that too-big T-shirt, which makes it even sexier. She's damn hot.

I want her. But I'm waiting, trying my best to be patient. We need to talk like two responsible adults about to embark on a serious relationship. And we need to eat, because I've barely eaten all day and I'm starving.

The pizza arrives less than thirty minutes later and we eat our dinner sitting cross-legged on the floor in front of my coffee table, laughing as we watch a dumb comedy movie on TV. It's a distraction we both need after the serious conversation we had in my truck. I hadn't meant to take it there, it just sort of happened—not that I regret it.

I hope she believed me when I told her I think she's amazing. I really do admire the way she handles herself in the face of adversity. She's so fucking strong, and I've felt mostly weak my entire life. Feeling sorry for myself and running from my problems has gotten me nowhere.

Being with Fable, even for just that short week, changed me forever. Made me realize I can be strong. I might relapse and fall back into old habits, but being with her again is the reminder I need to keep going.

Keep being strong.

We polish off the pizza and the movie ends, since we came into it more than halfway through. We both realize the only thing left to do is talk and she's quiet, chipping off the bright red polish that covers her short nails. Her hair hangs in front of her face and I study it, realizing the shade is different.

"Your hair is darker," I say out of nowhere.

She glances up at me with a small smile. "You finally noticed."

"When did you change it?"

"A few days ago." She focuses her attention on me instead of her chipped-up nails. "Promise you won't get mad?"

Okay, that's weird. "Promise."

"My boss asked that I change it. He said my old color made me look cheap."

Anger fills me. "He sounds like an asshole." My impression of him lessens with every thing I learn about the guy.

"He's really not, because you know what? He was right. I'm a natural blonde, but I started highlighting my hair in high school. I kept on bleaching it and damaged the hell out of it, too. So Colin took me to a salon, had them cut off a few inches and darken the color. Now I'm like a new version of myself."

"I liked the old version, too," I say stiffly. "You don't wear as much makeup, either."

"I gave that up after I came back from Carmel. I was just hiding behind the eyeliner, you know." She shakes her head. "Do you like the new me?"

"I like everything about you," I say. "The old you, the new you. All of you."

She smiles and scoots closer to me. "You say the sweetest things."

"I mean every word."

"I know." She braces her hand on the edge of the coffee table and gets on her knees, coming in so close she brushes her knees against my thigh. "I love that about you. You never, ever hold back what you want to say when it comes to me."

Turning my head, I meet her gaze. She used the word *love* so casually and it makes me wonder. Makes me remember what Dr. Harris said. How Fable should be worth the risk if I really am in love with her.

And I know without a doubt I'm in love with her. I can't deny it.

"Tell me what happened today," she whispers, her pretty green eyes sparkling in the dim light the lamp is throwing on us. "With your dad."

I sigh, wishing we didn't have to go there. Yet knowing it's necessary to keep our relationship honest. "My dad came here a few days ago to visit me."

She looks taken aback. "Really?"

"Yeah. He announced that he was divorcing Adele."

Her eyes narrow at the mention of Adele's name and I love that. Her immediate defense of me against the woman who irrevocably damaged me is mind-blowing. "That should be a *good* thing."

"It is." I blow out a harsh breath. "Then he called me this afternoon and said he was reconsidering his decision."

"Why?"

"He says when he went home, they sort of . . . reconciled." I don't go into detail the way my dad did. I figure Fable doesn't want to know all of that other bullshit I wish I could forget.

"Can I be honest?" she asks.

"Please do." I need her opinion.

"Your dad is an idiot if he goes back to her."

I laugh softly. "Trust me, I already know this."

"Why would he even consider it?" She wrinkles her nose and it's so cute, I lean in and kiss her there.

"Because she's a master manipulator and she has my dad's number." Which must be sex and lots of promises that will most definitely be broken.

"So your dad got your hopes up in thinking she'll forever be out of your life and then ruined it all by saying he's getting back together with her." Fable leans back on her haunches, resting her clenched hands in her lap. She looks ready to punch someone. "And you panicked and called your psychologist for an emergency session on a Sunday afternoon. She sounds like a miracle shrink if you ask me."

Sort of like my miracle girlfriend, though I don't say that. How'd I get so lucky to have not just one but two supportive women in my life? "You nailed it."

"I'm so sorry, Drew." Reaching out, she touches my cheek, her fingers gently stroking my skin. "Did it help, talking everything over with her?"

"Yeah." I close my eyes because her fingers on my face feel

so damn good and I want to savor her touch just a little longer. I sense her moving closer, feel the brush of her lips against mine, as light as a feather, and I remain perfectly still, afraid to move for fear of breaking the spell that's suddenly come over us.

"Would it help talking to me?" She kisses me again, her lips capturing my bottom one only, giving it a little tug before she releases it.

Damn, that felt incredible! Last night and this morning with her had been amazing, but I rushed it in my need to be inside her. She deserves more than that. She deserves to be kissed for hours.

"It always helps, talking to you." I reach out before she can pull away; though my eyes are still closed, I know exactly where she is. I curl my hand around her nape and haul her in, our lips perfectly aligned, her breath hot and sweet against my mouth. "Maybe we should talk more later, though. I'm sort of all talked out."

She braces her hands on my chest, her fingers gripping the fabric of my shirt. "If you're trying to avoid a serious conversation by using sex as a distraction, I might have to protest."

I crack my eyes open to find her smiling at me. "Really?"

Slowly she shakes her hand, sneaking her fingers beneath the hem of my T-shirt so she can stroke my stomach. "Not really," she murmurs before she leans in and captures my lips with hers once more.

We *should* talk. I know we should. There's still so much to tell her. But I can hardly think when she's in front of me, touching me, kissing me. I want to drown in her.

So I do. Just for a little while. I touch my tongue to hers

and she parts her lips easily, letting me in. My grip tightens in her hair, pulling a little so her head arches back, her pretty neck on display. She moans and I break the kiss, running my mouth down the length of her throat, licking and nibbling the fragrant flesh.

She whispers my name and the sound sends a zing straight to my dick. I've waited for this all day. Thought about doing this all damn day to her, with her. I'm a man obsessed.

"Maybe—" Her breath hitches when I bite her earlobe. "Maybe we should talk a little more before we do . . . this."

"Do what?" I lift my head so I can study her beautiful face. Her cheeks are pink, her lips swollen, her eyes glazed. I'm teasing her and she knows it.

A little smile tickles the corner of her lips. "You know what." She tunnels her hands up beneath my T-shirt, her fingernails grazing my skin, and I shiver. "You're being a bad boy, Drew. I didn't think you had it in you."

"You bring it out of me." I pull her toward me and she falls into my lap, wrapping her legs around my hips. I think this is our favorite position. I know it's my favorite position tonight, what with her wearing only those panties and my shirt. I can feel her heat even through my jeans, and I groan when she rocks against me.

"Hmm, what else can I bring out?" She's tugging at my shirt and I hold my arms up, letting her tug it off me. Her gaze runs greedily over my chest as she licks her lips and I stifle the groan that wants to escape.

She's trying to kill me. I know it.

"I've missed you." Her words surprise me and by the look in her eyes, I think she surprised herself. "Being with you. Seeing you. Touching you. It's hard for me to wrap my brain around the fact that we're sitting here together and it's not a dream."

"It's definitely not a dream." I touch her face. Gently trace her lips. She's trembling; I can feel the subtle tremors vibrate beneath my fingers and I bring her lips to mine, connecting them, connecting us, for a long, quiet moment.

No tongues, no passionate, out-of-control kissing. Just our mouths touching; we're inhaling each other's breaths as we absorb each other. I need this connection. I think she needs it, too.

Maybe we need each other too much. But I can't worry about that now. Not when I have the woman I love in my arms, wrapped all around me.

CHAPTER 10

The best proof of love is trust.
—Dr. Joyce Brothers

Fable

I enter my apartment humming. I never hum. But I'm so freaking happy I feel like I could break out in song at any given moment. Considering I sing like crap, I think it's safer to hum a song I heard on the radio when Drew drove me home.

I can feel the smile on my lips and I brush my fingers over them, as if I can wipe it away. Doesn't work. Touching them reminds me of the way he kissed me before I climbed out of his truck. The way he looked at me when he asked if he could see me tonight. I have the day off work, but he has to go to school. He'd been ready to ditch class for me so we could spend the day together. I forced him to go, though.

Such a stern, bossy girlfriend I am.

The apartment is dark, all the curtains and blinds closed despite it being a gorgeous day outside, and I walk by every window, yanking open curtains, cracking open blinds. The kitchen sink is full of dirty dishes and I blame Owen, making a mental note to have him wash them all when he gets home from school.

When I start down the hall, I notice my bedroom door is open. An eerie sensation settles over me, making me uneasy. I never leave my door open. It's always firmly closed. If I could lock it, I would. It's not that I don't trust Owen or Mom. It's all those jerks my mom brings over, though lately it's just one jerk.

And my brother's friends aren't real prizes either. I remember the boys I knew in junior high. Hell, the girls, too. I was just as bad. We all stole like crazy, lifting makeup and candy from the local supermarket. Freaking stupid.

Imagine my surprise when I stop in my doorway to find it's my mom in my room, going through the jumble of stuff that litters the top of my dresser. Resting my hands on my hips, I clear my throat and she gasps, whirling on me with her hand pressed against her chest.

"Fable! When did you get home?" She fans her hand in front of her face like she's some Southern belle about to faint from the wretched heat. "You scared the life out of me."

"Good." I flick my chin in her direction. "What are you doing in here?"

She sneers at me, the Southern belle act evaporating like smoke. "No, 'Hi, Mom, how are you?' Since when did you get so rude?"

"About the same time you started neglecting us completely." I enter my room, already weary from the fight. My high has come crashing down and I'm left facing the reality that is my shitty relationship with my no-good mother. "Why are you going through my stuff?"

"I lost something." She tilts her nose in the air, a sure sign she's lying. "A ring of mine has gone missing."

Like I'd steal her crappy jewelry. "What are you trying to say?"

"Did you take it?"

"Why would I take your old-ass jewelry?" She's probably pawned or sold everything off anyway. She has nothing of any value anymore. I don't have anything either, but I never really did.

I do have a stash of tip money in my room, though. Hidden in a sweater pocket deep in my closet.

"Christ, you're a brat," Mom mutters, shaking her head as she starts for the door. "Can't even have a decent conversation with me."

"You just can't barge into my room and go through my things," I call after her. She needs to know her boundaries. More than anything, she needs to know she's not welcome in here.

"I can, too." She turns on me, her expression indignant, her green eyes, so much like mine though a little faded and a lot jaded, blaze fire as she glares at me. "This is my apartment. The lease is in my name. I own all of this stuff. I bought everything in here for you. If I want to go through it, I have every right."

"Give me a break. The furniture is hand-me-downs from relatives and friends. All the stuff in here, the clothes and the cheap jewelry and everything you see?" I wave my fingers around. "I bought it with money I earned. And your name may be on the lease, but I'm the one who pays all the bills every month. So don't act like a righteous bitch who can take everything from me just because you're my mom. I'm an adult. You don't own me."

I release a shuddering breath, surprised at my outburst. I can't believe what I just said to her. I've been holding that in for months. Hell, for years. And now I'm so angry, I'm literally shaking.

Where's Drew's miracle shrink when I need her?

"How dare you talk to me like that!" Mom whispers, her voice rough, her jaw tight. "You are the most ungrateful child ever. Fine, if you're such a high-and-mighty princess who can support yourself without me, then go find your own damn place to live."

"I've been thinking *you* should be the one to leave instead. You can't afford this place on your own and you know it. You don't even have a job. At least I pay the rent and take care of Owen." I hate her. I didn't realize the depths of my hatred for her until now but this conversation, everything she's saying, how she's acting, it all seals the deal.

She's awful. A spiteful woman who couldn't give a crap about me or Owen. All she cares about is herself.

"You can't kick me out of my own house." She straightens her shoulders and pushes her bleached blond hair away from her face. My mom looks tired. Old. Small and mean. Her eyes are hazy and I wonder if she's drunk. Or high.

She disgusts me. I can hardly stand looking at her. Yet . . . I also feel sorry for her. She's my *mom*. Only forty-two years old and look at her, with her crappy life and her crappy boyfriend, going nowhere fast. I've been scared for years I'll end up exactly like her.

But I'm nothing like her. I have ambitions and dreams. I'm just putting them on hold until Owen is old enough to take care of himself.

"Go back to Larry's, Mom. Go stay there and leave Owen and me alone, okay? Do you need money? Is that why you're digging around my room? I'll give you money. Just . . . let us be." I go to the kitchen where I left my purse on the counter and dig through it, finding my wallet and pulling out a wad of dollar bills from last night's tip money. "Is this what you were looking for?" I ask her when she follows me into the kitchen, holding the cash out toward her.

She snatches the money from my fingers and stuffs it into the front pocket of her jeans. "I won't refuse it."

Great. Doesn't even bother with a thank you. She's a real prize.

"Maybe I should stick around until Owen comes home." Mom leans against the kitchen counter, trying her best for nonchalance. I know she's really trying to get á rise out of me. Again. "I need to spend more time with my baby boy."

I refrain from rolling my eyes, but just barely. "He's going to his friend's house after school."

"What do you mean?"

"I mean, he's working on a class project with his friend after school. He won't be home for hours." I'm totally lying. They worked on the project last night. But I don't want her lurking around here waiting for Owen and freaking him out. He's uncomfortable around her.

Pretty sad when a kid doesn't like being around his mother because she's so removed from his day-to-day life.

"Great. So I'm not around, you're not around—what kind of trouble is he getting into if we're all too busy for him? Stupid kid," she mutters, shaking her head.

That does it. How dare she criticize Owen? "He's a *child.*

135

What do you expect him to do if no one is around to supervise him?"

"Well, where are *you*?" she accuses.

"I'm working!" The words explode from my chest. "Where the hell are *you*? Oh, I know, you're out drinking and doing drugs with your asshole boyfriend. Maybe you're sleeping in all day when you should be out hunting for a job? When you should be, you know, staying at home so you can be here for your son? Don't blame me for your inadequacies as a mother. It's not my fault you have better things to do."

I'm riled up all over again. No one else does this to me. No one. I'm usually the calm in a storm. I'll rush to someone's defense in a heartbeat, but I don't get worked up easily. I'm also loyal to a fault.

My loyalty to my mom disappeared years ago. I can't count on her. No one can. She always acts like the victim and blames everyone else for her mistakes. She can't own up to the fact that she sucks as a mother and she's lazy.

So I don't mind reminding her of both.

"I won't tolerate your disrespect. I am your *mother*," she stresses.

"Then act like one." My voice is calm. Like scary calm. I cross my arms in front of my chest, practically daring her to step into the role she's supposed to embrace every day of her life. Knowing full well she won't.

"I don't need this sort of abuse." She grabs her purse from where she left it on the coffee table and slings it over her arm, heading toward the door without looking at me once. "You can go to hell, Fable."

She slams the door behind her and I fall apart. Just . . . completely fall apart like a crying, out-of-control baby. I curl up on the couch and press my hands to my face, my tears soaking my palms. My entire body is shaking, I'm so angry, so frustrated, so . . .

Ugh. There are too many emotions coursing through me to try to sort them all out. I've gone from the most extreme high to the most extreme low in a matter of minutes, and my mind and my heart can't take it any longer.

Despite my anger, it feels good to cry. It's a release from all the built-up resentment and tumultuous emotions that have been swirling within me. I don't know how long I've been sitting here, crying until my chest aches and my eyes sting, when I finally throw back my head, exhausted, and stare up at the ceiling.

My mom hates me and I hate her. I have to reconcile that fact and come to terms with it. I need to protect Owen from her, too. I should probably get serious about finding another apartment, because I wouldn't put it past Mom to pull some stunt and somehow screw us out of living here.

There's a lot to do, but what else is new? I take care of everything and everyone. It doesn't even occur to me that I could ask for help from Drew until this very moment. One text message, one simple word, and he'd drop everything and come running to my rescue.

Wouldn't he?

How I hate that I doubt him even a little bit.

Drew

I'm in the midst of planning a special night for Fable when I get the call from the one person I dread talking to more than any other. I'm so caught up in searching for the right place to take Fable to dinner tonight, I don't bother checking who's on the other end when I pick up my cell and answer with a distracted hello.

"Andrew." *Fuck me sideways.* The sound of Adele's voice sends icy shivers down my spine. "I can't believe you answered."

"It was a mistake, trust me." I pull the phone away from my ear, ready to end the call, but I can hear her frantically saying my name, begging me not to hang up.

Like an idiot, I bring the phone back to my ear, silently waiting for her explanation.

What the hell could she have to say to me? Why am I giving her a chance to explain anything? Am I doing it for my dad? Because I sure as hell have no reason to talk to her ever again. Not after that bomb she dropped on me the day Fable and I left Carmel.

Vanessa's not your sister, Andrew. She's your daughter.

I close my eyes against the memory. How downright excited Adele had sounded when she made that outrageous declaration. I've talked about Vanessa with Dr. Harris. She knows the circumstances that surround Vanessa's death, my guilt over leaving her alone. How it's my fault she's dead. How my affair with my stepmom might have resulted in her birth. My sister, my daughter . . . Hell, I still don't know what to believe.

There's also that underlying fear that Adele will confess all to my dad and he'll hate me for what I've done. The threat of divorce makes people do crazy things to keep their marriage together. It also makes people do outrageous things to break up their marriage for good.

Adele is a loose cannon. I'm scared to death she'll reveal

all my secrets and I'll look like the world's worst son. The very last thing I want to do is disappoint my dad.

Too late for that. I've disappointed him countless times and most of the stuff I've done, he doesn't even know about.

"Your father wants to leave me," she finally says.

I crack open my eyes, stare blearily at the blurred laptop screen in front of me. "I thought you two already kissed and made up."

"I know he went to see you this weekend. The question I have is, why? It's not like you two are close anymore. What did you promise to tell him? Did you talk about me? What did you say?" She sounds panicked—and completely self-absorbed.

Typical.

"We hardly talked about you at all, not beyond him explaining briefly that the two of you were having trouble and he's ready to file for divorce." I can't believe I'm explaining myself to her but as sick as it sounds, we're in this secret together. Both of us have plenty to lose if it's revealed.

"You're lying. You're trying to convince him to leave me and I won't allow it, Andrew. You're just as guilty in this situation between us as I am. I refuse to take the fall for it." Her voice is low, full of ice-cold venom.

"His reasoning for leaving you has nothing to do with . . . us." I choke the last word out. There was never any *us* with me and Adele. More like her dragging me under and me helpless to fight it. "It has to do with you screwing around with some golf pro."

She sucks in a harsh breath. *Guilty.* "Is that what he told you?"

"I shouldn't be having this conversation with you." Damn

139

it, why am I still talking to this bitch? "I'm hanging up now. Don't bother calling me again."

Before she can get another word out, I end the call, throwing the phone across the room so it hits the wall and bounces on the carpet with a satisfying thud.

But I'm still not satisfied. I'm mad. At myself for answering the damn call and listening to what she had to say. At Adele for contacting me when I explicitly told her I refused to talk to her ever again.

I broke my own rule, though, didn't I? So how can I blame her when I'm just as guilty?

My phone dings from where it sits on the floor and I go pick it up, dreading to see if it's a text from Adele.

But it's not.

Are you out of class yet?

Despite my anger, I smile and answer Fable.

Yeah. What's up?

Can you come get me?

I'm typing my answer when another text from her comes through.

I understand if you're busy. I just . . . need to see you.

Worry crashes through me and I tell her to give me ten minutes.

She's waiting for me at the foot of the stairwell that leads to her front door and I pull up beside her. She climbs into the truck and slams the door, staring straight ahead as if she can hardly look at me, and I'm quietly freaking out.

"Are you okay?" I slip the truck into park, my nerves doing somersaults in my stomach. She's not acting right.

A sigh escapes her and she slowly shakes her head. "I got into a fight with my mom."

"Just now?"

"A few hours ago." She hangs her head, staring at her lap. "I said terrible things to her. What's worse is I don't regret it."

"Hours ago? Fable, why didn't you call me sooner?"

She shrugs. "I didn't want to bother you."

Holy shit. Does she not get it? I'd go to the ends of the earth for her after everything she's done for me. For how selfless she is, how she always, always comes to my rescue . . .

Reaching out, I settle my hand on her shoulder and give it a gentle squeeze. "I can't help you if you don't let me in."

Fable releases a shuddering breath and finally looks at me. Her skin is pale, her expression emotionless. "I'm used to doing things on my own, you know? I've never had anyone on my side. Not really."

"Not Owen?"

"He doesn't count since he's just a kid."

"Well, he definitely came rushing to your defense when he punched me yesterday," I point out.

A little smile appears and she rolls her eyes. "He was sorta amazing when he did that, huh?"

"My jaw still hurts." I run my hand over the spot where his fist connected with my face.

"I'm sorry." She doesn't sound sorry at all and I let it go. If she were my sister and some jackass had broken her heart, I would've done the same thing.

"Fable." Her gaze jerks to mine once more. "I want to be there for you. Always. I know I haven't proven myself to you yet but I will. I swear. I want to make a promise to you."

She clears her throat, looking nervous. "What sort of promise?"

Reaching across the center console, I grab her hand and lace our fingers together. "No matter what, from this day forward, I'm here for you. You need me and I'll come running."

Her lips part as if she's going to say something, but then she presses them together with a wince. "I want to believe you, I do. But I'm afraid you'll leave me again. And I don't know if I could take that."

I squeeze her hand tight. "What can I do to prove to you I won't leave? Tell me. I'll do it."

"You'll do anything?"

"Anything." I nod furiously, my heart aching. If she rejects me, I'll lose it. But I've also asked for it. She's fragile right now. Me walking back into her life, the fight with her mom, her worry over her brother . . . She takes on so much. There's only so much a person can handle before she reaches her breaking point.

She releases a harsh breath. "I want to pretend we have a normal, fun relationship. No worries, no stress. I want to forget about my mom, how I'm going to pay the bills, where I'm going to find a new place to live—"

"Wait a minute." I cut her off. "You're looking for a new place to live?"

"I've thought about it," she admits. "The rent's a lot here since it's a three-bedroom and my mom's never there. She uses our place for storage more than anything. I want to find a cheaper place for just Owen and me."

My mind is spinning with ideas, all of them involving Fable and her brother moving in with me.

She'd laugh in my face at the suggestion. We've been back together—if you could call it that—what? A couple of days? No way would she move in with me.

"But I don't want to worry about any of that right now," she says firmly as she pulls her hand from mine. She waves it in the air, as if dismissing all of her problems with a flick of her fingers. "I'm sick of worrying and being stressed out over money, what Owen's doing, if he's getting good grades, if he's lying to me. Worrying about my mom and what she's doing and why she hates us so much."

"She doesn't hate—"

"She hates us," Fable repeats, interrupting me. "She hates me especially. We're a burden to her. If she could make us disappear, she probably would."

Damn. We always focus on my problems, but she's just as much of a mess as me. Her mom sounds like a world-class bitch.

"Forget about her. I am." She smiles, but it doesn't quite reach her eyes. "Let me pretend for just a little while we're normal. That we don't have issues and secrets and problems, that our lives are easy and we're just two people who are falling for each other."

I've already completely fallen for her. I thought she felt the same way. "If that's what you want, I'll give it to you. I'll give you whatever you want."

The smile grows, lights up her eyes. *There's my girl.* "Thank you," she whispers.

Unable to take it anymore, I touch her. Thread my fingers through her hair so I can cup the side of her head and bring her lips to mine. "Why are you thanking me?"

"Thank you for getting me. And for wanting to make me happy." She closes her eyes when I kiss her and I study her face, her thick eyelashes, her tiny nose. "We're probably avoiding the inevitable, but I'm tired of dealing with the heavy stuff. I'm jealous of people without problems."

"Everyone has problems," I point out.

She opens her eyes. "As heavy as mine? As heavy as yours?"

"Point taken."

CHAPTER 11

I'll never forget the things you said to me. Not because they mattered, but because they made me feel like I did.
—Unknown

Fable

Drew made good on his promise. From the moment we agreed we'd pretend for a little while that we're just two normal people in a new relationship, that's exactly how he's treated me. No mention of my mom, his dad, Adele, our problems, our past. Nothing.

We've spent the last twenty-four hours together doing nothing but talking. And kissing. Lots and lots of dreamy, long, and delicious kissing. Which of course leads to touching, and then that leads to sex.

Lots and lots of sex.

We haven't left his apartment since he came to pick me up. I called to check on Owen and made sure he was okay. Again, he was at Wade's. He asked if I was with Drew and I told him yes.

He proceeded to both cheer me on and warn me. Owen loves the idea of me being with a football player. He hates the idea of me being with a guy who broke my heart.

He's conflicted—we all feel that way, I think.

But I pushed the conflict aside and focused on the positive. Drew with me. Over me. Inside me. Whispering hot words in my ear when he pulls me in close. How he touches me so reverently, the way he holds me when we sleep. Not that there's been much sleep going on . . .

I was able to trade out my shift today so I could spend one more full day with Drew, but tomorrow, reality waits. He has to go to class. I have to spend time with Owen before I go to work. Drew has to meet with his shrink.

Sometimes, I really hate reality.

Being with him constantly like this, I can't concentrate. Since he's walked so completely back into my life, I've been in a constant state of arousal I can't control. I have never been so . . . needy. I look at him and he's all I can think about. Funny how I believed for a fleeting moment that I was interested in Colin.

The way I feel for Drew can't compare to any glimmer of attraction I'd had for Colin.

We're at a restaurant now, Drew and I. He ran out of food in his apartment and we were starving, so we finally made our escape. Plus, I thought it might be good to be out in public like real people versus naked and rolling around in his bed all day and night.

Staring at him from across the table, I realize pretty quickly that being out in public like real people is totally overrated.

"What do you want to order?" His head is bent, his dark hair tumbling over his forehead as he peruses the menu. I wonder when he last got a haircut. I like it long. It's easier for me to run my fingers through and grip when I kiss him.

"I don't know." I sound breathless, I feel breathless, but he doesn't notice. He props his elbow on the table, absently scratches his temple with his index finger, and I remember exactly what that index finger did to me earlier. How he circled my nipples with that finger, how he slipped it between my legs, drenched it with my wetness, and then brought it up to his mouth, licking it, tasting me, his gaze never leaving mine . . .

I'm squirming in my seat like some sort of horny freak. And the man is clueless.

"I thought you said you were hungry." He glances up, his gaze catching mine. "What are you in the mood for?"

You, I want to tell him, but *jeez.* I had him not even an hour ago. What's wrong with me? I go without Drew for a couple of months and now I act like I need him every minute of every day.

"I don't know." I open the menu to check out my options. I've never eaten at this restaurant. It's close to Drew's apartment and I'm rarely in this part of town. "What's good here?"

"Fable." His deep, quiet voice makes me glance up and I find him watching me, his dark brows drawn, a little frown curving his mouth. "Are you okay?"

He's got both elbows propped on the table now, his hands clasped together, and I want those hands on me. His black long-sleeve shirt clings to his arms, accentuating his bulging biceps, those broad shoulders, that wide chest. I've explored every inch of his body the last few days and it's still not enough. I can't believe he's really mine.

And I can't believe I'm his.

"I'm not very hungry," I admit.

His frown deepens. "You're the one who wanted to come here."

I shrug, feeling silly, my gaze locked on his hands. They are so big. Long fingers, wide palms, a little rough, a little smooth. I love how they touch me, sometimes gentle, sometimes with force. I like it best when he wraps my hair around his fingers and tugs. Oh God, I really love it when he does that . . .

I want those hands on me. Now. "I guess I'm not as hungry as I thought." My stomach is fluttering with nerves. I don't want to eat. I want Drew. I feel sort of crazed with it. Like I need to have him as much as possible before he slips through my fingers and I lose him forever.

But I'm not going to lose him. We're in this together. I need to remember that—and believe it.

"You're being weird." Worry fills his eyes. "Are you mad? Did I do something?"

Just his breathing—that does it for me. "I'm not mad. I'm, um . . ." I let my voice trail off, feeling like an idiot.

"You're what?"

"I'm looking at your hands," I admit with a little sigh. Can I admit out loud that I'm horny? That would sound ridiculous.

Those dark brows shoot up practically to his hairline. "Why?"

My cheeks are hot. I squirm in my seat again. "I'm . . . remembering what they did to me earlier."

The frown is gone, replaced with a wicked smile that sends my body temperature skyrocketing. He leans across the table, his voice so low it vibrates through me and settles between my legs. "Maybe we should go back to my place so I can do that to you all over again."

Oh my God, that sounds like the best idea ever. "Maybe we should."

The smile never leaves his face. In fact, it grows bigger. My quiet, hesitant Drew has morphed into some sort of cocky sex god. "You don't want to order anything?"

I slowly shake my head. "Can't we just get pizza again? Later?" We had it last night, too. "From somewhere different this time. You know, just to mix it up. Or maybe Chinese? I love Chinese."

He laughs, the sound husky. "You said you wanted to get out of the house for a while because you worried we were becoming addicted to each other."

"Is that what I said?" I honestly can't remember. What's wrong with being addicted to each other? Aren't we still in this pretend mode where we're normal people who like to have sex without hangups or issues? I wonder if Drew has ever had sex like this. Carefree and so . . . normal.

"Yep." He nods.

"Maybe I like being addicted to you," I admit softly. We haven't said we loved each other yet. I can't work up the nerve. Maybe he can't either. Silly, considering how consumed with love I am for him. He is just . . . amazing. Sweet. Attentive. Funny. Smart. Sexy.

I understand him. He understands me. We're perfect for each other.

Maybe we're *too* perfect together. Too perfect doesn't really exist. This could all be a façade. Just like our week together over the Thanksgiving break.

That week *felt* fake, though. Surreal. There were real, grounding moments, but for the most part, we were caught up in an act. Maybe we're pretending right now, too, but I'm trying to be as real as I can with him. Without the baggage and the heartache and the trouble hanging over us. For at least a little while.

It'll all come crashing down upon us soon. That's a reality I don't want to face quite yet.

He reaches across the table for my hands and takes them in his. "I really like being addicted to *you*."

The smile I send his way is so big it hurts my cheeks. We are so in this addiction together.

For once, I know I'm not alone.

"Let's go home and play true confessions," I suggest because I'm feeling silly. "Nothing heavy, though. We can keep it light and easy."

"True confessions? I'm intrigued."

"You should be," I say coyly. "It's going to be a sexual true confessions."

He stiffens the slightest bit and I squeeze his hands in my grip. We need to be open with each other and while the sexual connection we have is amazing, I know sometimes he holds himself back. I understand why. Sort of.

That's where we're complete opposites. I was the type who gave it away just so I could feel something, anything, for a little while. He'd rather box himself up and feel absolutely nothing.

"Fable . . ." His voice trails off and his smile fades. "I don't know if I'm up to that yet."

"It won't be anything crazy, I promise." I lean over our

linked hands and bring them to my mouth, pressing a lingering kiss to his knuckles. "No pressure. Just fun."

"Just fun?" He brushes his thumb over the top of my hand
and my entire body reacts.

"Always fun," I whisper.

Drew

I'm curious where Fable thinks she's taking this true confessions game she mentioned. Curious enough to agree to leave
the restaurant without ordering, earning a strange look from
the waitress when we do.

Feeling a little nervous, too, since I'm not the most comfortable when it comes to talking about sex. Fable is the first
girl I've ever really wanted. I've been forever damaged by
what happened with Adele. I've had sex since then, but it was
always quick. Meaningless. Never with the same girl twice.

After a while, it became too complicated. So I avoided
girls. It was easier that way.

Our agreement to pretend to be normal has given me
some freedom. I'm able to let go—at least temporarily—of
some of the issues that constantly plague me and enjoy my
time with Fable. We hardly leave my bed. We've remained
naked pretty much the entire time.

It's also been pretty fucking incredible.

"Let's play strip true confessions," she suggests as we
enter my apartment. The chipper sound of her voice makes
me burst out laughing.

"Strip true confessions?" I scratch my head as I shut and
lock the door.

She turns to face me, her bright smile stealing my breath. "We confess, then we take off a piece of clothing."

"Didn't we already plan on taking off our clothes?"

"Of course, but this makes it much more interesting." Grabbing my hand, Fable leads me back to my bedroom. She tugs me down with her so we both sit on the edge of the bed and she turns to face me, her expression solemn, those pretty green eyes beguiling. "Now, I'll go first. We must confess something sexual that we've never done. Or something we've always wanted to do. And then we take off one piece of clothing when we're finished. Are you game?"

I have no idea where she's going with this, but I'm curious to hear what she has to say. "I'm game."

"Perfect. Okay." She blows out a harsh breath and drops her gaze. "This is more nerve-racking than I thought."

If *she's* nervous, I'm in huge trouble. She's much more open sexually than I am. Though the more time I spend with her, the more I'm coming around.

"It's just me," I remind her and when she glances up, I offer her a reassuring smile. "I'm not going to judge you."

"I know," she says softly. "All right, I'm going for it. I've never been taken from behind before."

I mock frown. "Taken?"

She rolls her eyes. "You know . . . I've never done it doggy-style. God, that sounds gross, phrasing it like that."

It sounds arousing as hell but I school my expression, going for serious. "I'm sure that could be arranged. Me taking you from behind, doggy-style."

Her cheeks color a pretty shade of pink and she shrugs out of her zip-up sweatshirt, tossing it on the floor. She's only wearing a white tank top with a black bra beneath it. Jesus, she's hot. "I'm sure it could. Okay, your turn."

"Uh . . ." There are a lot of things I could confess.

"Don't be shy." She smiles, all pure, sweet seduction. "Come on. Out with it. Pick an easy one."

"I've never slept all night with a girl. Until you." I yank my sweatshirt off and throw it on top of hers on the floor.

"Aw." She leans in and gives me a quick kiss. "I love that I'm your first," she murmurs against my lips before she moves away from me.

She's a lot of firsts for me. It's embarrassing to admit just how many.

"I've never had sex outside." A wistful look crosses her face. "I think that would be incredibly romantic. Under the stars, a cool breeze over hot skin. Maybe on the beach, by the ocean . . ."

"Sand getting in our asses," I add because I can't help it—that's my first thought when I hear "sex on the beach."

Fable smacks me on the arm. "You're such a guy. Way to kill the romantic mood."

"You knew it would happen." I rub my arm, watching as she takes off one sock. "Only one?"

"An article of clothing a confession, right?" She shrugs, looking smug.

I'll remember this. But then again, do I want to confess that much?

"I've never had phone sex." I take off a sock just like she did.

"Me either." She takes off her other sock and giggles. "This is silly."

"It was your idea," I point out.

"Yeah, yeah." Fable nibbles her lower lip. "This one's crazy. I'm afraid you'll freak out when I say it."

"No going back now. You have to tell me," I urge. Hell, it's supposed to be my turn, but I'm letting her skip right on by me.

"Fine, you asked for it." She takes a deep breath. "Lately I've been thinking about getting my nipples pierced."

I'm stunned. "Are you serious?"

She nods and bends her head, letting her hair fall in front of her face. "Is that crazy?"

Sort of. She's full of surprises. I like it. Hell, I like *her*. A lot. "Don't you think it'll hurt?"

"Yeah, but I can deal with a little pain." She keeps her head bent. "I've heard it feels good to have them tugged on during . . . you know."

Okay, my girl is trying to drive me crazy. I've never thought of nipple rings as particularly sexy before, but the thought of me tugging on a tiny silver hoop with my lips and tongue and hearing her moan . . .

I get hard just thinking about it.

"Would you ever get your nipples pierced?" she asks, lifting her head so her eyes meet mine.

"Uh, I doubt it," I croak, then clear my throat.

"It's just a thought. I doubt I'll go through with it either." She slowly lifts the hem of her tank and takes it off, revealing her toned stomach, her enticing black satin bra. I want to grab her and kiss her. Screw these true confessions. "Your turn," she whispers.

Studying her cleavage, I start to sweat. "I've, uh . . . never done the dirty-talk thing before."

"Isn't that the same theory as phone sex?" She frowns.

"Not really."

"Hmm." She taps her smirking lips with her index finger. "So you're saying you'd like it if I leaned over and whispered in your ear that I want to suck your cock?"

I swallow hard. "Hell, Fable."

Her smile grows. "You would definitely like that, wouldn't you?" She gets on her hands and knees and crawls toward me, nuzzling my cheek with her nose, her mouth close to my ear. "Drew," she whispers. "Do you know how wet I get just looking at you?"

I swallow hard, slipping my arm around her waist so I can bring her closer to me. "Are you trying to kill me?"

"Maybe." She laughs, the sound sexy as hell, and I tackle her, pinning her beneath me so she can't get away. I thrust my hips against hers and her eyes darken. "Ooh, I can tell I am totally getting to you."

"All this true confession talk. A man can only take so much." Lifting up, I take off my shirt, pleased when I catch her drinking me in with her greedy gaze. She has no problem letting me know how much I turn her on and I love it. "I'm thinking I need to see just how wet you really are."

A little sound of pleasure escapes her and she clamps her lips shut. "Why don't you do some investigating and find out?"

CHAPTER 12

Love is composed of a single soul inhabiting two bodies.
—Aristotle

Fable

After playing our silly, sexy game of true confessions, we tease each other like crazy, taking off each other's clothes between lingering kisses and possessive caresses meant to ignite. I love this playful side of Drew. He's funny, he's sweet, and he's sexy as hell. When he said he wanted to see just how wet I really was, everything inside me went loose and hot. And when he proceeded to yank off my sweatpants and slip his fingers beneath my panties, I nearly came right then and there.

Being with Drew, naked and open like this—I've never experienced anything like it. I've never felt as close to another human being in my life as I feel to Drew Callahan at this very moment.

I'm pinned beneath him, trapped, but there's nowhere else I'd rather be. His soft hair brushes against my chest as he makes his descent down my body, sending a scattering of gooseflesh across my skin. His hot mouth is everywhere, searching me, and I feel like I'm floating on a cloud, completely lost, too caught up . . .

"Look at me, baby." I open my eyes, startled by the endearment. He rarely calls me anything but my name. "Watch me," he whispers.

I do as he asks, breathless as he drops tender kisses in the valley between my breasts, across my belly, all the while his gaze never leaving mine. Reaching out, I thread my fingers through his hair, stroking his head, and he covers my breasts with his mouth, drawing one nipple between his lips with a slight tug. I close my eyes, too overwhelmed by the delicious sensation of his mouth so intimately on my flesh, and I hold him close. Spreading my legs, I accommodate his big body more fully as he presses against mine.

This is exactly what I've been wanting between us. No walls, no barriers. He finally seems as open to me as I am to him and I love it.

I love him.

He braces his upper body above me, his hands pressed into the mattress on either side of my head. I meet his gaze, my heart fluttering as if it could take flight, when I notice the expression on his face. It's as if he's at war with himself and what he should do next. "What's wrong?" I ask, scared he's going to say or do something that will break this magical moment between us.

"I have a confession to make." He hangs his head, almost as if he's embarrassed. "I've never done this before."

I frown. "Um, I hate to break it to you, but we've definitely done this before. Together. More than once."

Chuckling, he meets my gaze once more. "I mean—shit, I don't know how to say this."

"More true confessions, Drew?" Reaching out, I touch his cheek, my fingers lingering on the stubble that lines his jaw. I like the way his bristly cheeks feel against my own when he kisses me. It's sorta hot. He is all sorts of hot. "Don't be shy. Just say it."

He leans in, his mouth at my ear, his breath warm against my cheek. "I've never gone down on a girl before," he whispers.

Okay, now I'm shocked. I rest my hand on his chest and push him away slightly so our eyes can meet once again. "Seriously?"

"Seriously." He nods. I notice his cheeks are ruddy and my heart squeezes.

God, he is so stinking cute and he's all mine. Mine, mine, mine. We're pretending we're perfectly normal and we're not. We're both all sorts of messed up.

But I don't care if he's troubled and has dealt with an endless amount of bullshit at the hands of a woman so disgusting I can't even *think* her name, let alone say it. I still want him. All the time. Desperately. I know he's damaged. I also know he's trying his best to work through the damage and become a whole person again.

More than anything, I know he needs me. And I need him. I love him. And Drew loves me. Even though we haven't said it to each other yet, I know deep in my heart it's the truth.

"If you don't want to do it, you don't have to." I'm giving him an excuse to back out because the last thing I want to do is pressure him. He's dealt with enough pressure in his life. Our game of true confessions was hard for him. I knew it would be. But I think it helped us become closer.

A sexy smile curves his lips and I'm momentarily breathless at the sight of it. "Oh, I want to, Fable. More than you can possibly imagine."

Now it's my turn to become embarrassed, and I feel my cheeks heat. "So what are you waiting for?"

"I just . . . wanted to warn you. In case I somehow screw it up." He lowers himself so his body covers mine, his mouth against my neck. He's kissing and nibbling me there, driving me crazy with the way he touches me, and I close my eyes, losing myself.

Finding myself. With him.

He's somehow worried he's going to go about this all wrong, but he doesn't know that no matter what, he can't possibly screw this up. That everything he does, everything he says, how he touches me, is all so perfect, it's scary. He's all I ever want. All I'll ever need.

Drew maps my body with his hands and mouth, his tongue . . . God, his tongue. He licks me everywhere, tasting me, savoring me, until I'm writhing beneath him, my entire body on fire. He skims his fingers along the insides of my thighs so lightly I shiver. My entire body is shaking in anticipation as he kisses the sensitive flesh of my stomach, my hips, my thighs . . .

And when he finally, finally delivers that first tentative lick between my legs, I moan so loud I'm almost embarrassed.

But I'm not. How can I be, when the man I love so much is overwhelming me with pleasurable sensation after pleasurable sensation? He searches me intimately with his tongue, slipping one long finger deep inside me, and another shivery moan escapes as I arch against him.

It's too much. It's not enough. I both want to come and make it last and when he increases his pace, I know I'm dangerously close to splintering completely apart.

"Tell me where, baby," he whispers against me as I'm

shuddering and gasping, my fingers clenched in his hair. "Tell me how you like it."

"Higher," I choke out and he moves higher, his tongue flicking against my clit, his finger deep inside my body. Oh, shit, that is *it*. It's perfect, just perfect where he's touching me, licking me. *Right. Fucking. There . . .*

With a ragged whisper of his name falling from my lips, I'm coming. The waves wash over me again and again, sweeping me under, banishing my thoughts so all I can do is feel.

And then I feel him. Drew. Looming over me, his big hands gripping my hips as he positions me, and without warning, he slides deep inside my body. I gasp at first contact, going completely still as he fills me completely. He dips his head, his mouth crushing mine, and I can taste myself on his lips, his tongue.

I don't care. God, it arouses me even more, and within an instant our bodies are a frenzy of movement as we rock against each other, into each other, taking us higher and higher until we're both panting, sweating, heaving masses of tangled flesh.

He presses his forehead to mine, his breath hot in my face, and I open my eyes to find him watching me. "Fable." He swallows hard and closes his eyes, breathing so deep his bare chest brushes against mine. "You feel so fucking good."

I'm completely undone. So is he. I feel like we're both going to absolutely die if we don't come at this very instant. Together. Orgasm number one is already a distant memory. Orgasm number two is threatening to take over and I wind my legs around his waist, sending him deeper.

His thrusts increase, become more urgent, and I move

with him. Encouraging him with murmured words, stroking his back with my fingernails, resting my palms on his muscular backside so I can push him farther. Our bodies are smashed so close together, I feel like we're a permanent part of each other.

I've heard those sorts of declarations before. Where two become one and you can't tell where one begins and the other ends, blah, blah, blah. I always thought it sounded like a bunch of romantic crap.

But I feel that way right now with Drew. As if our bodies are entwined, bound so tight we could never, ever come apart. His heart is mine.

And my heart is his.

I breathe his name across his lips as I begin to tremble. This orgasm is different from the first one. It starts low in my belly, radiating through my muscles, my bloodstream, until my entire body is shaking. He keeps moving, keeps thrusting, hard, harder, driving my climax on until he strains above me, consumed by his own orgasm.

I'm captivated by the powerful display of his tense muscles and I run my hands across his shoulders, down his chest. His skin is hot, his flesh unyielding, and tears form at the corner of my eyes at the swell of emotion that threatens to take over me.

The need to express my feelings for him is so overwhelming, I'm afraid I might burst. I don't want to say it first. He may have written it in a note, but he's never, ever said those words out loud to me. I want him to say them.

I need him to say the words first.

Squeezing my eyes shut, I inhale deep, trying to calm my

racing heart. Drew drops a lingering kiss to my forehead before he pulls away and climbs out of bed. I assume he's throwing away the condom I never even realized he'd slipped on and I roll over on my side, hugging myself as I curl up into a ball.

My emotions are a jumbled mess. What the hell just happened? We've had plenty of sex the last few days, but this time I feel like I was hit by a semi truck.

"Hey." He rests his hand on my bare shoulder. "Are you all right?"

"Yeah." I keep my back to him as he slides into bed with me. He wraps an arm around my middle and hauls me in close, so my back is nestled to his front. He's still breathing hard, too, and I snuggle deeper into the pillow, closing my eyes on a soft sigh when he starts raking his fingers through my hair.

I really love it when he does that. And he knows it, too.

"Does it bother you? What, uh, happened to me?"

The question is so out of nowhere, I turn in his embrace so I can see his face, look into his eyes. "What are you talking about?"

"What you found out. When you were with me at my dad's house. Does it bother you?"

"Of course it bothers me, but not in the way you think." I touch his cheek, forcing him to meet my gaze. "I hate what you've endured. I hate what she did to you and how it makes you feel guilty. More than anything, I hurt for you. Your pain is still so fresh and I wish I could somehow take it away."

"You do take it away. You make me feel like a real person. That it's okay to be so free like this. Together. Sexually." He closes his eyes, breathing deep. "You make me feel normal."

Here I am being selfish and wishing he would just tell me he loves me, and he's still going through all of these turbulent emotions. Worrying that I'll think less of him because he's been abused. Yes, abused. He can call it an affair or whatever the hell else he says happened with Adele, but she molested him.

I wish he could really see that.

"Drew." I brush my fingers through his too-long hair. "No matter what, we're in this together. I'm not going to run. Whatever we discover, whatever happens, I'm going to stand by your side and support you."

He opens his eyes. "I have no more secrets with you. At least none that I know of. I've bared my soul to you. I've got nothing to hide."

"Neither do I," I confess softly. "Yet here we still are. Together."

"Together." He smiles faintly. "Can I tell you something? It's been bothering me that you don't know this. I have to get it off my chest."

Wariness creeps over me and I try to shove it away. "What is it?"

"I know . . ." He huffs out a breath. "The day Vanessa died, I know you think I was inside with Adele . . . but it wasn't like that. We were having an argument."

"Oh?" I try my best to remain neutral but anger grows inside me, like a slow, simmering pot threatening to boil over at any minute.

"I was telling her she had to leave me alone. She tried her best to convince me to, uh, you know, but I refused." He closes his eyes again, pain etched all over his handsome face. "I just didn't want you thinking less of me. That I was off fooling around with my stepmom while Vanessa drowned. It wasn't like that. Not at all."

My heart hurts so much. His pain is like a living, breathing thing and I wish I could take it all away. Curling my arms around him, I crush my body to his, scooting up on the mattress so his head can rest on my chest. I press my lips to his forehead and kiss him, the tears flowing freely down my cheeks. "I'm sorry she did this to you. I hate her."

He clings to me much like I cling to him, his face pressed against my bare breasts, and I swear I feel dampness on my skin. Like he's crying. Which only makes me cry more. "I love you," he murmurs against me. "I love you so much, Fable."

My heart cracks in two, both at his pain and at his beautiful, much-needed declaration. "I love you, too."

I've never felt more complete.

Drew

"I told her I loved her," I blurt out of nowhere.

Dr. Harris nods, no emotion on her face whatsoever. As usual. "What did Fable say?"

"She said she loved me, too." I look at my hands, remembering earlier this morning. When I woke Fable up by kissing her softly all over her naked body, the rising sunlight casting her skin a golden hue. Our bodies came together lazily, our whispered I-love-yous fueling me completely.

Our two days pretending the outside world didn't exist ended on a perfect note. Now we're both back to reality.

"Do you believe her?"

Doc's question surprises me. "I think I do."

"Mmm-hmm."

Shit. "It's hard to believe someone loves you for who you are when they've seen all your faults and know all your secrets."

"But doesn't that make it even more believable? Fable's seen everything. She knows everything. Yet she still wants to be with you?"

"I guess so." I shrug and change the subject. "Adele called me a few days ago."

"And what did she have to say?"

"She accused me of poisoning my dad's mind with reasons why he should divorce her."

"Is she right?"

"No. I told him he had to make that choice for himself. I'm not about to give him advice on how to handle her," I say vehemently. My emotions turn into chaos every time I think of the woman. It's exhausting.

"And are they still reconciling?"

"I don't know. I haven't talked to my dad since he told me he might change his mind about the divorce." I don't bother telling Dr. Harris how Fable and I ignored everyone else and pretended we were normal. She'd probably say we were just avoiding the inevitable and accuse me of trying to have an unhealthy relationship with unrealistic expectations.

Yep, I've been to more than my fair share of shrinks when I was younger, before the really bad shit started. I know the drill. Luckily enough, I really connect with this one. She gets me. She doesn't push and she doesn't judge.

"It's hard, isn't it, being in a relationship? With all of your extra baggage, do you think you can be there for Fable when she needs you?"

Ouch. One of those tough questions the doc is famous for.

"I want to believe I can be there for her. She's strong. Sometimes I think she's stronger than me, emotionally."

"But doesn't she have her own set of problems? We all do, you know. And I remember you mentioning she doesn't have the best home life."

I lean back against my chair, sprawl my legs out in front of me. "Her mom is selfish and never around. She has a little brother who's fourteen and she worries about him a lot." I go on to tell Dr. Harris how Owen punched me when he realized I was the one who supposedly broke his sister's heart. I'd forgotten to mention it the last time we saw each other, I'd been so wrapped up in my father's non-divorce announcement.

"I'm starting to see why the two of you are drawn to each other," Dr. Harris says.

Glancing up, I catch her smiling at me and I frown. "What do you mean by that?"

"Your experiences are somewhat similar. You both come from a broken home, you both carry heavy responsibilities and unnecessary guilt. You have money and she doesn't, so there's one difference. You run from your problems and it seems that she confronts them, from what you've told me."

"She's the strongest person I know." I wish I had even half of her strength.

"Don't you think she ever feels weak? Powerless?"

I've never seen Fable anything less than mighty and strong. "I don't know."

"I'm sure she does. You need her, right? So don't you believe she needs you just as much? Her life can't be easy. She has responsibilities, a job, a brother to take care of, and a mother to take care of as well. Whom do you take care of, Drew?"

I swallow hard. "Myself." There's no one else I have to worry about. I'm not good at taking care of other people.

Look at what happened to Vanessa. She died on my watch.

"Do you work?"

Why is she asking me this? She already knows the answer. "School is my job. And football."

"But you're taking a lighter load this semester. And the football season is over," Dr. Harris points out gently.

"Are you trying to make me feel guilty for not having as much responsibility as Fable does?" It seems like she's purposely trying to make me angry.

"No," she says slowly. "I'm trying to make you see that she's probably going to need you. Do you think you have the capability to be there for her?"

"I don't . . ." My voice trails off when I see the pointed look Dr. Harris is giving me. "Yes. I can be there for her. I have to be. I love her. That's what people who are in love do. They support each other."

"You're right. Relationships aren't easy, especially for people who still feel somewhat . . . broken."

"Are you saying you think I'm broken?" I'm immediately on the defensive.

"Not at all. I said people who *feel* they are broken. Don't you feel that way still?"

I'm quiet. That's answer enough, I'm sure.

"Just because you feel like you're broken doesn't mean she views you the same way. Fable sees all of your potential. All of your strengths, and she believes in you completely. Otherwise, she wouldn't be with you. Right?"

"I hope so."

Dr. Harris sets down the iPad that she uses to take notes

MONICA MURPHY

and smiles at me. "Just remember that your relationship with Fable is still in that fresh, euphoric honeymoon stage. Cherish her. Enjoy her. But never forget you need to be there for her through the good times and the bad. And I'm saying this in a rather subjective way, Drew: I believe that girl is good for you. She can help you heal."

I can hardly contain my smile. "Are you saying Fable has your approval?"

Doc laughs. "I shouldn't be talking to you like this, you know. I'm losing sight of my objectivity. But from everything I hear you say about her, that would be a resounding yes."

CHAPTER 13

If I want her, I need to fight for her.
—Drew Callahan

Fable

I cruise into the restaurant late in the afternoon humming under my breath, offering a hello to the bitchy chick who works the hostess's desk. Her jaw about drops to the floor and I smile blithely at her, thrilled that I threw her off her catty game.

Nothing can get me down today. I'm on a complete Drew high.

Heading toward the back, I go to clock in and see Jen's already hanging out in the small employee lounge area, sipping on a Starbucks Frap and watching me. "Fancy you coming back to work," she drawls.

"I trade one shift with someone and it's suddenly I don't want to work? So unfair." I stash my purse in one of the lockers provided to keep our stuff safe and twirl the lock, keeping my back to Jen for fear of any judgmental staring on her part.

"Colin wants to talk to you. He asked me to tell him when you got here," she says quietly.

I turn to face her, fear turning my blood ice cold. "Is he going to fire me?"

"No." Jen doesn't offer any other sort of explanation.

"What's going to happen, then?"

"He's going to ask if you take this job seriously. He sees a lot of potential in you, Fable. He wants you to eventually take it to the next level here."

"What the hell does that mean?" Give me a break. I'm a freaking waitress. Yeah, from what I can see so far, the tips are fabulous. Better than any other place I've ever worked. But there's not a lot of room for growth at The District. I'm not stupid.

"You know how T goes around helping him open restaurants and training the staff? Colin has huge plans. He wants to open up a bunch of Districts all over the state and eventually the west coast, turning it into a chain. And he needs more training staff."

"I've been here only a couple of weeks," I point out incredulously.

"I told you, he thinks you have potential."

"You've been with him longer. Why wouldn't he choose you for his new training person? Or any of the other girls who work here?"

"I don't . . . like to travel." Hmmm, there's something she's hiding, I can tell. "And the other girls, they're just here to get dressed up and look pretty and pick up guys. They view this job as a way to get spending money and keep Mom and Dad happy while they nearly fail college. They don't have future aspirations for the food industry." Jen shakes her head.

"Well, I don't have future aspirations for the food industry either," I retort. Hell no do I want to work at a restaurant for the rest of my life. I hate this sort of thing. I'm doing it because it's all I know.

"Well, what *are* your future aspirations?"

Funny thing is, I haven't a clue. I always talk about having hopes and dreams and wanting to get the hell away from this small town. But what do I really want to do? What do I want to be when I grow up?

I haven't a fucking clue.

"Is she here—oh." Colin stops short as he strides into the room, looking totally surprised to see me standing there. "Fable. I was looking for you."

"I heard," I can't help but say, earning a death glare from Jen.

"Have a minute? I'd like to talk to you." He smiles, his stance relaxed, all that easygoing don't-worry charm buzzing all around him. He looks damn good in dark jeans and a white button-down shirt he left untucked, the sleeves rolled up to reveal strong, tanned forearms.

I may be in love with Drew, but I can appreciate a handsome man when I see one.

"Am I in trouble?" I ask, making sure Jen wasn't lying.

"Not at all," he says quickly, his voice smooth.

I raise a brow, letting him know I don't quite believe him. "Shouldn't I be preparing the tables for the evening?"

"Jen has it under control for now. Besides, I only need to take up a few minutes of your time. Then you can go polish glasses to your heart's content." He chuckles and presses his hand to my lower back when he approaches me, guiding me to his office, his hand never leaving me.

I shrug away from his touch the second we walk into his office. He shuts the door behind us, rounding his desk and pointing a finger toward an empty chair. "Have a seat."

Sitting on the edge of the seat, I tap my heel against the bare wood floor. We're wearing the lace shirt/black shorts getup again and I know when Drew picks me up from work, he's probably going to attack me.

Dirty girl that I am, I can't freaking wait.

"What happened with the shift change, Fable?" Colin asks once he settles in behind his desk.

"I had something come up." I shrug. "Something personal."

He raises a single brow. "Is everything all right?"

"Oh, yeah. Everything's fine."

"I don't mind when my employees switch out their schedules as long as everyone's covered and as long as people don't make a habit out of it. I do have some concerns, though." He rests his folded arms on top of the desk, his expression solemn. "Are you happy here?"

I'm taken aback by his question. "Um, yeah."

His eyes harden. "Really?"

"What are you digging at? I mean, I've only been working here a few weeks. If you're not happy with me, then go ahead and fire me." I perch farther on the edge of my chair, ready to take flight if need be.

"You automatically assume the worst, don't you?"

This little meeting is getting ridiculous. "Listen, say what you need to say and get it over with. I'm not in the mood for a bunch of games tonight."

"Fine. Get over your pissy attitude and I'll tell you everything you need to hear."

My jaw drops open. I can't believe he just called me pissy. But he's right. I am. "What's up?" I ask weakly.

"I know you've only been here for a few weeks, but you impress me. A lot. You only need to be told once what to do and how to do it, and you have it under control. The customers like you. T thinks you're fantastic and I value her opinion above that of anyone else in this place." Colin leans across his desk, as if he really wants to get his message across. "I want to give you more hours, but I won't do it if you're going to bail on your shifts all the time."

"I won't bail on my shifts," I say automatically.

He smiles. "So you'll take the increase in hours."

"Absolutely."

"I'm giving you a sixty-day probation period. Once that passes and I'm satisfied with the job you're doing, you'll automatically receive a raise."

My eyebrows shoot up. "Really?"

"Really." He nods. "I plan on opening up a few more locations in the Sacramento area over the next twelve to eighteen months. I need people who are able to train my new employees the way T does. Is that something that interests you?"

I'm like Jen. Travel is near to impossible for me, what with Owen in school and my mom never around. But I can't say no, can I? The restaurant biz definitely doesn't interest me long term but I need a steady, good-paying job, especially if I really go through with it and get an apartment for just Owen and me. What Colin's talking about sounds like my every current financial wish come true.

"Um, possibly?" My vague answer doesn't please my boss at all. He's frowning at me big time. "Look, I have a little brother and our relationship with my mom is . . . complicated."

His bunched expression smooths out completely. "We'll discuss everything further once we get closer to the possibility of my needing you for training purposes. Truthfully, the plans for the restaurants are just that—still in the planning stages."

"Sounds amazing," I say weakly, because it does. This guy is ambitious as hell and I can't help but admire him.

"It will be, trust me." The grin he flashes me is so bright it momentarily blinds me. "Now get back out there and help Jen. We have three reservations tonight, all big parties."

Groaning, I stand and hurry out of his office, my feet already aching, and I haven't even really started working yet.

"Do you work tomorrow?"

I grab my purse out of the locker I stashed it in and shut the metal door with a loud clang. I'm exhausted. Tonight's shift was rough and I can't wait to go home and collapse into bed. "No, thank God."

"Me either. Look." Jen glances around, as if she's afraid someone's going to catch us talking. Weird, considering we're all alone in the room. "There have been some things going on in my life and I'm dying to go out and blow off my steam, you know? So you want to go with me tomorrow night and grab some drinks? Maybe have a girls' night out?"

My first response is to say no. I don't want to miss out on one night with Drew, which is ridiculous and needy, but damn it, he only just came back into my life. I want to spend every moment I have with him.

Then I catch the look on Jen's face, the worry and need in her gaze. Does she not have any other friends to ask? Or is she just like me, with really no friends at all?

"Sure," I say before I can talk myself out of it. "Where do you want to go?"

The smile that appears is worth my few hours away from Drew. I think this girl needs my friendship more than I realize. "I don't know, La Salle's?"

I smack her lightly on the arm. "Good one. I don't think so."

"How about Jake's? It's always hopping."

"Well . . . you do realize I'm underage." I used to have a fake ID but I lost it. After a bouncer made me sign a piece of paper to make sure the signature matched it one night about a year ago when I was with some loser dude on a date, and it didn't match. I was done for. He snatched that license from me and I haven't bothered to find another one since. "So I'm not much fun on the go-out-and-get-drinks deal."

Jen laughed and shook her head. "I forgot. You act so much older than twenty, you know? You're like an old soul."

"I don't know whether to take that as a compliment or an insult." I wrinkle my nose.

She laughs some more. "It's definitely a compliment. We can go out to dinner. I'll drink and you can watch me."

"Ooh, sounds fun," I say sarcastically, but I really do mean it.

"I'll text you details tomorrow." Jen slings her purse over her shoulder, studying me. "You don't mind, do you? I know you have that guy in your life now."

I squirm, suddenly uncomfortable. I'm not prepared to

talk about Drew with anyone yet. "I can stand to be away from him for a few hours." *Maybe.*

"Are you sure?" Her gentle voice and twinkling eyes tell me she's teasing, but I also wonder if she's worried I'll bail on her for a guy, which I have no plans in doing. Drew and I don't need to spend every waking moment together.

Though sometimes it sure feels like we do. Being away from him is hard. Silly, considering he's been back in my life for only a matter of days, but we share such an intense connection, it's hard to ignore it.

"By the dreamy look on your face, I'm going to guess this guy must be pretty special." Jen nudges me. "You can tell me all about him tomorrow night."

"Yeah," I agree with a laugh, but I doubt I will.

What I share with Drew is still a little too special to blab about with my new friend.

Drew

I watch Fable exit the restaurant. She's with the same girl who worked with her the night of Logan's party. Tall, with dark hair and olive skin, she's the complete opposite of Fable in every way. It's sort of funny, watching them talk animatedly with each other. A yin to each other's yang.

My heart squeezes in my chest when I see Fable laugh and shake her head. She looks happy. The happiest I've ever seen her. I'd like to think I'm responsible for some of that happiness.

I know she's made me the happiest I've ever been.

She waves goodbye to her friend and walks across the

parking lot toward my truck. I'm struck anew by how beautiful she is, her smile growing on her face as she comes closer. She's wearing those damn shorts again, the ones that are way too short, and this time she's added black tights to the mix. They make her legs look incredibly long.

And incredibly hot.

Pushing away from the side of the truck, I meet her halfway, slipping my arms around her and pulling her in for a quick kiss. She's warm to my cold since I've been standing outside for the last ten minutes, and she brushes her nose against mine before she pulls away. "You're freezing," she murmurs.

Her voice alone warms me up and I open the truck door for her without a word, pushing her inside by cupping her backside, making her squeal. I slam the door and round the truck, eager to take her back to my place, though I have no idea where she wants to go. She probably has to get home. She has responsibilities, after all.

And I have none, as my shrink so kindly reminded me.

"Where to?" I ask casually once I slip behind the wheel.

"I should probably go home." She won't meet my gaze, and I wonder why.

"No problem." I throw the truck into gear and pull out of the parking lot, turning onto the street. "Busy night?"

"Exhausting. Thank God I'm off tomorrow."

"We should do something." I don't have school and she doesn't work. We could stay in bed all day and I'd be perfectly content.

"Um, about tomorrow." She sounds hesitant. Even a little nervous. "My friend Jen, the girl I work with? She asked if we could hang out together tomorrow night. Go to dinner and have drinks. Stuff like that. You don't care, do you?"

I care a lot. I'd rather she never left my side, but I'm being completely unrealistic. And also thinking like a jealous ass. "I don't mind. I mean, I'm not your keeper."

She's watching me. I can feel her eyes on me though I face straight ahead. "It'll only be for a few hours. I get the sense Jen doesn't have many friends. I don't either. It's nice to find one who doesn't think I'm out to fuck her boyfriend behind her back."

I have to look at her now, shocked at the harsh way she just spoke. "Did you used to do that? Fuck other girls' boyfriends behind their backs?"

She shoots me an icy stare. *"No."* A sigh escapes her. "Fine. I made one mistake. Only because he lied to me and said he didn't have a girlfriend. I was a sophomore in high school and he was a senior. Gorgeous. Popular. Played on the football team, sort of like a weak copy of you. We went out on a few dates. He was always sneaking me around, never taking me out in public or with his friends, but I didn't care. I was too far gone over him."

This story is going in a bad direction. I can feel it. "A weak copy of me?" What, does she have a pattern? A type she prefers? Is she saying I fall under that type?

"You know what I mean." She waves a hand. "He was my first. I gave up my V card to him because I was stupid, thinking it would bring us closer and he would fall totally in love with me. Then I find out he has a girlfriend, right after I had sex with him. He was totally using me because she wouldn't mess around with him, so he ran out and found the first dumb girl who would."

I both feel sorry for her and infuriated with her that she would do something so careless. "So, what, you were fifteen when you were first with that guy?"

"Yeah."

"How many guys have you been with, Fable?" Okay, now I totally sound like the jealous asshole boyfriend. I don't want to be that guy. I know she needs to get her past off her chest and it shouldn't matter. It shouldn't hurt me. I didn't know her then. We were both different people then.

But knowing about her past does hurt. I can't deny it.

"You're going to automatically assume the number is out-rageous, aren't you? I really didn't expect you to pass judg-ment on me like everyone else in my life." She crosses her arms in front of her chest. "You disappoint me, Drew. I fig-ured you were better than that."

Fuck. How do I respond? I've blown it completely. Now she's pissed. I can practically see the steam rising out of her ears. She refuses to look at me, too. Instead she chooses to stare straight ahead for the rest of the ride to her apartment, her jaw hard, her eyes narrowed.

From happy to angry in a matter of minutes, that's what I just did to her. And why? Because I'm feeling a little posses-sive of her time and I want her to spend it all with me? Am I that insecure? I've never had a real girlfriend before. I've never been someone's boyfriend. Twenty-freaking-one years old and I'm a complete, clueless idiot when it comes to rela-tionships and how to make them work.

I pull into the parking lot of her apartment complex and her hand is already on the door handle. She looks ready to leap out of the vehicle while it's still in motion, she wants to get away from me that badly. "Fable, wait."

Hitting the brakes, I wait for her to respond, but she doesn't. Her back is to me, her body poised to take flight and escape right out the door. I've hurt her and I hate that.

"I'm sorry," I say, my voice soft. "I didn't mean to pass judgment on you. I have no right to do so. You accept all my faults, so it's the least I can do for you."

She turns to glare at me. "Because I accept your faults, you'll accept mine? Is that all this is? If so, I need more from you, Drew. This isn't some tit-for-tat sort of deal. I need your trust. I need you to believe that I want to be with you and only you. And my past can't shade our present or our future. My past has always followed me, and you know what sucks? Most of the stories out there are completely untrue. I make a few wrong steps, a few bad mistakes, and it turns into me ruling a multiyear slutdom over all the guys. Through high school, outside of high school . . ."

I remain quiet, absorbing her words. She's right. I can't let her past bother me or darken our future. If I do, I'm just setting us up to fail.

"I'm not perfect," she murmurs. "No one is. But I'm not going to pay for my mistakes every time you get mad at me or jealous. Going out with Jen tomorrow night isn't about me trying to flirt with other guys or anything like that."

"I never said it was."

Her eyes soften the slightest bit. "So what's the problem? Why are you acting like this?"

"I'm not good at this sort of thing. I'm fucking it all up and I don't know why." I tap my fingers against the edge of the steering wheel, unsure of what to say next, feeling edgy as hell.

She holds all the cards in this argument right now. I'm scared she's going to say I'm not worth the trouble.

"Using that as an excuse isn't going to fly forever, you know. After a while, it'll just get old."

"What are we doing, Fable?" I ask incredulously.

She shrugs. "Having our first fight as a couple?"

I want to laugh, but I don't. "I mean this. Us. What's going on between us?"

"If you have to ask, that scares me," she answers warily.

"Are we really a couple? Are we in a relationship? We haven't defined it yet."

"Do we need to? Can't we just take it day by day?" She turns away from me and stares out the window. "I'm tired. Maybe we shouldn't talk about this now."

Panic rises within me. "But . . ."

"I think I want to be alone. I'm super tired and the last few days have been sorta overwhelming." She opens the door and climbs out of my truck, bending over so she can meet my gaze through the still-open door. "I'll call you tomorrow?"

It feels like she's leaving me for good. My throat's dry and I can hardly force any words out, I'm so worried this is it. With my luck, I'll never see her again. "Yeah," I croak before she slams the door. "Call me."

She offers me a tiny smile before she lets the door close. And then she turns and walks away.

Taking my heart with her.

CHAPTER 14

If I had a flower for every time I thought of you . . . I
could walk through my garden forever.
—Alfred, Lord Tennyson

Fable

"Wake up." I yank the covers from Owen and he tries to grab
at them, rolling onto his back with an agonized groan.

"Shit, Fabes, what are you doing here? And why are you
waking me up like some sort of drill sergeant?"

"Ha, if I were a drill sergeant I'd have a whistle blasting in
your ear and be commanding you to run some damn laps." I
thwack him on the leg with my index finger and thumb, dropping the comforter back on him in a pile. "You're going to be
late for school."

He cracks open his eyes and glances at the clock on his
rickety bedside table. "It's not even seven yet. Why the hell
are you up? What are you even doing here? I thought you'd
stay the night with your new lover boy again."

Yeah, well, so did I. I'd even contemplated asking Drew to
stay with me so I could be here for Owen last night. But that
petty argument we got into ruined all those plans.

"I wanted to stay home and talk to you." I sit on the edge of his bed, glancing around his room. It's a disaster, not that mine is much better, but at least I don't have smelly socks lying all over the place and a pile of dirty clothes in the middle of the room that I swear is waist high. "You need to douche this room, and soon."

"Did my big sister use the word 'douche'? Now I think I've heard it all." He sits up and rubs the back of his head. "I can't believe you ditched your new man for me. You must want to talk about some serious shit."

"Why must you continue to use such foul language?" I sound like a mom. I should be used to his constant cussing. And really, I have no room to judge. I've had a foul mouth for years. It was my first act of rebellion against my mother and I never let up.

"Gimme a break. You curse like a sailor." He stifles a yawn and scratches his bare chest. "What do you want to talk about?"

"I've been thinking." I pluck at a loose thread on his worn comforter. I really wish I had more money so I could buy the two of us nicer things. "I want to find a different apartment."

He's quiet for a moment and I look at him, see the shock and disbelief written all over his face. "You want to move? And leave me with Mom all alone?"

"No." I shake my head. "No, no, no. I would never do that. I want us to leave Mom. I want the two of us to live to-gether." When he doesn't say a word, I forge on. "She's never here. She's always with her new boyfriend and she doesn't have a job anymore, so she can't pay rent. I'm paying for everything, and trust me, it's hard. I don't make a ton of money. I work freaking part time, though my new boss is willing to give me more hours."

"That's great."

"It is, but we still have too much apartment here. I bet I could find a two-bedroom in a better neighborhood for way less money. What do you think? You want to do it?"

"I'll go wherever you go," he says, but I can hear the hesitation in his voice.

"But what?"

"But . . . I'm only fourteen. Aren't there legalities or whatever about that sort of stuff? Like, won't Mom have to make you my guardian or something if I go and live with you?"

"Why would she need to? Let's not pretend that she wants us around here so bad. She won't care if you come live with me."

"She might." He drops his head, bunching the comforter up in his lap.

Crap. He wants to believe Mom actually cares about him. After all, he's just a kid. No one wants to face the realization that their mom doesn't give a rat's ass about them. I still don't like facing it. But I've put up a wall against the pain and tell myself it doesn't matter. I don't need her.

"Owen." I grip his knee and he looks up, his gaze meeting mine. We both have the same eyes as Mom, though I always thought his were prettier. He has the thickest, darkest lashes I've ever seen, and I don't know where he got them from considering his hair is a dirty blond. Girls are going to go crazy for those eyes someday, if they aren't already. My brother is handsome. Cocky and full of attitude. I feel sorry for any girl who falls for him. "I want you with me. I don't want to do this alone."

"What about Drew Callahan? Wouldn't you want to move in with him? Isn't he rich?"

I grimace. "I have no idea what's going on with Drew. But you and me? We're blood. We're family. I'm not about to leave you. We're all each other has."

"What's Mom gonna do? Don't you think she'll get mad?"

"I doubt it. This way she doesn't have to worry about us and she can go live with her boyfriend. I can find a nicer place that's smaller and pay less rent. It's a win-win for us all." I can't think about Mom getting upset with me for wanting to do this. Why should she care? I'm making her life easier.

"What happens if it doesn't work out for her and Larry the Loser? Then where will she go?"

"Owen." I grip his knee tighter. "She's not our responsibility. She's an adult. She can take care of herself."

He tilts his head, screws up his lips. Looking far older and world-weary than any fourteen-year-old should. "I just worry about her. I worry about you, too. I'm supposed to be the man of the house."

My jaw drops. "Who told you that?"

"Mom. A long time ago. She said I had to watch out for the both of you and I promised I always would. I haven't done the best job of it, but I swear, I try."

My heart breaks for this kid. He's gone through so much at too young of an age. He's seen too much. Grabbing his shoulders, I bring him in for a quick hug, not holding on to him for too long since I know he'll just wiggle out of my grip anyway. "We'll take care of each other, okay? It's not all on me or all on you. We'll share the load."

"I'll help you with whatever you need, Fabes. I'm on your side. I promise." He clings to me and I hug him close, savoring it for a little while longer. I love him so much. I hate that he's conflicted between Mom and me.

"Go take a shower," I tell him once I get up off the bed and start out of his room. "And when you get home today, I want you to clean this room. It sucks."

His laughter follows me down the hall as I head toward the kitchen. I've been up for over a half hour, lying in bed, staring at the ceiling. Thinking of looking for an apartment today, talking to Owen about it, maybe gathering up the courage to talk to Mom about her moving out.

Trying my best to not think of Drew.

What the hell happened last night, anyway? Our fight had started out of nothing. I tried to be honest with him and he got all macho-man-how-many-guys-have-you-fucked-anyway on me. I accept him for who he is, flaws and all, so why can't he accept me?

I get irritated just thinking about it. So it's best I don't.

A knock sounds at the door and I scowl. Who the hell is here at seven in the morning? Stomping over to the door, I look through the peephole but I see nothing. I throw open the door and peek to the left, then the right. No one's there.

Then I glance down and find a gorgeous bouquet of wildflowers sitting on the thin, faded doormat. The vase is full of a riot of colorful blooms; I can't identify any of them beyond their pretty colors. I know in an instant who they're from.

Grabbing the vase, I clutch it in my hand as I step farther outside, my gaze steady as I study the parking lot. But I don't see his truck. I don't see any indication he's been here at all other than the flowers in my hand.

How the heck did he get them here and then disappear? I

know he's fast on the football field, but come on. Where did he go?

"Who the hell was knocking—oh, Lover Boy."

I turn to see Owen grinning at me, wearing a stained T-shirt with some unknown and I'm sure crappy band's logo on the front and black faded skinny jeans. We walk back into the apartment together. "That's what you're wearing to school?"

He glances down at himself. "I'm not going to the prom. Gimme a break. Hey, you got any smokes?"

"Owen! Promise me you're not smoking." The guilty look on his face says it all. If the flowers weren't so beautiful, I'd hurl the vase at him, I'm so pissed. "You're too young to smoke. It's a horrible, nasty habit."

"*You* do it."

"Not all the time. I mostly quit." Yeah, that sounds lame as hell.

"I only smoke every once in a while," Owen whines. "It soothes my nerves."

"Such a bullshit answer. I'm sure if I dug around in your room right now, I'd find some weed, too. Am I right?" I raise a brow, just daring him to deny it.

His eyes widen the slightest bit right before he goes for pure defiant nonchalance. "Oh, who cares? You act like you've always been on the straight and narrow. I bet you've smoked a few bowls in your life."

Not really. Drugs don't do much for me. I smoked a joint here and there through high school, but cigarettes were my major vice. The occasional keg party would do me in, too. Make me do stupid things. That's why I avoided them after a while. "I'm twenty, you're fourteen. There's a difference be-tween what I'm doing and what you're doing."

"Such crap," Owen mutters as he walks away from me, heading toward the couch where his sweatshirt is flung over the back. "I'm outta here."

I set the vase down on the kitchen counter, my pleasure at receiving the flowers evaporating when I realize I've not only just gotten into a huge fight with my brother, but I did the same thing with Drew last night.

Who's the one with the problem, hmm?

"Owen, look. I'm sorry." He stops at the door, as if he's waiting for me to further explain myself. "I just hate to see you make a bunch of stupid mistakes like I did. I wish you could learn from me."

"I'm going to do what I do no matter what, Fabes. I wish you could see that." He turns to face me, looking like a raga-muffin in his faded black sweatshirt streaked with bleach stains. Who the hell does his laundry? Oh, that's right, he does. "I'm not a bad kid. I get decent grades. I only skip class sometimes. And I have good friends. So I smoke here and there. So I get high and forget about my troubles for a while. Is that so bad?"

Yes! I want to shout at him. *I want you to be perfect and well behaved and never give me any problems. I don't want you doing drugs or smoking or drinking or fooling around with girls. I want you to be eight years old forever.*

"Maybe we can talk later?" I suggest. "I should be here when you get home from school."

"What else is there to talk about? You've already made up your mind. We're moving without Mom, you hate that I smoke, and you think I'm a fuck-up. Whatever." He leaves the apartment without another word, slamming the door behind him, and I'm left standing there, so shocked my mouth is hanging open.

Holy. Crap. I've stepped in it all over the place. Why am I so confrontational lately? What the hell is my problem?

Regret settles over me and I sit heavily on the creaky bar stool. Way to go and screw up that conversation. Clearly I'm the one with the bad attitude. I keep picking fights with my favorite people. Not the smartest move I've ever made, that's for sure.

I run my finger over one of the soft flower petals. It's a bright, sunny yellow, the complete opposite of my morose mood.

Look at me. A man leaves me flowers on my doorstep and I'm all mopey. I should be the one apologizing and he's the one making grand gestures. No guy has ever brought me flowers. Ever.

My gaze catches sight of a small cream-colored envelope nestled among the blooms and I snatch it up, opening the envelope with trembling fingers.

Fable is . . .
Faithful
Amazing
Beautiful
Loving
Exquisite
I'm sorry.
   —Drew

A wistful sigh full of longing escapes me. I think he's trying to slowly tear me apart so he can be the only one who puts me back together. His words kill me. Slay me dead.

And they fill me with so much hope, I don't know how I could have ever doubted him.

Drew

My head is throbbing when I wake up, my brain foggy. I lay awake in bed most of the night, replaying my conversation with Fable. Unable to figure out exactly where everything went wrong, but since I'm a world-class screw-up, it had to be my fault.

I finally gave up pretending to sleep and climbed out of bed, threw on some clothes, and went to a local supermarket. Found a beautiful arrangement of wildflowers and bought it without thinking twice. Yeah, maybe I should've got her some roses since they're twice as expensive and supposedly are more romantic, but they didn't seem Fable's style.

The note made me work a little harder. I wanted to get it just right. No way could I use the word "marshmallow." She would've killed me. I'd like to see her use it on me again. The one time she did, I almost blew it and didn't show up.

But if she ever did use our code word again, I'd love to see that moment of sweet surprise wash over her when I come to rescue her so fast, her head spins.

Instead, I write her a little poem using her name. Much like I did for my tattoo, though this one is simpler. Sweeter. All about her.

Once I got back home, I crashed out. Woke up hours later with the hangover feeling, the sun's light deathly bright in my room. Feels like the day is already half over and when I check my phone, I see that it almost is.

I also see I have a bunch of text messages from a certain someone.

Drew is . . .

Delicious

Real

Extra sexy and . . .

Wonderful

My heart threatens to crack. She wrote me a poem back. I can't fucking believe it. I text her a response:

You got the flowers then.

She replies immediately.

I love the flowers. Thank you.

A smile forms on my lips as I answer her.

You're welcome. Did you like the note?

I loved the note even more. I think you're a closet romantic.

My smile grows.

Only for you.

She doesn't answer, and I wonder if I somehow screwed up.

Then I get pissed at myself for always thinking I screwed up. She finally texts back:

What are you doing?

I'm still in bed.

I pause. Should I say what I really want to say next? *Aw, fuck it.*

Thinking of you.

I send the text, my heart rate increasing. I hope she's forgiven me. I'm dying to see her.

Are you naked, Drew? Because I could totally get on board with that image.

MONICA MURPHY

I burst out laughing at her text and quickly reply.

You want me naked? That can be arranged.

I'm only in sweats, not even wearing any underwear. That I'm thinking like this almost makes me want to laugh.

Also makes me want to suggest we indulge in some of that phone sex/sexting thing we talked about a few nights ago, which sort of blows my mind.

But with Fable, I'm willing to do just about anything.

Only if I'm naked with you.

A few words typed on a screen and I'm hard as steel. Damn, this girl.

My doorbell rings and I go completely still. Who the hell is that? I head toward the door and open it, shock rendering me frozen when I find Fable standing on my doorstep, her cell phone clutched in her hand. A wicked smile curves her lips and I let my gaze wander over her.

She's wearing bright pink cotton shorts and a black long-sleeve T-shirt that clings to her breasts and makes them look huge. Her hair is pulled back in a long braid, wild blond strands brushing her cheeks. Her face is devoid of makeup with the exception of some gloss slicking her lips, making them extra shiny. Extra kissable.

My girl is gorgeous. Those shorts should be criminal. They're like a lethal weapon. I swear if I keep staring at her legs I'll keel over from witnessing too much hotness.

"I keep getting these crazy messages from some random guy." She holds her phone up. I see the last message I sent her on the screen, along with her accompanying reply. She's just as guilty. "He says he wants to get naked with me."

I lean against the door. If she wants to play this game, fine.

I'm up for it. Might make things more interesting. "Hmm, weird. Why would anyone want to get naked with you?"

She rests her hands on her hips. "I don't know. Looks like *you're* almost naked."

Glancing down at myself, I scratch my bare chest. I can feel her eyes on me and I look up, watching her as she blatantly checks me out. Just like I blatantly checked her out only moments ago. "I assume you've accepted my apology?"

Her expression changes in an instant. Those pretty green eyes dim and her mouth softens. "I'm the one who should apologize. I feel like I've been picking fights all over the place."

I grab her hand and yank her inside, shutting the door behind her. Without giving her a chance to think, let alone escape, I pin her against the door and hold her there with my body, my hands on her waist. Her skin is warm, I can feel her heat through the thin barrier of her shirt, and I want her.

Beneath me, over me, with me. Always.

"Who else are you fighting with?" I slip my fingers beneath the hem of her shirt so I can touch soft, pliant flesh.

"My brother." A shaky breath escapes her. "I'm sorry we argued last night, Drew."

I love how she always cuts through the bullshit. There are no lingering misunderstandings or grudges. We argue, we challenge each other, we apologize, we move on.

"I'm sorry, too." I lean in closer and inhale the subtle scent of her shampoo. She smells so good. Everything about her smells amazing. She's warm and fragrant and soft in my arms, her breasts nestled against my bare chest, her arms wrapping loosely around my waist. "Wanna have makeup sex?"

She giggles just before I rain kisses along her slender neck.

MONICA MURPHY

The giggles turn instantly into a low moan and she slides her hands up my back, her nails skimming my skin. "I would love to have makeup sex."

Before she can say another word, I lift my head and settle my mouth on hers. I'm hungry for her sweet lips, her tongue. I devour her, holding her in place as I cup her head with my hands, my fingers tangling in her hair, ruining her braid. She whimpers against my mouth, her hands diving beneath the loose waistband of my sweats, and I hear her murmur of pleasure when she discovers I have no underwear on.

"You are so bad," she whispers, her tongue darting out to lick my lower lip as she shoves my sweats down so they fall in a heap around my ankles. I step out of them and kick them out of the way, my tongue doing a slow search of the inside of her mouth.

No one who knows me would ever consider me a bad boy. I left that image up to other guys, always happy to stay in my good-guy place. Girls preferred bad boys, so I walked the straight and narrow.

Plus, I flat-out didn't like feeling bad. Being full of secret shame does that to a person.

Fable makes me want to be bad for her, just to hear her say it. Her pleased tone is unmistakable. I think she likes corrupting me.

My mouth never leaving hers, I grab her ass and lift. She twines her legs around my hips, clinging to me, the heat of her burning my dick through the thin fabric of her shorts. I frantically tug at them, dropping her so her feet fall to the ground only so I can push her shorts and lacy panties off, she helping me the entire time.

Regret flashes through me as I watch the delicate scrape of fabric fall to the floor. I'd have to linger over those pretty lace panties next time. I'm too eager, too caught up in the moment to take it slow. I needed to be inside her. Now.

"Drew." She pants my name against my lips as I lift her back up, those sexy legs going around my hips, her ankles digging into my ass. "I want to feel you."

"You're feeling me right now, baby." Oh hell yeah, she's feeling me, and I'm feeling her. She's so slick and hot, the head of my cock nudges against her folds and all I want to do is plunge inside her. Fuck her until I can't see straight and I'm coming so hard I can't think.

"I mean . . . oh God, I can't think when you do that," she whispers, her voice trembling when I thrust against her, nice and slow. "I'm on the pill, Drew."

"That's awesome." Yeah, no babies for us. We can barely handle each other, let alone throw a kid in the mix.

She tugs on my hair, getting my attention. "I mean, I want you inside me with no barriers. No condom."

I stare into her eyes, my breaths coming in ragged pants, my skin already glistening with sweat. And I haven't even been inside her yet. I'm so worked up, so ready to do what-ever she asks me to do, I don't give her suggestion a second thought. I'm fully on board.

"That sounds like a great plan," I say as I slide inside her. "Ah, fuck." Closing my eyes, I lean my forehead against hers, hear the thunk of the back of her head making connection with the door. But she doesn't seem hurt. More like overcome with sensation, just like I am.

Without the condom on, the heat of her, snug and wet, it's

all a million times more intense. I could buck against her once and probably come like a geyser.

Instead I take a deep breath and stay completely still. She's so tight, so hot, and she shifts against me, making me groan and squeeze her hips hard to prevent her from moving any further.

"W-what's wrong?" She sounds confused.

I open my eyes to see her troubled gaze. "You keep moving like that, I'm done."

"Moving like what?"

"Just . . . moving." She does it once more, a subtle thrust of her hips, her legs tightening around me, sending me deeper, and I groan again, moving my forehead away from her so I can press it against the door. "I can't take it."

"Why?" She runs her hands through my hair, her nails scratching lightly along my scalp, and I shiver.

"I'll come so fast, I'll embarrass myself."

She's slowly sliding up and down, riding me as best she can. "I want you to come fast. I want to watch you lose control. I find it . . ." She sets her mouth against my ear and releases a shuddering breath. "Extra sexy."

I smile despite my agony and lift my head to look at her. She's quoting her poem to me and I love her for it. "We've only started. What about you?"

"Come for me, Drew." She's grinding against me now, and I'm grinding back as if I have no control over myself. "There's plenty of time for us to do this again this afternoon, right?"

"Right," I agree because at the moment, I'll agree to just about anything, she feels so fucking amazing wrapped all around me, her top and bra still on, the lower half of her body completely bare.

Rectifying my neglect, I push her shirt up, exposing her white lacy bra that offers a glimpse of her hard pink nipples beneath, and I groan. I'm going to lose it. I run my fingers along the edge of her bra, feel the tremble ripple beneath her creamy soft skin from my touch.

"I love you, Drew," she whispers. I watch her, entranced by the expression on her face. Her eyes are closed, she's biting her lower lip as I continue to touch her, as she continues to ride me, and I'm completely and totally overwhelmed.

"I love you, too," I murmur against her swollen lips just before I kiss her, my tongue thrusting in her mouth much like I thrust deep inside her body. Continually, again and again, trying to convey all of the feelings, the love and the need and the want I have for her.

Her little cry tells me she's closer than I thought and I increase my pace, spilling myself inside her within seconds. She's coming, too, her body gripping my cock tight as she convulses around me, and I open my eyes. Watch her fall apart, intoxicated by the flush of her skin, the little anguished sounds she makes, the way she feels, the way she smells.

Clutching her close, I run my fingers through her messy hair, touching her, calming my racing heart. She is my everything and I swear at this very moment, I will never let her go.

CHAPTER 15

Stand up for something you love. Even if it means you stand alone.
—Unknown

Drew

My cell's nagging ringtone wakes me up and I lift my head, glancing down to find Fable snuggled against me, warm and naked and fast asleep. Her arm is draped over my stomach, her cheek pressed against my pecs, her silky-soft hair in my face. Hell no do I want to answer that call. Whoever it is can wait.

I have my girl sprawled all over me, fast asleep. Why would I want to end this anytime soon? My phone stops ringing only to start again and I reach out, grabbing it from my bedside table to see who it could be.

The word *Dad* flashes on the screen and I answer the call, trying my best to keep my voice low so I don't disturb Fable. "Hey."

"Can you talk?" He sounds frantic. Freaked out and upset.

"Sure, give me a minute." I disengage myself from Fable's

grip and she murmurs in her sleep when I slide away from her. Quietly I climb out of bed, grab my sweats, and slip them on before I head out into the living room. "What's going on?" I ask.

His breathing is ragged before he starts speaking. "Adele cheated on me. I know it. I've seen proof. We're finished. Through. I won't put up with her lies any longer."

I fall onto the couch, my skin going ice cold at his words. "What sort of proof have you seen?"

"I followed her. She went to the country club, told me she was going for golf lessons. Some lessons." He snorts. "She met up with the golf pro, dragged him into a private room, and kept him in there for hours. *Hours.* When they finally came back out, he had a shit-eating grin on his face and she had a fresh-fucked look about her." He groaned. "I confronted them."

"Ah, Dad." My heart hurts for him. At his pain, the humiliation of what he must have endured. And for him to confront Adele and her piece on the side . . . damn, he must've been enraged.

"She went crazy, son. Crazy. Crying, hysterical, full of denials. All of them lies, all of them."

"Where are you now?"

"At the house. I kicked her out. Left the country club, raced home, and tossed all her shit out onto the lawn. She followed me, raged at me in the front yard, and swore she was going to call the cops. So I did it for her."

Closing my eyes, I scrub my hand over my face. My dad's imploding marriage was one big fucked-up mess. "You called the cops?"

"Sure did. And I asked them to escort her off the premises since she wouldn't leave. Considering my name is the only one on the mortgage, I think legally I have that right even though we're married. Hell I don't know." He pauses. "I met with my lawyer today and we're proceeding with the divorce. The papers are being drawn up. She should be served in the next few days. I'm done."

"Really." My voice is flat and full of doubt. I can't help it.

"Really. I know you probably find it hard to believe, but I'm dead serious. She has wronged me so completely, there's no way she could ever come back from that. I can't trust her. I'm done."

If he knew what happened between Adele and me, he'd probably be done with me, too. I can hardly stand the thought. Besides Fable, he's all I have. "Has she bothered you lately? Like in the last twenty-four hours?"

"No. I haven't heard from her at all. I figure she's staying with her fucking golf pro. Let her go see how uncomfortable her life will be, living with a punk-ass kid working a shit job? She'll figure out real quick he wasn't worth screwing up our entire marriage over." The bitterness in Dad's voice is overpowering. I don't know if I've ever heard him sound so angry.

"If you need to get away from all the crap, come up here and hang out with me. I have the extra bedroom or you can grab a hotel room. Spend some time with me, clear your mind," I offer. Fable probably won't be pleased. She's not a huge fan of my dad, but I'll worry about her later. I need to help him. He sounds off. Consumed with anger, and that can't be healthy.

"I appreciate the offer, but no way am I leaving this house.

With my luck she'd move her pretty ass back in here and never leave. Then she'd get me on squatter's rights or some such shit. I can't have it. I'm staying put," he says determinedly.

I bite back the sigh of relief that wants to escape. "Well, know the offer still stands."

"I appreciate it, son, I do. I just can't believe . . ." His voice trails off and he releases a shuddering breath. God, I hope he's not crying. "I can't believe she would do something like this to me. After everything we've been through, everything we've shared together, she goes and does something like this. It's unbelievable."

There's nothing I can say. I can't console him. I want him to run as far and as fast away from Adele as he can. But he loves her. For whatever reason, he loves her, and now he's hurting from her betrayal.

Imagine if he found out what I did to him. I think of Vanessa. I still don't know the truth. No way do I want to go to Adele and demand the truth. She'd tell me one thing and Dad another.

Sick, twisted bitch.

I talk to Dad for a few minutes longer. More like let him rattle on for a while over how much she betrayed him while I listen and make the appropriate noises where needed. He can't stop talking about it. He's starting to repeat himself, saying the same things over and over, his voice full of fire, his anger and sadness so strong I feel it settle over me like a heavy, wet blanket.

But then I glance up and catch Fable standing in the hallway, her hair sticking out all over the place, my dark blue comforter wrapped around her naked body, her expression hesitant.

"Dad, I gotta go. Call me if you need me." Before he can reply, I end the call and go to her, slipping my arms around her and pulling her in, the bulky comforter preventing me from getting too close. "Hey, you're awake."

"I woke up when you slipped out of bed." She rests her hands on my bare chest, stroking my skin. "Is everything okay?"

"Yeah." I wish she would drop the damn comforter so I can touch her for real. "It was my dad. I guess the divorce is back on."

Her hands still. "And that's a good thing, right?"

"Definitely. I want her out of our lives for good. There's been a lot of back-and-forth, though. I don't know if I believe him."

"What happened to make him want the divorce again?" she asks.

"He caught her cheating on him. As in, he followed her and watched her hook up with a guy, then confronted her." Dad's acting like a man possessed, but I guess when a person's been wronged so completely by the one he loves, that person can tend to do crazy things.

"Wow. Sounds awful."

"I know. My dad . . . he's really upset." I smooth my hand over her hair, trying to tame the wayward strands. I desperately want to change the subject. "You look pretty in my comforter."

Fable rolls her eyes, but her cheeks turn a delicate pink. "I think you'd say I look pretty in anything."

"You're right." If I could, I would forget about all of my

problems and lose myself in her. She's the only thing that feels right and normal in my entire universe.

"I should go," she says softly. "I promised Owen I'd be home when he's done with school. Plus I'm going out with Jen tonight and I need to get ready."

Jealousy flares in my gut and I tamp it down. I'm being ridiculous. Like a macho asshole who never wants to lose sight of his woman, and that's not cool. I trust her.

I just don't trust any other guy who gets near her. I mean, look at her. She's beautiful and she's all mine. One mistake on my part, though, and I could lose her. Look at what happened last night.

I push last night's argument firmly out of my mind. Dwelling on my mistakes is pointless.

"Okay." I kiss the tip of her nose. "How did you get here, anyway?"

She shrugs, a little smile curving her lips. "Jen came by my apartment to pick me up earlier so I could go get my paycheck from the restaurant. Once I was there, I jogged over."

"You jogged?" I had no idea she had it in her. Though her body is bangin', there's no denying it, she's never mentioned she likes to run.

Of course, there's plenty I don't know about Fable. She's still a mystery to me. One I want to examine and take apart, learn every bit of piece by piece.

"Yeah." She leans in and presses her lips to the center of my chest. My heart skips a beat, as if it could literally feel her kiss. "I have all sorts of secret talents."

"I'll say," I mutter, enthralled with the way she's touching me. So easily, as if we've been together forever.

Laughing, she withdraws from me and starts toward my

bedroom. "Maybe if you're lucky you'll discover more of my secret talents later tonight," she calls from over her shoulder.

I frown. "What are you talking about?"

More laughter. The musical sound washes over me, filling me with happiness. "You'll see."

I'm left still pondering that remark hours after she leaves.

Fable

I feel good. The best I have in ages. Jen and I went out to dinner at some new place downtown where they serve the best appetizers ever. We laughed and laughed as we gushed over the delicious food, knowing Colin would absolutely kill us if he caught us in there.

We were coconspirators, and that was fun. The only time I've ever felt truly part of a team is with Owen and somewhat with Drew. With Drew, our relationship is still so new, so fragile, I'm afraid sometimes to push too hard.

Tonight, I plan on pushing hard. Tonight, I feel free.

"So tell me more about your hunkalicious boyfriend." Jen's dark eyes are sparkling. We're at one of the local college hangouts. It's two stories, the bottom level a very casual restaurant/burger joint, the top level a huge bar and dance floor. They don't let anyone underage upstairs, which totally bums me out. I'm literally writhing where I sit in the booth, my body overtaken by the muted throbbing beat that comes from upstairs.

"What do you want to know?" I play coy on purpose, stirring my straw in my glass of soda. I sort of wish for harder stuff. Jen's a little buzzed—I can see it in the flush in her face, the light in her eyes. I'm less than six months away from my twenty-first birthday, and not that I'm a party girl or anything, but it'll be nice to be able to booze it up whenever I want.

"How'd you meet?"

Such a simple question that requires a not-so-simple answer. "It's sort of hard to explain."

"He's gorgeous, you know. And popular as hell, you little shit. You told me he was no one I knew. Everyone in town knows Drew Callahan." Jen sips from her drink, her lips curved in a smirk. "Is he amazing in bed, or what?"

Jen gets a little liquored up and she's making all sorts of crazy statements. I don't even know how to answer that. I'm used to girls accusing me of stealing their boyfriends, not of friends asking how my boyfriend is in bed.

"Your cheeks are red, so I'm guessing the answer is unbelievable." Jen shakes her head, a wistful expression on her face. "I miss sex."

I'm taken aback. I totally had it pegged that she and Colin were doing the nasty, as my brother so eloquently states it. "By that statement, I guess you're not having it?"

"Nope." Jen shakes her head. "I know what you're thinking. I bet you assumed Colin and I are together."

I still say nothing, not wanting to voice my suspicions.

"Well, we're not. He's just a friend." She glances around, as though someone's lurking in the background and might hear us. "If I told you something, would you promise to keep it a secret?"

"Sure." I swear I have a sign around my neck that says *excellent secret keeper*.

Jen leans across the table ominously and lowers her voice. "Colin was my older brother's best friend."

I frown. "Was?"

A pained expression crosses her face. "My brother died. In Iraq."

"Oh." I reach across the table and give her hand a squeeze. "I'm so sorry."

She shrugs, though the hurt is still in her gaze. "It was a few years ago, and everyone was completely devastated, especially Colin. Danny's death . . . threw my family completely off. We all splintered apart and I ended up running away. I couldn't go back home. There was just no way I could stay there with all that pain and misery surrounding me. So I ended up here. Working dead-end jobs, trying to keep my head above water."

Sounds familiar. At least I'm not alone. I'm thankful for having Owen, and even my mom to a point. She's awful, but she hasn't flat-out deserted us.

"I was working one night a few months ago and Colin just . . . walked in. Like out of nowhere. Told me he'd been looking for me, he had a job lined up and a place to stay if I wanted it. I figured he worked for The District, you know? Was like the restaurant manager or whatever. When I realized he owned the place—that he owns multiple restaurants and he's filthy rich—I couldn't believe it. He's done so much with his life." The dreamy look on Jen's face was unmistakable.

She's crushing majorly on her dead brother's best friend. I freaking knew it. I just didn't realize they had a past connection. A really strong connection that runs deep.

"Are you in love with him?" I ask quietly.

"What? No!" Jen shakes her head, trying her best to make a quick recovery.

But I know a liar when I see one.

"He's like family to me. Like another big brother," she insists, her eyes locking with mine. "Don't tell anyone, okay? I don't want any of the girls at the restaurant to know. Plus, Colin doesn't want anyone to know either. He doesn't want to look like he plays favorites."

"But you live with him. Everyone knows it."

"He's done this sort of thing before. Letting his employees live with him." She shrugs. "He just wants to make sure everyone's okay and has a roof over their head. He asked me about you, wanted to make sure you weren't living in a shack somewhere."

"He knows where I live." I proceeded to tell her how he texted me, then came by my place to pick me up.

"See how nice he is? He just wanted to help you out."

Jen's so enamored of Colin he can do no wrong. I always wondered at his motives with me. Not that he was ever sleazy, but he was certainly extra attentive. Far more attentive than any other boss I've ever had.

But maybe Jen is right. Maybe he looks out for those he worries about. I can't fault him for that. He's like a protective big brother.

"Enough talking about me. Let's talk about you and your sexy boyfriend." Jen grabs her glass and sips from her drink, all easy-breezy again. "I'm surprised he let you out of his sights tonight."

"I deserve a girls' night out, don't you think?"

"Of course you do. So do I. So does every girl." Jen grins

when the music changes to a fast, heavy beat that has me moving in my seat again. "Did I happen to mention I know the bouncer upstairs?"

"No. Really?" I stop seat-dancing. "Think he'd let me in up there?"

"As long as you promise not to order anything from the bar, I bet I could convince him." Jen laughs when I clap my hands in excitement. "I didn't figure you for a dancer, Fable."

"I love to dance." I just rarely do. When do I have time to go out clubbing? Oh, and who with? "I work a lot, so I don't get out much."

"Well, let me work my magic and get you in there. This should be fun." Jen whips her phone out of her pocket and starts texting, presumably the bouncer upstairs. I glance around the room, waiting anxiously for her to figure out a plan. She's so nice, so easygoing and fun. I'm so glad I agreed to go out with her tonight. I needed this. Needed a taste of freedom, a taste of friendship.

Noticing Jen's still tapping away at her keyboard, I pull my phone out and send off a quick text to Drew. He replies within seconds.

Having fun?

As much as I can without you here.

Which is sort of the truth. All of a sudden, I miss him.

Give me a break.

I smile as I type a question.

Do you like to dance?

Not really.

I laugh softly. I'm not surprised. He is so not the dancing type.

"The bouncer can get us in," Jen says, breaking through my Drew-induced mental fog.

I glance up from my phone with a grin. "You're kidding."

"Nope. But we need to get up there now, before the floor fills up and they start turning people away." Jen tilts her head toward my hand, where I'm clutching my phone. "Texting Hunkalicious?"

Why does everyone call Drew nicknames? Owen and Lover Boy. Jen and Hunkalicious. I should call him something like Drew Bear or Drew-bee. Something silly and dumb and just for me. He'd probably die of mortification if I tried.

"Maybe," I say with a shrug.

She smiles. "You should have him come pick you up."

"But what about you?"

Jen shrugs. "I'm going to swing by the restaurant before I go home. Colin just messaged me and asked me if I would."

Ah, I get it. Colin snaps his fingers and Jen comes running. I can sort of relate.

Focusing all my attention on my phone again, I type out a quick message to my hunkalicious boyfriend.

You should come and watch me dance.

Where are you?

I tell him, ending it with, Want me to tell you what I'm wearing so you can find me?

Baby, I could find you anywhere is his immediate reply.

Smiling so hard my cheeks hurt, I tuck my phone into the front pocket of my jeans and smile at Jen. "Let's go upstairs."

CHAPTER 16

The real lover is the man who can thrill you by kissing your forehead or smiling into your eyes or just staring into space.

—Marilyn Monroe

Fable

The room is small and dark, jam-packed with people. I can hardly move, it's so crowded, but I don't care. I've got my arms above my head and my hands in the air, the lights that hang over us flashing in time to the beat of the music. I'm dancing my ass off, my hair sweaty, my legs aching.

Such a great night, I'm overwhelmed with how much fun I'm having. I feel fucking fantastic.

Jen is dancing with me and she's surprisingly good, full of an innate rhythm that encourages me to step up my game. A group of guys crowded around us earlier, trying to get us to dance with them, but we turned in to each other, like we were on some sort of date. I wanted to discourage them and she did, too, so thankfully we were on the same page.

We danced together, bumping and grinding against each other a little bit because she's buzzed and so am I, though not on alcohol. For once in my life, everything feels right on track. Like nothing is standing in my way.

I've turned into a total cliché again. But this time I'm a positive one. I might start singing cheesy eighties anthems because I feel like nothing's gonna stop me now and all that crap.

The guys step back and form a semicircle around Jen and me as we dance, hooting and hollering and generally acting like perverts. We encourage them, swaying our hips, thrusting out our chests. I'm not even dressed that sexily. I went for casual with my jeans and a cute plaid shirt I found on clearance at Target, leaving it open with a white tank underneath.

Casually cute, I guess, because who am I trying to impress? Originally, my guy wasn't supposed to be here.

He still isn't here.

Another song comes on, this one slow, and everyone on the floor seems to vacate all at once. Jen and I send each other a silent message and we exit the dance floor as well, heading toward the bar. Jen scoots her skinny ass in between a crowd of people and somehow garners the bartender's immediate attention, ordering us both a glass of ice water.

When she finally hands me the drink I chug it, the cold water soothing my parched throat. The lights have gone completely dim as a few couples slow dance together, most of them hardly moving, their feet shuffling as they focus on groping each other instead.

I'm thankful for the break, but I also miss Drew. Seeing the dancing couples lights a deep yearning within me. We've been dancing for over an hour. I thought he would be here by now, so where is he?

"I need to get going soon." Jen pushes her damp hair away from her forehead. "Is your boyfriend coming to get you or what?"

"I thought so." I glance around the room but I can't see anything. It's too damn dark.

"Huh." She sips her drink. "No way am I leaving you here alone waiting for him. I can drive you home."

"You don't have to—"

Jen cuts me off. "I picked you up; I can definitely take you home. Don't worry about it."

"Cool. Thanks." I nod once, my shoulders stiff. I refuse to be disappointed. I also refuse to text him. He knows exactly where I'm at, so what the hell is taking him so long?

Maybe his dad called him again and needed to talk. Maybe he was going through a tough time over his dad's anguish with the divorce and I'm being completely selfish wondering where he is. Maybe . . .

"Let me finish my drink and I'll be ready to go," Jen says, interrupting my thoughts.

"Okay." I drain my ice water and set the glass on a nearby table, ignoring the girls sitting there, who shoot me a dirty look. Though it was probably rude, what I just did, I couldn't care less. I'm irritable.

They're whispering loudly, probably griping about me and hoping to catch my attention, but I ignore them. I don't need a bunch of catty bitches' crap tonight.

The song ends and the lights brighten, flooding the dance floor. One of the most popular songs on the charts comes blasting on and everyone heads out to the floor, including Jen and me since we got caught up in the mass wave.

"One more dance!" she shouts at me, and I nod in agreement.

The insult girls are dancing close by, shooting Jen and me rude glares, and I turn my back to them, trying my best to enjoy this last song. My nerves are shot, though. The mean girls killed my buzz and I should've insisted on leaving before the song started.

But Jen's into the music, a giant smile on her face as she waves her hands in the air like she just don't care, yo.

I smile at my own mental joke and throw my hands up in the air, mimicking her. The music slowly starts to work its magic, taking me over until all I can feel is the pulse of the bass and the heartfelt lyrics running through my mind. I'm about to be completely swept away with the chorus when I hear one of the mean girls gasp behind me.

"No way! Is that Drew Callahan?"

Glancing over my shoulder, I catch sight of him standing on the opposite side of the room near the door, as if he'd just entered. He's squinting as he scans the room, searching for me, no doubt, which sends a flutter of anticipating nerves through my body. He looks cute as hell in a white long-sleeve shirt with a button placket at the neck, the sleeves pushed up to reveal his strong, sexy forearms. And jeans, of course, that mold to his thighs and remind me of just how muscular they are. His hair is hanging in his eyes and he pushes it away, flicking his head in irritation.

Pressing my lips together, I want to sigh like a little school-girl with my first crush. My man is so damn fine I can hardly stand it. He still hasn't found me, though. In fact, he looks mighty irritated as he pushes through the crowd, his gaze constantly scanning, and a warm sensation washes over me as I keep moving, my attention half on the girls gushing about Drew and watching him.

"He never goes anywhere," one of the girls says. "God, he's so fucking gorgeous it hurts just looking at him."

I'm tempted to turn and scratch her eyes out, but I restrain myself. After all, I'm the one who had him naked and between my legs earlier today. Drew Callahan belongs to me.

"Oh my God, he's looking this way!" another one screeches.

He's staring right at me and I can feel the sizzle of his smoldering gaze from clear across the room. Tossing my hair over my shoulder, I send him a sultry smile, hoping like crazy I don't look like a fool.

Drew sends me a delicious smile right back. But he doesn't come toward me. I can still hear those girls going on and on about him. They need to know he's mine. I'm desperate for them to know he's mine.

So I watch him. And I want him. But no way am I going to approach him. He has to come and get me first.

"Your boyfriend is here!" Jen shouts in my ear.

Nodding, I never take my eyes off of him as I continue to dance to the throbbing beat. "I know!" I shout back.

"He's looking at you like he wants to gobble you up." Jen laughs as she moves away from me.

Heat flares between my legs. He is totally looking at me like he wants to eat me up. Unable to stand it, I crook my finger and give him the age-old sign that I want him to come to me.

"Look, he's coming this way!" One of the mean girls

screams as he makes his way across the crowded dance floor straight toward me.

I wait in breathless anticipation as he approaches. He's taller than most of the people here and he stands out. Or maybe that's because I notice no one else but him. The way that white shirt he's wearing stretches across his shoulders and chest. How much I love his longer hair. The way he's looking at me when he stops directly in front of me, his gaze dropping to my mouth for one hot, lingering moment before he lifts his lids to meet my gaze.

"Hi," he says, but I can hardly hear him. It's more like I have to read his lips. His sexy, gorgeous, irresistible lips.

So I loop my arms around his neck and give him a sweet kiss on that irresistible mouth. "Hi," I whisper, my lips brushing his.

He settles those big hands on my butt and tugs me closer. I can literally hear the horrified gasps coming from the group of mean girls standing behind us, and I hang my head back and laugh triumphantly.

It feels really good to be the girl who gets the guy for once.

Drew

It took me forever to escape my apartment. Dad called twice to gripe about Adele and whatever else she was doing. I didn't want to hear it. But I sensed that he needed to unload, and so I let him. Until finally I checked the time and realized Fable was probably waiting for me at that stupid club she's at.

She's probably good and pissed at me for keeping her waiting, too.

I finally drive myself over there and get inside, which is no small feat. I had to promise I was only going in to snag my girlfriend out of there and then we were leaving. The line to get in was huge. The guy manning the door figured out who I was real quick and was a major football fan, so I lucked out.

Now I have a warm, sexy woman in my arms, smiling up at me like I'm God's gift. She's snug against me, her fingers playing in my hair at the nape, her body still moving to the music. Driving me out of my mind.

"I thought you weren't going to show!" she yells at me. The music is so loud I can barely hear her.

Leaning in close, I murmur in her ear, "Sorry, my dad kept calling."

She nods, her fragrant hair brushing against my cheek, making me inhale sharply. "I wondered if that was the case."

The friend she's with touches Fable on the arm and tells her she needs to go. We both wave at her and she leaves, threading through the crowd until it swallows her up. The song changes, still fast though not as hyped up as the previous one, and Fable swivels her hips, the smile on her face alluring.

Sexy as hell.

"I missed you." She brushes her chest against mine and I feel like I'm going to shatter. Both from being turned on and the earlier tension I dealt with over the stupid divorce. I wish he hadn't called. He ruined my mood. My girl senses it, too. Her smile turns into a frown. "What's wrong?"

I shrug, not wanting to dwell on a bunch of bullshit tonight. I want to focus only on her. "I'm absorbing other people's problems and stress, which I know is ridiculous but I can't help it."

Her frown softens but it's still there. She probably feels sorry for me and I don't want her to. I want her free and beautiful and flirtatious. Fable behaving like this makes me feel free. "I can help you with that," she says, her voice full of promise.

I dip my head to hear her better. "You can?"

"Oh, yeah. You need to learn how to let go of all your troubles." She whispers the words in my ear, the sound of her sexy voice sending a jolt of lust straight through me. "You chasing me here is the first step."

I settle my hands on her hips and pull her in closer. The music is loud, the room is stifling, and the crowd is thick. But with Fable's arms slung around my neck, her body close to mine, it's as if we're the only two people in this room. "First step to what?" I ask, confused. My brain fries when I'm with her.

She trails her fingers lightly down my nape and I shiver. "First step to acting like two normal people who are madly in love and can't keep their hands off each other," she murmurs right before she kisses me.

I drown in the taste of her, in the feel of her sinful body snug against me. I slide my hands back and forth over her ass and she whimpers, the sexy little sound sending a zing straight through me, making me hard.

Damn. I want out of here. It's too public, too crazy to indulge like this with her. We're completely surrounded by people and the song changes yet again, to a popular song that's been overplayed on the radio, though no one here seems to care.

Including my girl. She's withdrawn completely from my

217

arms, a little smile teasing her kiss-swollen lips, and she starts moving to the beat. "Dance with me," she shouts over the music.

I slowly shake my head, my gaze dropping to her hips. The way she moves, as if she were born to dance. She knows I'm watching, too, and she puts on a show, just for me. I watch the sway of her hips in those too-tight jeans, how she thrusts her chest out as she lifts her arms above her head. The white lace of her bra peeks above the neckline of the tank she's wearing beneath the plaid button-down shirt and without thought, I grab her. Let my hands rest on her waist as she moves against me.

"You don't dance?" She arches a brow and I do the same in return as my answer, standing completely still while she keeps moving. Her hips shift beneath my palms and she turns around, brushing her ass against my front, making me harder.

Glancing over her shoulder, she offers me a sultry smile but doesn't say a word. Just keeps dancing while I keep my hands on her. I pull her closer. Closer still until her back is nestled to my front and I slip my arms completely around her, my hands pressed flat against her stomach. I smooth them down, to the tops of her thighs, and I swear I feel her tremble beneath my touch.

She looks up at me, her eyes gone wide, her lips glistening as if she just licked them. We've been playing a game since I got here and I'm ready to claim my prize.

Her. She's all I want. All I'll ever want.

I never believed in the fairy tale, even when I was a little kid. My life has been full of tragedy since my mom died. My illusions were shattered completely when I was fifteen years old. I became such a shell of my old self, I never believed anyone could truly accept and love me. It sounded pitiful when I admitted to Dr. Harris that I firmly believed I would go through my entire life alone, but it was the truth. I felt completely unlovable.

Disgusting. Shameful.

Being with Fable, all of those old, harsh feelings are slowly evaporating. She loves me for me. She knows every single dark and horrible thing that's happened to me in my life and she doesn't care. She wants to help me, stand by me, be there for me no matter what.

She flat-out wants . . . me.

I'm probably thinking too fast, wanting to move way, way too fast for her comfort, but having Fable in my arms at this very moment, smiling up at me from over her shoulder, I know without a doubt that this is the girl I want by my side forever. She's embedded herself so completely into my life and my heart, I can't imagine being without her.

It's just that simple and that complicated, all at once.

"Let's get out of here," I whisper in her ear and she nods once, her hair brushing against my face. She smells amazing, her cheeks are flushed, and all I can think is how fast can I get her home so I can have her naked beneath me.

Taking her hand, I start to guide her off the dance floor, noticing a group of obvious sorority girls watching us as we go. Fable turns and flips them the bird, sticking her tongue out at them, and I yank on her hand hard to get her out of there before she starts a fight.

"What the hell was that for?" I ask her as we walk down the back stairs and push open the door that leads out into the parking lot.

"They were giving me shit. Saying catty stuff about me.

Next thing I know, you walk into the room, and they all flip out." She smiles and squeezes my hand. "They thought you were smiling at them but really you were smiling at me."

I shake my head. "Who gives a shit what they think?"

"Me. I do. I'm always looked down upon. They're practically creaming their panties over the fact that you showed up and I loved knowing you didn't give a shit about them. You came there for me." She pulls me to her and lifts up on tiptoe so she can kiss my cheek. "Letting everyone know you're mine makes me feel good."

I feel exactly the same way. I entwine my fingers through hers, and we walk toward my truck quietly, my mind racing. How do I tell her I want her in my life for always? Should I even bring it up, or would it scare the crap out of her? The last thing I want to do is put pressure on her.

But I don't want to lose Fable either.

I hit the keyless remote and the doors unlock, both of us slipping inside the truck's cab. Fable pulls her cell out of her pocket, a little gasp escaping her as she hits a button on the screen to make a call.

"Where are you?" she asks the moment whoever is on the other end answers. "What do you mean the place is empty?"

I watch her, see the worry and concern wash over her face, the way she white-knuckle grips the phone as she holds it to her ear. My skin prickles with uncertainty and I'm curious as hell over what's happening and who she's talking to.

Knowing whatever it is, it can't be good.

"I'll be right there. Yeah, I'm with Drew. I'll have him drive me straight over, okay? So don't leave." She pauses. "Ten minutes, tops. Stop panicking, Owen. We'll be there."

She ends the call and turns to look at me, her eyes wide with fear. "Owen's at the apartment. He says it's empty."

I frown. "What do you mean, it's empty?"

"Like almost everything is gone except some of our personal stuff. The furniture, all our things, the food in the kitchen—it's all gone." She nibbles on her lower lip, lost in thought.

"Were you guys robbed?" I can hardly wrap my head around what she said. It made no sense.

"No, no way." She shakes her head and laughs, though she's definitely not amused. More like she sounds distraught. "I think—I think my mom did it. I bet she packed up all her shit, had her loser boyfriend help her, and moved everything out without telling us."

I grimace as I pull out of the parking lot and turn toward Fable's place. "Who the hell does that sort of thing?"

"My mother." She leans her head back against the headrest and sighs. "I told you how I wanted to move out and take Owen with me, but I hadn't gathered up the courage to tell her yet. Guess she took care of that, didn't she?"

"But what you're saying, it's like she . . . abandoned you."

"She abandoned us both a long time ago. I've come to terms with it. Owen hasn't. He still believes our mom loves us and wants to take care of us. He's young; he'll figure it out someday."

The bitterness in Fable's voice makes me hurt for her. We both come from really screwed-up situations. With parents who don't seem to give a shit about us, but in radically different ways. I wish I could help heal her heart. She may say the way her mother treats her and Owen doesn't bother her, but I know she has to be lying. It probably hurts like hell.

My father's indifference and neglect hurts me to this day. My mom's death—I sometimes feel like she abandoned me, and it wasn't even her fault. That's how irrational my thinking is.

And I can't even go into what Adele's done to me. I'm completely fucked up from the mind games she played on me for far too long.

The moment we pull into a parking slot, Fable's already out of the truck, running toward her apartment building. I follow behind her, taking a little more time, only because I want her to get in a few private moments with her brother first.

When I finally walk into the apartment, I'm shocked. The place is literally empty. No furniture remains in the living room. The table and chairs are gone from the small dining nook. Every cabinet door is hanging open in the kitchen.

Owen and Fable are leaning against the kitchen counter. She has her arms around him and his face is pressed against her shoulder. Tears are streaming down her face, but she doesn't look sad.

She looks majorly pissed.

"I hate her," she says vehemently. "I can't believe she would do this. She took my bed, Drew. She took Owen's, too. And all the furniture in our rooms. They dumped out all our stuff that was in the drawers and left everything in a pile on the floor."

"How could she have done this, hauled everything out of here so fast?" I glance around the empty room, amazed that everything's gone. I've only been inside her apartment once, but I remember it crammed with a bunch of stuff.

"She has friends. Or I'm sure her loser boyfriend has a ton of friends. I bet they plied them with beer and they hauled everything out as fast as they could." She shakes her head. "Owen and I both left before six."

And it's past eleven now. "So they had at least five hours."

"It's amazing how fast you can work when you need to." Her mouth screws up into an angry twist.

My arms literally ache to comfort her. Pull her into a hug and tell her everything's going to be okay. But she's too busy taking care of her brother, and right now he's her number-one priority.

Feeling helpless, I walk down the hall and glance into Fable's room. There's nothing but a pile of clothes and miscellaneous stuff lying on the floor, as she'd mentioned. Same with Owen's room, though his is an incredible mess. Her mom's room is completely empty.

This is truly some of the craziest shit I've ever seen.

An idea comes over me so perfect I stride back into the living area, excited to tell her. It's the perfect solution to their now very major problem.

"I want you to move in with me."

CHAPTER 17

True love isn't easy, but it must be fought for. Once you find it, it can never be replaced.
—Unknown

Fable

Shock washes over me at Drew's words. "You can't be serious." Owen pulls out of my embrace, his body stiff. His eyes are swollen and his cheeks red from the crying. He was in a total state of panic when he called. So freaked out over what Mom did, I could hardly understand him at first.

"I'm dead serious." Drew takes a few steps toward me but stops just before he reaches me. He can probably feel Owen's animosity. It's rolling off him in huge waves. "I have the space. Owen can even have his own room."

"Where will Fabes sleep?" Owen asks, his look pointed, his expression fiercely protective.

I rest my hand on his tense arm. "Stop. Drew is trying to be nice."

"Or he's just using you for free sex. Maybe make you his little woman once you move in with him and not let you go anywhere or do anything. Don't do it. I don't want to move in with him," Owen says vehemently.

I don't quite understand Owen's hostility. Though maybe it all stems from when I was an emotional wreck after I came back from Carmel and Drew ditched me. He's run before . . .

Just like Mom.

I'm tempted, though. So, so tempted to say yes. But I need to prove my independence, not move from my mom's to Drew's without ever experiencing time living on my own.

"You don't have to make the decision now," Drew says softly, his gaze pleading. "But you don't want to stay the night here. The place is empty. There isn't even a bed to sleep on."

He's right. Even though I know Mom is responsible for taking everything and we weren't robbed, I'd feel creepy staying the night here. The apartment feels too hollow. Almost violated.

"I don't want to stay here," I murmur to Owen, grabbing his hand and squeezing it. "Besides, we have nowhere else to go. Drew's apartment is nice and he has a spare bedroom."

"I'm sure his apartment is badass. I still don't want to stay there," Owen retorts. He's so angry, so hurt by what our mother has done to us, my heart breaks for him.

"Come on. Do this for me." Owen glances up, his gaze meeting mine. "I love him," I whisper. "He'd do anything to help me. To help *us*. I know it."

Owen rolls his eyes and yanks his hand from mine. "Fine. We'll stay there. But I refuse to move in with him, Fabes. You hardly know his ass."

"Owen, stop." I can't put up with his attitude right now. Drew is being nothing but kind and generous. Owen is probably using his rudeness as a defense mechanism to cope or whatever, but I don't want to deal with it. I can hardly wrap my head around what our mother has done.

Her mental abandonment has scarred me for life. Her physical abandonment will probably fuck up Owen's head forever.

I hate her. So much I can hardly see straight, let alone think rationally.

At this very moment, I need Drew's support more than ever.

We get Owen settled first. Drew has a futon in his spare room, which he must use as an office, if the desk and computer are any indication. I help Drew make the futon into a bed, spreading out the extra blankets while Drew goes and grabs some pillows. It feels very domestic and sweet, and I know I could get used to this.

But I refuse to let myself. I can't get all sappy and silly now. My brother needs me. I need to be strong and figure out what the hell I'm going to do next.

"Do you need anything?" I ask Owen when he walks into the room, his expression defiant. "A glass of water, or maybe some Tylenol?" He'd cried on the drive over to Drew's house, sniffling in the backseat of Drew's extended cab. I wanted to comfort him so bad but knew he would refuse it.

"Something to eat, maybe?" Drew suggests as he walks into the room with three fluffy pillows.

"I'm fine," Owen says sullenly. I send him a pointed look and he adds a muttered thank you to appease me.

"Do you want to talk?" I ask him quietly, both of us stepping out of the way so Drew can dump the pillows on the futon.

Owen shakes his head. "I'd rather be alone, Fabes. I just want to fall asleep and forget this ever happened."

"It'll just be there ready to face you again once you wake up," I remind him. We can't avoid this, even though I'd love to. It's staring me right in the face. I need to figure out what to do, where to go next.

"Thanks for the slap of reality." He sighs and shakes his head. "I know you're mad at her. But . . . I'm not. I'm worried about her. She won't answer your calls, and that sucks."

I'd tried to call her from the apartment and on the way over to Drew's. It went straight to voice mail. I left her a text. No reply, and that was over an hour ago.

The woman is doing everything in her power to avoid us. There's nothing we can do about it, either. No way am I going to call the cops on her. She's our mom.

"She's fine." I wave a hand. I have no doubt in my mind she's perfectly safe. Probably chugging a beer and laughing her ass off at how she pulled one over on us. "She'll answer tomorrow, I'm sure of it."

A lie. I have no idea if she'll answer me or not. For all I know, this is the last we'll ever hear of her.

It wouldn't bother me whatsoever, either. I'm so done with this bullshit she puts us through. The emotional ringer we're forced to deal with every time she flits in and out of our lives. I put up my walls long ago, but Owen is still open and dying for Mom to love him. Really love him.

She doesn't know how. And he hasn't realized it yet.

Drew exits the room without a word, closing the door behind him, and I appreciate what he's doing for us so much. He's nonintrusive while I try to deal with my brother. He's been nothing but gracious, opening his home up to both of us, giving Owen whatever he needs to ensure he's comfortable here.

He's amazing. And when I'm finished talking to Owen, I'm going to go to Drew and beg him to put his arms around me and just hold me.

I need him so badly right now. But first, I need to take care of my brother, who needs me more.

"What if she's *not* fine?" Owen asks, his voice trembling. "What if something really did happen to her and she's hurt and helpless somewhere? Or . . . worse? What then, Fable?"

The image his words conjure in my brain—no. There's no way she's a victim in all of this. She had a hand in it. I can feel it all the way in my bones. "I know you're worried. But I need to be honest with you. She doesn't care about us, Owen. Not like you want her to. She's too wrapped up in her own problems to realize how much you need her. How much you want her around. She'd rather run off and go get drunk and hang out at the bar with her boyfriend."

Owen stares at me, his cheeks red, his eyes filling with tears. "You don't know shit. Maybe she doesn't want to be around us because she knows how much you hate her."

I flinch. "I'm not the one to blame here. She can't stand the fact that we're close. She's jealous and it's so stupid, because she can't see how much you crave that sort of closeness with her. She's our mother, yet she treats us like we're nothing more than a pain in her ass."

"Maybe to you she acts that way, but never to me. She loves me!" He's yelling, the tears are coursing down his cheeks, and he swipes them away angrily. "Go on believing she's a bitch. Maybe *you're* being the bitch this time, Fabes. Did you ever think of that?"

I'm stunned. I can't believe he just said that to me. I'm this close to falling completely apart and damn it, I need to be the strong one. "You're upset," I say quietly. "I understand. Why don't we get a good night's sleep and we can talk tomorrow."

"Whatever." Owen turns away from me and crawls onto the futon, fixing the pillows and then pulling the blankets over him, his back to me. He's so stiff beneath the covers, he looks like he could shatter.

"I love you, Owen," I murmur just before I close the door.

He doesn't even bother with a reply.

Drew

I'm pacing my bedroom, waiting for Fable to come back. A million questions are running through my brain and I'm afraid to ask her any of them. We were having an amazing night. And now this . . .

If her mom really did ransack their apartment and take everything they pretty much freaking owned, leaving her kids only their clothes and personal stuff, then she's incredibly selfish and callous. Owen is heartbroken. Fable's so angry I'm afraid she's going to lose it at any moment, though she has this weird calmness about her, too. I've never seen her like this before, though hell, it's not like we've been together long.

This entire relationship of ours has been a whirlwind from day one. I can't imagine my life without her. I'm also trying my best to be there for her. She's not necessarily pushing me away.

But she's not really including me, either.

What the hell can I do for her anyway? I suggested she contact the police but her vehement "no" indicated that was the wrong thing to say. I feel helpless. No one can get hold of her mom. Owen hates me and views me as some sort of bad guy hell-bent on breaking his sister's heart—again. The only thing I can offer is a place to stay, and even with that, I feel like I somehow fucked up by making the suggestion.

I can't win. I sound like a selfish baby, but damn. I want Fable to know she can depend on me no matter what. I'll be her rock, her support, whatever she needs. I would do anything for her.

Unfortunately, I don't think she fully realizes that yet.

What seems like endless minutes later, she's slipping inside my bedroom, closing the door softly behind her. Her shoulders slump forward as she leans against the door, her expression one of utter exhaustion.

I want to comfort her but she's put up an invisible wall. One that says she can do this on her own, thank you very much.

Fuck that. I'm gonna tear down that wall, no matter how long it takes.

"How's Owen?" I ask.

"He hates me." She closes her eyes, a weird little smile appearing. "He blames me for our mom ditching us. Says that maybe if I wasn't such a bitch, she wouldn't have left in the first place."

"*What?*" I practically shout and she opens her eyes, glaring at me.

"Ssh! He'll hear you." Pushing away from the door, she walks toward my bed and collapses on top of it, burrowing her head in the pillows. "I don't want to talk about it now, Drew. I just want to go to sleep."

She's acting odd, but I'm not about to call her on it. She's upset. Yet again her life has been turned completely upside down.

"Do you want to change into something more comfortable?" I ask.

Her shoulders shake like she's laughing. She still won't face me. "Are you trying to use some sort of line on me? Let me warn you up front. I'm not in the mood."

"Fable." Like I would expect anything from her tonight. "I'm not trying to get in your pants. I want to take care of you."

"Fine." She rolls over onto her back and undoes the snap on her jeans, shimmying out of them. Despite my not wanting anything from her—and I swear I don't—I can't help but stare at her legs, not to mention those lacy pink panties she has on that are barely covering her.

Swallowing hard, I glance down, trying to gain some composure. I shouldn't act like a pervert in her time of need, but I look at her and I want her. It's an automatic reaction.

I glance up to catch her shrugging out of her shirt and tossing it on the floor. She reaches beneath her tank and undoes the clasp of her bra, pulling it off from under her top in that magical way girls have. The bra is white and lacy, a little scrap of fabric that falls from her fingertips. She's wearing just the tank and the panties, her nipples pressing against her top, gooseflesh rising on her skin, and I release a shuddering breath. Tell myself to get the hell over it and do the right thing.

"Cold? I can grab an extra blanket . . ."

"No." She shakes her head and bounds up from the bed,

tugging back the comforter and sheet so she can slip beneath them. "I'm just really, really tired."

I stand there, not knowing what to do. She's giving off a weird vibe. I know she's upset and she has every reason to be. Not only did her mom pull a really crappy move, but Owen blames her for it.

Her back is to me, her blond hair a mess around her head, and I want to go to her so bad. But I'm afraid she'll reject me. "Are you coming to bed?" she asks, her voice soft.

She just made up my mind for me. "Yeah," I say, removing my clothes until I'm only in my boxer briefs. Turning off the bedside lamp, I get into bed and pull the covers over me, wondering if I should reach for her.

I decide to stay on my back and stare up at the ceiling instead, my arms folded behind my head. She's quiet, she's hardly moving, and I think she might've already fallen asleep.

"Drew?"

Guess she's still awake. "Yeah."

"Thank you for letting us stay with you." She rolls over to face me and I turn my head so our gazes meet. "You didn't have to do that."

"What the hell?" I'm irritated. Does she think I'd let her deal with this on her own? "Of course I had to do that. Where else would you two go?"

She shrugs one shoulder. "I would've figured something out. I bet Colin would've taken us in. I hear he lives in a freaking mansion. I'm sure he has plenty of room."

Fuck me! I can't believe she would say that. The guy was a total dick to me that night I first saw her, making me believe he had something going on with her, and now she's saying she would've moved in with him like it was no problem?

"I don't want to inconvenience you," she continues. "First thing tomorrow before I go to work, I'm going apartment hunting."

"Why do you do that?" I ask, my voice so low, I sound like I'm growling. But damn it, I'm pissed. "Why do you act like you never want my help? Like you can't count on me to come through for anything?"

"Seriously?" Her voice rises. "When have you *ever* come through? I can't count on anyone. No one. I've always taken care of myself. I'm not about to become dependent on you now."

"Why the hell not? We haven't been together long enough for me to come through for you when the going gets tough. But I'm here now. Offering everything I have to try to help you and you act like you could give a shit." My blood is boiling. I'm infuriated that she's treating me like this. A voice inside my head whispers I need to tread lightly, but screw it. The gloves are coming off. I need to tell her how I feel before I explode and really lose my shit.

"I said thank you," she whispers.

"Yeah, like I held a gun to your head and forced you to say it," I return, flicking my gaze away from her so I can stare at the ceiling once again.

She's quiet, I hear the rustle of the sheets and comforter, and I glance at her out of the corner of my eye to see she's curled into a ball, her shoulder shaking. A sob escapes her and she slaps her hand over her mouth.

God, she's crying. Probably over how I just yelled at her, like I'm some sort of jackass.

"Come here," I whisper, gathering her in my arms. She comes to me easily, curling her arms around my middle as she rests her head against my bare chest. Her tears dampen my skin as I smooth her hair away from her forehead. I whisper soft words of comfort close to her ear, hating how despondent she sounds. She's crying hard, her entire body shaking. I fear her heart might be breaking in two.

"I—I don't know what to d-do," she sobs. "I can't believe she left us with nothing. That she didn't tell us she was leaving."

"It's going to be all right." I tuck a strand of hair behind her ear, run my index finger down the side of her throat. "I swear, I'll help you with whatever you need."

She takes a deep, shuddering breath. "It's not that I'm ungrateful. I just . . . I don't know how to do this. Accept help from someone. I've always carried this load on my own. It's hard to believe someone wants to share the burden."

"Whatever I can do to help, I'm here. You don't have to rush out and find an apartment right away." I slip my finger beneath her chin and lift her head. Her cheeks are streaked with drying tears and black smudges ring beneath her eyes. She never washed off her makeup and she looks so lost, so pitiful, I lean in and brush a soft kiss to her lips. "Take your time. Find a good place for you and Owen to live."

I'd rather they stay with me for the long term but I don't want to push. Having her brother living here with us would be . . . uncomfortable at first, but Fable is literally all he has.

"Okay." She nods, as if she's trying to convince herself. "Okay, you're right. I do need to take my time and not pick the first apartment that's available." She closes her eyes, presses her lips together. "I don't have any furniture. She took it all. Even my bed! I've had that stupid bed for years. It's not even that comfortable. The mattress is all lumpy."

I kiss her again. "She's crazy, baby. Bat-shit crazy for taking everything like she did, and so quickly, too. I honestly don't know how she did it."

"I don't know either. It makes no sense." Fable opens her eyes. "*She* makes no sense. I tried to stop figuring her out years ago, but then she goes and pulls a stunt like this and I'm left trying to piece together exactly why it happened."

"Stop thinking about it." I kiss her lips one more time, then drop a kiss on her cheek, her nose, her forehead. "We'll worry about it tomorrow. You need to get some sleep."

She nods, her eyes sliding closed, and she squeezes her arms around me. "I'm sorry."

"I'm the one who's sorry. I shouldn't have yelled at you."

"I think I needed it." Her voice is already fading and she nuzzles her face against my chest. "You feel so good, Drew. I love you."

My heart eases. I'm reassured by her sweetly spoken words. "I love you, too."

CHAPTER 18

Most of the shadows of this life are caused by our stand-ing in one's own sunshine.
—Ralph Waldo Emerson

Drew

"So she's moved in with you."

"It's temporary," I'm quick to tell Dr. Harris. I know what she's thinking. What everyone will think, though it's not as if I know a ton of people. We're moving too fast, Fable and I.

But it's been less than a week since her mom abandoned her and Owen. I just can't kick her out. They have nowhere to go. Besides, I like having Fable living with me. Owen and I have come to a somewhat uneasy truce. I know he's not my biggest fan, but the kid is polite, keeps his room clean, and doesn't give me any trouble. Not that I believed he would.

He's a good kid. Fable's raised him right.

Doc is tapping away at her iPad. Probably noting how worried she is that I'm living with Fable. "Are you all getting along?"

"For the most part." I can't lie to her. "There was tension at first, most of it coming from Owen. He's hurt that their mom did this."

"Understandable."

"He blamed Fable at first."

"Also understandable. We sometimes look to put the blame on others because we don't want to believe the truth." She looks at me pointedly. "We also tend to blame ourselves."

I know all about that. I get it. "They've hashed stuff out, but it's still a little tense between them. So that means it's a little tense between Owen and me. But overall, he's a nice kid. I feel bad for him." I remember being a teen. My entire world changed in the blink of an eye. I lost all my innocence, my childhood forever.

This betrayal by his mother has taken Owen's childhood away from him for good.

"Has the mother resurfaced at all?"

"Fable finally received a text from her a few days ago." And it had infuriated her. Only two sentences, it sent Fable into a funk that had her stewing the rest of the night.

I'm so sorry. Someday I hope you'll understand.

Fable deleted it immediately, calling her mom every horrific name she could think of.

"Your relationship is already a delicate one. Doesn't this situation put unnecessary stress on the two of you?"

"If we can get through this, we can get through anything, don't you think?"

Dr. Harris offers me a kind smile. "One would think. Such a momentous move while in the early stages of your commitment to each other can also turn everything sour. Are you afraid of that? Of losing her after finally getting her back?"

I'm always afraid of losing Fable. The fear stays in the back of my mind 24/7. Most of the time I push it aside and focus on the present day.

"She needs me."

"And you need her, don't you?"

"I do." I take a deep breath. "You won't want to hear this, but I'd prefer if they lived with me. I like having her there. We don't spend every waking moment together since she's working full time lately and I'm in school, but I like . . ." My voice trails off.

"You like what?" Dr. Harris asks.

"I like having her in my bed every night. Waking up with her every morning. Just knowing she's with me gives me a sense of peace I can't remember ever having in my life." I rub my thumb against my knee. "I don't want her to leave."

"She will eventually. It sounds to me like Fable is a very independent person, right?"

"Yeah." I don't want to talk about her any longer. I don't want to think about her leaving me, even if it *is* just to live on her own.

As if she can sense me closing up, my shrink changes the subject.

"Have you heard from your dad?"

"He called right before I came inside. I didn't answer." I feel guilty for sending him straight to voice mail but I can't deal with another rant. And that's all he does when he calls.

Rants about Adele and how much she wronged him. How she humiliated him among their friends and his colleagues. He's the laughingstock of the country club, she's flaunting her young piece all over town. On and on it goes.

I'm over it. I'll be there for him, but he still hasn't filed divorce papers. I know deep down inside he's waiting for her to come crawling back and beg for his forgiveness. Fool that he is for her, he'll probably take Adele back.

I can hardly stomach the thought.

"He still doesn't know?"

She's referring to Adele and me. I shake my head.

"So she hasn't said anything?"

"Not that I know of." Cold fear grips my gut at the mere thought.

"Have you ever considered beating her to the punch?" When I frown, Dr. Harris continues. "Telling your dad before she does?"

"No way." I shake my head. "I could never work up the nerve to tell him that."

"It might be easier coming from you. Being honest with your father might take an incredible load off your chest. If he hears it from Adele first, she's won. You've allowed her the chance to tell him, to make up whatever story she needs to tell to make herself look better."

I study her, letting her words sink in. She has a point. I'm way too chickenshit to broach the subject with him, though. "I'll consider telling him first," I say only to appease her.

She smiles. "I'm glad."

The moment I leave Dr. Harris's office I check my phone. Two missed calls from my dad and one from Fable. I call her first.

"You'll never believe what happened." She sounds excited. Happy.

"What?"

"I think I found the perfect apartment. Oh my God, Drew, it's so nice! Two bedrooms, two bathrooms, at a newer complex. The rent's reasonable and the deposit isn't too outrageous. I went and checked it out with Jen and it's beautiful. They already ran a credit check on me and said they'd hold the apartment for me, but I have to come up with the deposit by Friday."

Shit. She's leaving me. "Where's it located?" If it's in a bad part of town, I refuse to let her move there.

"Here's what's even better about the apartment. It's not too far from your place. Like about two miles away, tops. On the other side of the shopping center with the grocery store you like to go to." She laughs. "I don't have any furniture, but I don't care. We'll figure something out. I can shop the Goodwill."

"Let me help you," I say automatically because I can't not make the offer.

"No," she says softly. "You've helped me enough already. The money I'm making at The District is outrageous. The tips have been amazing. That's what I'm going to use for the deposit to secure the apartment. I have some tip money stashed at your place, but not enough."

"You don't deposit your tips in the bank?"

"No. It's mostly all ones and fives. I like to keep my cash in the pocket of an old sweater. Did you know I had almost five hundred dollars stashed in that sweater in my closet when my mom went through the house? Thank God they didn't find it."

She's happy she found a place and I should be, too, but I'm not. I don't want her to leave. How can I tell her that without sound cloying or overbearing? "Are you going to my place now?"

"In a little bit. I have to go by and pick up my check. Then Jen will drop me off. Where are you?"

"Headed home," I say as I walk toward where I parked my truck.

"Oh, good. Owen should be there. He just called me and said he was being dropped off."

"Is moving going to change where he goes to school?"

She sighs. "Yeah. He doesn't mind, though. Says he wants a change, though he'll miss his best friend. I promised him they could get together whenever he wants."

"It'll work out," I reassure her.

"I hope so. I'll see you soon, okay?" She hangs up before I can tell her I love her and I stare at my phone's screen, wishing I had said the words.

Being with Fable has turned me into a complete sap.

My phone immediately starts ringing again. This time it's my dad. I answer it, steeling myself for the inevitable spew of words over his hatred for his wife. "Hey, Dad."

"Where's Adele? Have you seen her?"

I stop in the middle of the sidewalk, causing someone passing by to bump into me. "Why would *I* see her? What's going on?"

"I don't know. We . . . talked this morning. Then we started to argue and she brought you up. Said she needed to see you and took off in my fucking Jag. Have you seen her? Did she come there?"

"Of course I haven't seen her." Dread creeps over me, making my head spin. "Why would she want to come see me?"

"I haven't a clue. She said she had something to tell you."

He pauses. "Don't turn her away, okay? Please? Hear her out, whatever she has to say. I'm sure she's going to you to ask if you would help convince me that the two of us belong together." He sounds smug, funny considering only last night he'd been a ragged mess, practically crying over her cheating ways.

He's way off base with her wanting to talk to me. Adele knows the last thing I would do is hear her out over how much she and my dad are meant to be together. She wouldn't have the balls to do something like that.

There's something else to this story. Something I don't want to know.

"If you see her, call me. Promise?"

"I promise," I say before I end the call.

The entire drive back to my place, I keep a lookout for my dad's sleek black Jaguar, but I don't spot it anywhere. That type of car is a dime a dozen back home. Here, in this small college town that's filled mostly with Hondas and Toyotas, the car stands out like a glaring beacon.

Thank God I don't spot the Jag in my complex's parking lot, either. Relieved I dodged that bullet, I head toward my apartment, surprised to find the door unlocked when I enter.

Surprised even more to find Adele sitting on my fucking couch, Owen sitting next to her and looking incredibly uneasy.

"Andrew!" She stands, pushing her long dark hair over her shoulder. "You're home!"

I shut the door, my gaze going to Owen, who sprang up so fast from that couch he reminded me of a jack-in-the-box. He'll hardly meet my eyes, and I'm instantly taken back in time.

I remember how she used to spend all of her time with me. Flattering me. At first, she made me nervous. I wasn't used to that sort of constant, almost overbearing attention. But after a while, I started to crave it. She knew exactly what she was doing, how she was manipulating me to fall under her spell.

"Get away from him," I say a little too forcefully, shocking both of them. "Keep your fucking hands off him, Adele—I mean it."

She smirks, shooting Owen a long, sultry look. "He's a sweet, sweet boy, Andrew—reminds me so much of you that age. Tall and handsome, and so strong. He's going to be quite the looker someday."

I've never been tempted to do harm to a woman in my life. Yet at this very moment, if I could wrap my hands around her neck and squeeze the ever-loving life out of her, I'd have no regrets. "Go to your room, Owen," I demand.

He scurries off without protest, slamming the door so hard, Adele jumps, then titters nervously.

"You don't need to scare the poor boy. I didn't do a thing to him. You know I only have eyes for you." She comes close to me. I can smell the scent of alcohol emanating from her body. She has to be drunk.

Sidestepping her, I ignore what she said. She's just trying to get a rise out of me, as usual. "Where's Dad's Jag?"

She laughs. "I parked it on the street, behind this building. Pretty devious, right? I knew you would flip if you saw the car. Knew that your dad would contact you and ask you to look for me. Heaven forbid he actually do it himself." She plops down on the couch, her body draped across it. "You have a nice place here. Why does your little slut's brother live with you?"

"It's none of your goddamn business," I bite out. "You call Fable a slut one more time, I won't be held responsible for what I do to you."

"Such anger! You know, I'm surprised the two of you are still together. I didn't pick her as your type." She tilts her head and smiles. "You deserve someone so much prettier, a better match for you. You have so much potential. Too much to squander it all on a stupid girl like Fable."

Adele spits out Fable's name like it's poison. Fable does much the same with Adele's name. "I already told you, watch what you say."

She waves a hand. "What are your plans for the future anyway, hmm, Andrew? Do you plan on moving on to pro ball? I know that's your dream. I think you could do it. You've always chased your dreams and accomplished so much at such a young age."

What is she talking about? "I'm not discussing my future with you or what I plan on doing next. You need to leave."

Her eyes widen in feigned shock. "Why, Andrew, I can't believe you would say such a thing to me. Are you that eager to get rid of me?"

"Yes," I tell her bluntly.

We stare at each other blindly for a long, uncomfortable moment, until finally her eyes narrow and she rests her hands on her hips. "I'm going to tell him, Andrew. I'm going to tell your dad about you and me and what we did. What we made. Vanessa. There's nothing you can do to stop me, either."

It feels like all the blood is draining from my body. "Why would you do that?"

"I need to come clean." She shrugs. "I need to get my sins

off my chest, Andrew. You're my biggest sin. Did you know that? I've never done anything so wicked as what I did with you."

"Shut up." If I could slap my hands over my ears to drown out what she's saying like some sort of little kid, I would. "Just shut up."

"Truth hurts, doesn't it? Imagine what it'll do to your dad. Oh, it'll tear him up. Destroy him and his relationship with you. You'll lose him forever." She smiles. "I've already lost him. What does it matter if you lose him, too?"

"Get out," I tell her. I need her gone. Fable's due home any minute and I can't risk a confrontation.

"Don't be so quick to send me home now. I fully plan on telling your father everything the second I see him." She heads toward the door, her walk smooth, her head held high as if she were some sort of queen. The perfect image she must keep up has to be exhausting. I should know. I did much of the same thing for years.

"Why would you want to do that to him? To me? I thought you loved him." I don't understand why she needs to do this.

"I don't love him. He doesn't fulfill me. I stay with him for the beautiful house and the cars and the jewelry and the money. I don't think I've loved him for years."

This isn't my problem. None of what she's saying has anything to do with me. That she would be so cold, talking about my father, is hard for me to swallow, but I need to push past it all and get rid of this bitch.

But before I can so much as push Adele out of the apartment, the door swings open and Fable walks in, stopping short when she sees who's standing in front of her.

Fable

Seeing Adele in Drew's living room nearly sends me stumbling backward. Luckily enough, I'm able to gain my footing so I don't make a fool of myself.

Also luckily enough, I find my voice immediately. "What the fuck is *she* doing here?" I ask, looking pointedly at Drew.

Adele laughs her bitch cackle. "As crude as ever, I see. The epitome of class, aren't you, Fable?"

"At least I don't pretend to be full of class when so clearly you're not, considering you like to molest teenage boys." I slam the door, realization dawning on me, and I look at Drew. "Where's Owen?"

"In his room," Drew says, his voice gentle. "He's safe. I promise."

"You two treat me like some sort of common child molester out to pick up little boys off the street, when you couldn't be farther from the truth." Adele sends Drew a warm smile, which totally creeps me out. "He seduced me as well, you know. I mean, look at him. He's always been a beautiful boy."

The bitch just crossed a line, and now I'm crossing one right back. I don't know what's come over me, what possesses me to do something so crazy, and I know there will be an eventual price to pay.

But here I go. It's as though it's all happening in slow motion and I know I'm going to do it before I actually complete the act.

I launch myself at her. Take her to the ground so hard, I hear her scream of pain when her body hits the floor. I'm sitting on top of her, tugging at her long, sleek hair, trying to scratch her beautiful smug face like I've always wanted to do. I want to beat the crap out of her and leave her as bruised and battered on the outside as she left Drew bruised and battered on the inside.

Doing all that, I know I still won't be satisfied.

"Fable, Jesus, stop!" Drew is yelling at me but I won't listen. I'm ready to tear this bitch apart. I'm pulling her hair, scratching at her, cocking my fist back ready to punch her square in the face, and that's when Drew grabs hold of my arm, stopping my fist from making a connection with Adele's jaw. "Get off her. Now."

I'm shaking, full of rage and fear and adrenaline. Both of us are panting, the sound filling the otherwise quiet room. Adele stares up at me with her dark, mysterious eyes and I wonder what happened in her past to turn this woman into such a complete fuck-up.

"Fable." Drew tugs on my arm so I have no choice but to climb off Adele and stand. His fingers are clasped tight around my upper arm and we both watch as Adele gets up, the expression on her face nothing short of murderous.

"I should call the cops," she says, pointing her finger at me. "And press fucking charges, you lunatic bitch!"

"She didn't touch you," Drew says in that scary menacing voice of his.

"What are you saying? She was all over me!" Adele holds out her arms. I suppose there might be a few scratches there, but nothing I can see. "Look at me!"

"Get out. Just get out," he says, ignoring her outstretched arms, her plea for help. All of it. "Before I'm the one doing something I'll regret."

Her eyes go wide for the quickest moment, and then she's

gone. Fleeing the apartment like some sort of terrorist in flight after dropping a major bomb in the middle of a crowded room. The door slams behind her and I fall onto the couch, my entire body shaking with anger.

"Why did she come here?" I look up at Drew. Misery is written all over his face. His brows are drawn, his mouth a thin, grim line.

"I don't know. To tell me she's going to confess to my dad everything that happened between us? She claims she's going to tell him about Vanessa, too." He sits down heavily beside me, tension radiating off his body in waves. "Should I call him? Should I be the one who tells him first? Dr. Harris says I should."

I part my lips, but the words clog my throat. I still can't believe what I did. How quickly I jumped her, how bad I wanted to hurt her. I may act like I'm tough, but I never resort to violence. I never got in physical fights at school.

That woman makes me want to lose my mind.

"I can't make that decision for you," I finally say. I know it's harsh, but I won't be responsible for Drew telling his dad or not about what happened. He needs to come to that conclusion on his own.

"You're right. I know you're right." He blows out a harsh breath. "I don't know how to tell him, though. I'm scared."

I hook my arm around his shoulders, trying to give him comfort. He's stiff beneath my touch, though, and I end up running my hand down his back before letting my arm drop. "It'll be okay," I murmur. "Don't let that bitch bother you."

"Easy to say, not so easy to do." He looks at me. His gaze is bleak, his face pale. "She'll ruin everything, Fable. She's trying to destroy my life."

I stare at him. He's giving her so much control still. I thought he was starting to move past this. Clearly, she still has her claws in him. He looks terrified. "We won't let her, Drew. I'll stand by you no matter what. I'll support you. It doesn't matter what she says."

"What if she wants to take it further? What if . . . what if she wants to go to the media or whatever? Try to make me look bad around here, in the community. That will destroy me. Destroy my chances at a professional football career."

"Is that what you want?" He never talks about football much with me. He seems to compartmentalize all these different parts of his life and only reveal what he thinks I should see.

"Yeah." He hangs his head. "I don't know what else I would do. I'm a business major with a minor in finance. But I did that to please my dad."

"Hey." I rest my hand on his knee and give him a little shake. "It's going to be okay. Really."

Drew settles his hand over mine and gives it a squeeze. We look at each other as he laces our fingers together and then he's leaning in, kissing me, so softly, so sweetly I almost want to cry. Touching my cheek with his other hand, he breathes words against my lips that make my heart ache for him.

"I love you so damn much. I know this has happened fast and we're having to deal with a lot of shit, but if we can make it through this, we can make it through anything."

He's right. He has to be right. If I could, I'd beg him to take me to bed right now. So we could lose ourselves in each other, if only for a little bit.

But now's not the time. There are other things to consider first. And Owen . . .

"Where's Owen?" I ask after I break our kiss.

As if he's lurking behind his bedroom door just waiting to bust out, he enters the living area, stopping short when he sees the two of us sitting so close together. We haven't been very affectionate or grabby in front of my brother. It makes me uncomfortable, which is so stupid, but I know Owen doesn't approve one hundred percent of me being with Drew.

Crazy. I shouldn't care. I love this man sitting beside me. And I love the boy standing in front of us.

"That chick was creepy." Owen shakes his head, looking at Drew. "She said she was your mom?"

Drew stiffens beside me. "She's not. She's married to my dad. My mom died when I was little."

"Wait a minute." I disentangle myself from Drew and stand, going to Owen. "You met her? You talked to her?"

"She was in the apartment when I got home," Drew adds.

"With Owen? *Alone?*" I'm stunned. *What. The. Hell.* "Who let her in?"

"I did," Owen admits sheepishly. "She was waiting outside when I got here. She said she was Drew's mom and that she needed to see him, so I let her in."

"Oh my God." I'm reeling. "How long were you with her alone?"

"I don't know. Ten minutes?" Owen shrugs. "What's the big deal? She's weird, I'll give her that. But it's not like she did anything to me. You act like she'd want to feel me up or something."

I look at Drew. No way am I going to say anything to Owen about . . . that. "She's a little mentally unstable at the moment. Everyone's worried about her." *Ick*. I can't believe I just said that. I'm not worried about her. I wish she'd fall off the face of the earth and rot in hell forever.

"I thought I heard you two fighting," Owen said, shifting on his feet. He looks uncomfortable.

"We don't really like each other." I circle my arm around Owen's shoulders and lead him into the kitchen. I need to change the subject, and quick. "I have good news. I found an apartment for us."

"Really?"

He's so excited as I tell him all the details, hyperaware of Drew sitting in the living room, alone with his thoughts. I'm torn. Excited to find my own place for Owen and me, but sad to leave Drew. I need this independence. But I need Drew as well.

And he needs me—now more than ever. I hope I can be enough for him.

I hope we can be enough for each other.

CHAPTER 19

The truth is rarely pure and never simple.

—Oscar Wilde

Adele

I'm sick and tired of feeling guilty for the things I've done. I can't help who I fall in love with. Why is it such a crime, falling in love? My husband neglected me for years. His son reminds me so much of him . . . only better. Younger. More vibrant. Sweet and eager to please.

At first it was all for fun. When her husband loses interest in her sexually, a woman starts to feel less than. Ignored. Alone. I started flirting with Drew and he responded. Oh, maybe he was a little uncomfortable at first but the more we talked, the more time we spent together, the more he liked it.

The more he liked me.

Now he hates me. I don't know where it all went wrong. I don't understand his total disgust for me. I wish I could change it. I wish I could make him see I only want the very best for him. He has so much potential. He'll be a star someday. A bright, shiny star who for a brief moment, I held in my hands.

Only he slipped away and has no plans on ever coming back. The disappointment that floods me every time I think of him is so overwhelming, I can't dwell on it for long.

So I don't.

I've had affairs. Brief, meaningless dalliances with beautiful young men who make me feel good for a little while. Jonah the golf pro is my latest indulgence, and while he's magnificent in bed and eagerly attentive, he's also young and foolish and enjoys bragging to his friends that he's banging an older woman. They call me a cougar.

So crude, these boys are. Not my Drew. Scratch that—my *Andrew*. I'm the only one who calls him that. The only one who's allowed.

I drive around the backwater little town he lives in while he goes to college, getting lost on all the one-way streets while I try to find a decent hotel. The campus is nice, the downtown area eclectic, with lots of cute shops and restaurants. Other than that, the town is an absolute shit hole. If he remains here with that stupid, useless girl, he will go nowhere.

Thinking of her makes me want to vomit. I can't believe she attacked me. My head still hurts where she literally ripped the hair out of my scalp. The way she looked at me, the words she said! She hates me.

That's fine. I hate her, too. She's turned my beautiful boy completely against me, and the idea of her having sex with him makes me want to tear her apart.

Andrew is mine. He belongs to me.

I finally find a hotel and check in, handing over my husband's credit card. The price doesn't matter. Price never matters. Andy hasn't cut off my credit cards or my access to our bank account, none of it. No matter what I do, no matter what I say, he wants me back. I'm his favorite prized possession and the idea that I might belong to someone else fills him with worry.

He won't let me go. That's both reassuring and cloying. I need Andy for financial security. I want others for excitement and passion. My husband can no longer give me that sort of excitement, which is a shame.

I go to my hotel room, bringing with me the small travel bag I packed just for this special occasion. I'd hoped Andrew would let me stay with him, but he has that bitch girlfriend living at his apartment for the moment, along with her younger brother.

Who was a most interesting specimen, if I'm being truthful. He's handsome and young and full of attitude—I could sense it the moment I set eyes on him. Not necessarily my usual type, with his blond hair and green eyes, his slender build and wannabe bad-boy personality.

He has potential, though. Tremendous potential.

Setting my bag on top of the bed, I unzip it and reach inside, pulling out the small handgun I took from my husband's dresser. He keeps it there for protection. I brought it with me for the same reason. I'm about to do something that will change our lives forever and I'm not sure how others might react. I'm especially grateful I brought it, considering that stupid bitch is still in Andrew's life.

It might be a mistake making my confession, but I need to get this information off my chest. Andy deserves the truth. Andrew must face his truth.

I may have told Andrew that Vanessa belonged to him,

but I don't know if it's true. I want it to be true. I'd much prefer believing Andrew was her father. Unfortunately, I never had it confirmed. There is no absolute proof for me regarding her paternity. But now she's gone, and though it's wishful thinking on my part that Andrew would ever gift me with another child, I still hope for it.

Despite his hatred for me. Despite his fear and disgust for me, I still wish for him to be mine.

Forever.

CHAPTER 20

Mistakes are always forgivable, if one has the courage to admit them.

—Bruce Lee

Drew

When your phone rings at two in the morning and wakes you from a deep sleep, you know it's never good.

The ringing startles me and I reach for my cell where it rests on my bedside table, my heart thumping wildly. Fable moves away from me in her sleep, rolling over on her side, her naked back to me. I'm immediately cold without having her close and I glance at the phone, see that it's my dad calling. Again.

Reluctantly I answer, keeping my voice a whisper. "Hello."

"Drew. My God." He's breathing heavily and I restrain myself from blowing out an exasperated breath. I'm so over his drama I can hardly take another anguished phone call, another crying plea. "Is it true?"

It's as if all the blood drains from my body. You tell yourself you're prepared for a particular moment, a certain revelation, but when it happens, you're still knocked on your ass. "Is what true?"

"Adele told me what happened between you two." His voice lowers to an almost inaudible whisper. "Tell me, is it true?"

I don't know what he wants me to say. Yes, it's true or no, it's not? Fuck, I'm confused. "What did she tell you?"

"That the two of you had an affair going on for years? Tell me, son. I need to know. Is she lying to me? Please say she's lying."

He doesn't want to deal. Well, that's just great because neither do I. "Dad . . ."

"Don't beat around the bush. Just confirm it. Say yes or say no."

I exhale heavily, my heart aching, my stomach turning. "I . . ."

"Say it! Yes or no. It's as simple as that."

Right. It's so simple, admitting my deepest, darkest secret. "Yes," I say, my voice harsh.

Dad is silent for so long, I wonder if he's hung up on me. But then a burst of sound fills my ears, so ragged and pitiful, I almost don't recognize it for what it is.

He's . . . crying.

"I hate her," he sobs, his voice broken. "She's destroyed everything. My marriage, my son, my daughter. Oh God, I hate her so much."

I climb out of bed, never looking in Fable's direction. She might be awake by now, I don't know, but I need to concentrate on what Dad is saying.

At the moment he's sort of blowing my mind.

"I can't believe that she had an . . . affair with you. An *affair.*" He laughs, but it's hollow sounding. "She molested you. God, she's sick! I never want to see her again."

257

"You don't blame me?" I fall onto the couch, my head spinning. All these years I believed that if he discovered the truth, he would hate my guts.

"Blame you? How could I blame you? She said this started when you were just fifteen. Fucking fifteen!" He's crying harder. "I'm sorry, Drew. I brought her into our lives and I'm so goddamn sorry. I had no idea. No fucking clue she was doing that to you. How could I be so stupid, so selfish? So blind?"

"It's not your fault, Dad . . ."

"Stop right there, just . . . stop. It's all my fault. I should've paid better attention. I should've been there for you but I wasn't. I hate that. I've let you down." He takes a deep, shuddering breath. "It's over, son. My marriage is over. You don't have to worry about her being a part of our lives any longer. She's no longer welcome in my home, in my heart, in my life."

I'm crying, too. The tears are falling and I sniff, trying to gain some control over my emotions. That tight feeling I've been carrying in my chest for months—hell, years—is slowly but surely easing. My dad knows the truth.

And he doesn't hate me for it.

"When did she tell you?"

"She called me hours ago. I have no idea where she is. Did you see her? Did she come there? God, she's twisted! I swear she's obsessed with you."

"I saw her. Fable tried to beat her up when she found out Adele had met her younger brother."

"You're still with Fable? I thought you two broke up." He pauses for a moment. "Wait a minute, does *she* know what happened between you and Adele?"

"Yeah." My voice is a raspy whisper.

He's silent for a while, as if he needs time to process that bit of information. "Things must be quite serious between you two."

"She—she figured it out when I brought her home." Adele had been less than subtle. That my father couldn't recognize her crazy, possessive behavior showed how oblivious he really was to it.

"I'm an idiot. I hope someday you can forgive me."

His words take my breath away. "I—I feel the same way."

"There's nothing for me to forgive. You were innocent in all of this." A little sob escapes him again. "I'm so sorry, son. For everything."

We talk a little bit more and I promise to come see him soon. Hopefully going there without Adele present will remove the ghosts that haunt me in my old house. My dad needs me right now. I need to forget all those ghosts once and for all.

I end the call and go back into the bedroom to find Fable sitting up, leaning against the pillows, the bedside table lamp on its lowest setting. She has the sheet tucked around her, her shoulders bare and gleaming in the soft light, and she's twirling a strand of long blond hair around her finger, staring at the ends.

She's beautiful. And so understanding, so accepting of all my secrets, I don't know what I did to earn her trust and forgiveness. I love that she's in my life. That she wants to be with me despite it all.

"Is everything okay?" she asks, her voice hushed.

Going to my side of the bed, I settle in beside her. "That

was my dad." I take a deep breath and stare straight ahead. I'm almost afraid to look at her even though she knows everything. "Adele told him what happened."

"How did he react?"

"He doesn't hate me. He feels awful for what she did to me."

"See?" Her voice is quiet. "I told you he would be on your side."

She did. I hadn't believed her. "I guess you were right." I release a deep, shaky breath. "I can't believe how accepting of me he was."

"Did she tell him about . . . Vanessa?"

Frowning, I turn to look at her. How could I have missed that? "He never mentioned it. So I'm assuming no."

Fable lets the strand of hair she'd been twirling fall from her fingers. "Do you really think it's true? That she was your daughter?"

I shrug. This is the information that makes me the most uncomfortable. I don't want to believe it. That I could've been a father just . . . blows my mind. I have a tough time talking about it with anyone, even my therapist. It's a subject I don't want to face.

Especially since I haven't a clue if it's true or not. There's no way I can prove it either way. Vanessa's gone.

"I want to believe she's lying to me because it's easier." Fable moves closer to me, resting her head on my shoulder, and I slip my arm around her. Closing my eyes, I voice what I've been unable to say since the day Adele threw that bomb at me. "The day we came back here, after I dropped you off at your apartment, I called Adele. I demanded she tell me the truth. She said . . . she said she couldn't get pregnant with my dad so she decided to try with me. That she poked holes in the condom and she got pregnant. All it took was one time, she insisted. One freaking time. I hate her. I hate that she tricked my father and me. I hate what she's done to me. I hate that I let what happened between us control me for so long."

"I'm sorry," Fable whispers.

I close my eyes and trail my fingers across her shoulder, down her arm. I need to touch her. Having her close anchors me. Reminds me of how far I've come in so little time. "So am I. But I can't remain in the past. I can't let what she's done cripple me for the rest of my life. I need to let it go. Let her go, once and for all."

"Easier said than done." Fable lifts her head so she can meet my gaze. "It'll take time, Drew. I'm here, though. Even though I'm getting my own place, and I know you don't like that, I'll be here for you. I swear."

"You don't have to move—" I start but she cuts me off.

"I need to do it. I can't be dependent on you. Not like this."

"I want to take care of you," I whisper. "I can do it. I have money. You'd never need anything if you and Owen lived here with me."

She flashes me a quivery smile. "I know. And I love that you want to help and take care of me. But I need to learn how to take care of myself first." She lifts her head and brushes her mouth against mine. "I need to show Owen I can do this."

I touch her throat and she shivers. I slip my hand around her nape and bring her in closer to me, our mouths meeting, our tongues tangling. She melts against me, slipping her arms around my neck, the sheet falling away from her so I feel nothing but soft, bare skin.

After everything that happened today, my normal MO would be to run and hide. Pretend I don't exist. Focus on anything else but living. Feeling.

Now, all I want to do is feel. Feel Fable's mouth on mine, her hands on my body, her body moving against me. Press her into the mattress, explore her skin with my hands and lips, and push inside her, finding that connection with the one person who means more to me than anyone or anything in this world.

As I stare into her eyes while buried deep in her welcoming body, I whisper that I love her. The smile she offers me in response, tender and so full of emotion, unravels me completely.

She holds my heart in her hands. And for the first time in my life, I give it over to her completely.

Freely.

Fable Maguire owns me. And I know I own her.

Fable

Yesterday was one of the craziest days of my life. A whirlwind of emotions swept through me, from the highs to the lows and everything in between.

I found the apartment of my dreams. I tried to beat the shit out of a woman who almost destroyed the man I love. The man I love was nearly brought to his knees when his father discovered his darkest secret.

After the day we had, both of us were emotional wrecks.

Somehow I still fell into Drew's arms, too overcome to fight the powerful pull that tugs within both of us. That pull brings us together as if we can't resist each other.

It's a fact. We just . . . can't.

We made love slowly, quietly. No teasing, no urgency. Just a fluid, delicious connection of bodies until we were both spent, falling asleep in each other's arms like characters in the corniest movie you've ever seen on cable.

I'm the luckiest damn girl in the world. I know most girls would think I'm crazy. Drew Callahan is definitely not what's on the surface. He's troubled. He has issues, deep issues that aren't resolved yet.

I don't care. He's mine.

Despite being up half the night, I get up early and force Owen awake. Ply him with a real breakfast before I drive him to school using Drew's truck. I need a car. More than I need furniture or anything else, a freaking car would come in real handy. I can't depend on Drew or Jen driving me forever. Colin mentioned a few days ago that he knew someone who manages a local dealership and could get me a deal. I might take him up on that offer.

Smiling, I park Drew's truck in his assigned spot and shut off the engine. For the first time since I don't know when, I've surrounded myself with people who I can call my friends. Jen, T, Colin . . . Drew. The list isn't long, but it's getting there. I know my life isn't perfect, that I'll be facing more struggles. The issue with my mom is far from resolved.

But for once in my life, I feel like I'm in a good place.

The weather turned dreary overnight, but the dark clouds heavy with rain don't spoil my mood. The wind whips up, bending the little trees that dot the apartment complex property, and I climb out of the truck, forcing the door open against an extra-hard gust of air. I hit the keyless remote and start toward Drew's apartment building, when I hear a voice straight out of my nightmares.

"Well, look at you. Moving in with him. Driving his truck. Aren't you all cozy and snug in your seemingly perfect little life?"

I turn to find Adele standing before me, a smirk on her face. She looks odd. Still wearing the same clothes from yesterday, her hair's a mess, as if she hasn't brushed it, and her eyes are wide as she stares at me. A huge, expensive-looking dark brown leather purse is slung over her shoulder and she clutches it close.

Weirdly close.

"What are you doing here?" I try to keep my voice casual but she's freaking me out a little. Something's not quite right with this picture.

"Looking for you." She smiles.

A chill trickles down my spine at the sight of that weird smile. "Yeah, right."

"No, really. I wanted to talk to you. Maybe we should go somewhere and chat." She waves a hand behind her. "My car is around the corner. Let's go."

Like I'll just take off with her because we're best friends and all. The woman is delusional.

Slowly shaking my head, I start toward Drew's apartment. "I don't think so." She steps in front of me, halting my progress, and I glare at her. "Listen, I don't want any trouble. Just let me get by, okay?"

"No." Her smile grows. It's really creeping me out. "Drew can't save you now. You're coming with me." She reaches inside her bag and pulls out a handgun, aiming it right at me.

I blink slowly and throw my hands up in surrender, backing up a step. The woman is crazed. All that talk about your life flashing before your eyes right before you think you're going to die?

Yeah, that's happening to me at this very moment. Making me realize I've hardly lived my life at all.

No way am I going to let some greedy maniac bitch take it all away from me.

"Don't make a scene." The wind blows her hair across her face and she bats it away with her free hand, causing her to wave the gun around. I take another small step back, contemplating trying to run for it, but I have no idea if that gun's loaded or not. Or if she's a good shot.

I'd rather not take that chance.

"I'm not making a scene," I murmur, trying to keep my voice even. Calm. "What do you want from me, Adele?"

She throws back her head and laughs. Everything about her actions is exaggerated. Over the top. "I want everything you have. Well, not necessarily everything. You're an ugly little slut who deserves nothing, you know that?"

Her words are so full of venom I almost recoil. Instead, I stand my ground. "Let me get by. I'll forget this ever happened if you just let me go."

"No." She waves the gun again, pointing it right at me. "You know what I really want? I wish you would just . . . disappear. That would make my life so much easier. No more worrying about Andrew falling in love with a whore. I could

265

have him all to myself. I deserve him, you know. I created him. I made him the man he is today."

I don't argue with her. Have a feeling she wouldn't listen anyway.

"My husband hates me," she continues, clearly on a roll. "Did you hear about that? Of course you did. I try to be honest with him so he understands me better and instead he tells me he never wants to see me again. According to my husband, I destroyed both him and his son. And my daughter." Tears streak down her cheeks, a little sob escaping her. "Doesn't he see how much he destroyed *me*? How they both destroyed me after Vanessa's death? It's their fault she's gone."

I can almost—not quite, but almost—feel sorry for her. The death of any family member is horrible. The death of a small child must be absolutely devastating.

"Both of the Callahan men hate my guts and I have nothing to live for anymore. Absolutely nothing. It's all your fault, you know," Adele says matter-of-factly.

My jaw practically drops to the ground. And *I* almost felt sorry for her? "How is it my fault?"

"You came into his life and ruined everything. *Everything*. You made Andrew want to reveal the truth. You made him stay away from me. He was mine, you stupid bitch. All mine until you came along and stole him away from me."

He was never really hers. But you can't argue with crazy.

"You destroyed me, so now I'm going to destroy you." That gun is aimed right at me. "Let's take Andrew's truck. I like the idea of all of this happening in something he owns. This way, he'll never forget."

All of this happening—oh God, what is she talking about? "I'm not going anywhere with you."

She straightens out her arm, that gun coming dangerously close to me. "Go unlock the fucking truck right now."

I do as she asks, hitting the keyless remote again, the wrong button this time. The one that sets the horn alarm off.

"Stupid bitch," she mutters just as the door to Drew's apartment swings open. He's standing there, clad only in a pair of sweatpants that hang loose on his hips, and I see the greedy, lustful gleam that fills Adele's gaze when she sees him.

I think I'm going to be sick.

His eyes widen when he sees the gun in Adele's hand. He looks at me, panic in his eyes, his expression grim. "What the hell is going on?"

"Shut that fucking thing off!" Adele screams and I hit the button, silencing the car.

I turn my gaze on Drew, trying to convey everything I can to him in that one long look.

And then it hits me. I know exactly what I need to say that'll let him know this is serious. Not that a gun isn't serious, because holy shit, I hate her shaky grip, the way she waves that gun around. How completely unhinged she is. This bitch is close to losing her shit—and she wants me to take the fall for all her troubles.

"Hey, Drew," I say, raising my voice, tipping my head in Adele's direction. "Marshmallow."

CHAPTER 21

I'll be here for you. Always.
—Drew Callahan

Drew

I called 911 right before I opened the door. I don't know what compelled me to peek through the front window but I'm so fucking glad I did. Adele is standing there pointing a gun at Fable—*hell!* I almost bolted outside right then.

But I knew I needed to keep a calm head. Fable's life was at stake here. I needed to handle this right. So I told the emergency operator there was a crazy woman waving a gun around my parking lot and hung up.

Now the crazy woman is looking straight at me. I recognize that look. For a moment, I feel like I'm fifteen again. Trapped, with nowhere to go. Hating myself for what's about to happen. Wishing I were strong enough to tell her no. That awful helplessness is winding its way through me, paralyzing me for one long, agonizing moment.

And then my girl says the magic word, the one that automatically springs me into action.

"Adele. Put the gun down." My voice is firm. I don't want her to argue with me.

"No." Her voice is shaky, as is the smile she flashes at me. "She's ruined my life, Andrew. It's all her fault."

"It's not her fault. It's mine." I start down the sidewalk toward where they're standing. "I'm sorry for what I did to you."

She frowns. Tears dampen her cheeks; her eyes are filled with so much sadness. This woman is completely broken. Lost.

Yet I can't work up an ounce of sympathy for her. Everything that's happened to her, she's brought on herself.

"You're not sorry." Adele shakes her head. "None of you are. You don't care what happens to me. How I've lost everything. Where am I supposed to go now? What am I supposed to do?"

I focus all of my attention on Adele. I'm worried about Fable. I hate that Adele is pointing a gun at her. But I can't let the fear grip me. I need to save my girl. "A divorce isn't the end of the world."

"Yes, it is!" Adele wails, waving the gun around. "I'm ruined. I have nothing. Nothing to live for."

"Put the gun down," I say softly. She's scaring me. I chance a look at Fable and her posture is rigid, her shoulders back. She looks almost defiant.

But I note the fear in her gaze, the way her lips tremble subtly. She's scared as hell.

So am I.

"I should just shoot her now and put her out of her misery," Adele mutters.

"No!" I clamp my lips shut, pissed that I yelled at her. I just showed my hand and hope like hell it didn't register with Adele. "You'll go to jail. Do you want that? To spend the rest of your life in prison?"

Adele shrugs. "It doesn't matter anymore. Nothing matters anymore."

"Shoot *me*, then," I say, stepping in front of Fable. "If you're going to do it, shoot me. You can't blame Fable. She has nothing to do with any of this."

"She has everything to do with it. She stole you from me, Andrew. You were mine. You belonged to me. And then you left me. You found someone else. You bring her back home and flaunt her all over the place. She's pretty and young and gets to be with you whenever she wants." Adele aims the gun right at my chest. "I hate her!"

"You hate *me*," I remind her. "I'm the one who rejected you, who pushed you away. It's my fault."

Fable presses her fingers against the middle of my back. That one little touch fuels me, makes me stronger. Clears my head and allows me to focus on what I need to do.

Slowly, I reach out toward Adele. "Give me the gun."

She shakes her head furiously. "No."

"Give it to me."

"Fuck you!" She stretches out her arms straight in front, both hands gripping the gun tight, her index finger sneaking around the trigger. "Step out of the way, Andrew."

"No. Give. Me. The. Gun."

"Oh, God." Adele's voice cracks, her arms trembling, the gun wavering. "This isn't going to work, Andrew. I can't shoot you. I love you too much."

That's what I hoped for, though I hate her choice of words. She doesn't love me; she has some sort of weird obsession with me. "Then hand the gun over."

"I can't. I have to do this." She drops her arms, the gun hanging from her fingers at her side. "You give me no choice."

Fable presses closer to me, resting her head against my back. All I can think about is her safety. Forget me, forget Adele, forget everything and everyone else. I need Fable to be okay.

"Give you no choice for what?" I ask Adele.

"To do this. It's all your fault, Andrew. Never forget that." Adele places the barrel of the gun in her mouth.

And pulls the trigger.

Fable

Drew turns to me, buries his head against my hair as he clutches me so tight, I can't breathe. Seconds later, I hear the sound of a gunshot. It's so loud my ears are ringing. I can't hear a thing. All I feel is Drew wrapped tight around me, his chest heaving, his arms shaking as they hold me close.

"Fuck me, she just shot herself," I think I hear him say and I try to pull away from him.

But he won't let me go.

People start coming out of their apartments, the sound of gunfire no doubt drawing their attention. The ringing in my ears slowly lessens. I hear gasps, one woman yelling to call the cops.

Still Drew won't let me go.

"Don't look," he whispers close to my ear. "You don't want to see her. Don't look, Fable."

Worry clutches at my chest. Did he witness her doing it? I don't think so. He turned and grabbed me just before the gun went off. But I don't know. *God,* I hope he didn't see.

I don't think my Drew can take much more tragedy and sorrow. He's already endured enough.

Someone approaches us. I can hear footsteps and I glance up, catching sight of a guy who looks around our age. "Are you all right?" he asks.

Drew lifts his head and I glance up at him. I see the anguish, the sorrow etched all over his face. I also see tiny splatters of blood dotting his shoulders. *Oh, God.* "We're okay. Did someone call an ambulance?"

"Dude." The man tips his head to look past us and immediately looks away. "There's no need for an ambulance. There's no saving her."

I tighten my grip around Drew's waist. "Has someone called the police?"

"Yeah, they should be on their way," the man says, his face grim.

As if on cue, I hear the sirens in the near distance, coming closer and closer. They're going to want to talk to us. I so don't want to deal. I need to drop off my apartment deposit today. I need to go to work. Normal, everyday stuff.

But my life is far from normal. I could've been killed. I could be the one lying on the ground, blood pouring out of my body.

Drew saved me. He stepped in front of me and told Adele to shoot him. I can't believe he did that. That he would sacrifice himself for me . . . blows my mind.

Makes me realize just how much he loves me.

He finally relaxes his hold on me, and I pull away from him slightly so I can see his face. "Did you see her do it?" I ask. I have to know.

Slowly he shakes his head, his gaze never leaving mine. "I saw her put the gun in her mouth but I turned just as she was pulling the trigger. I couldn't watch that." He exhales on a shaky breath. "I hated her, Fable. But I couldn't stand there and watch her blow her brains out."

I close my eyes and press my forehead to his firm chest. "Thank you," I whisper. "You saved me."

"I'll always save you. You never have to worry about that."

I finally, finally believe him.

CHAPTER 22

Two people in love, alone, isolated from the world, that's beautiful.
—Milan Kundera

Seven months later

Fable

Drew and I were never believers in the fairy tale. We both had our own issues, our problems, our fucked-up home lives that blew all thoughts of happily-ever-after right out of the water. Once upon a time, we were cynics facing the world alone. Our story changed into that of two warrior cynics facing the world together.

Now, we own the happily-ever-after and we refuse to let that bitch go.

I watch him now, sitting on the sidelines of the football field. It's hot, even though it's only nine in the morning, and the summer sun is intense. I have a pretty nice tan already from sitting out here for hours watching Drew practice with his team.

He's sorta dreamy out there on the field. I love watching

him play. He's so talented, so in command of his teammates and his game play. Rumors are already spreading of how his chance at an NFL contract is getting closer and closer.

Once upon a time, that would've scared the crap out of me—the thought of him leaving me behind. Or maybe he'd want me to go along with him—and that would've scared me, too.

Now I take everything day by day. No need for panic. When the time comes for a decision to be made, I know we'll do the right thing.

Together.

I love how sweaty my man gets when he plays, too. Does that make me a freak? Oh, I put on a big show when he grabs me and hugs me after practice, complaining loudly how gross he is, all stinky and damp.

But I'm lying. I love it.

He's coming toward me now during a break, a big grin on his face, and I stand, offering him a big smacking kiss before I hand over a fresh bottle of water. He takes it from me, tears off the cap, and chugs every last drop within a few swallows.

Did I mention how sexy he is when he drinks? No? Well. I'm tempted to fan myself every time I watch him.

"Did you put on sunblock?" he asks, crushing the empty plastic bottle in his fist before he hands it back to me.

I clutch the bottle in my hand. "Maybe."

He taps the tip of my nose with his index finger. "You're turning pink. You need some."

His concern for me is slightly over the top. Since what happened with Adele, he's been very overprotective. From always being there to pick me up when my shift is over at work to slathering on enough sunblock to his satisfaction, he wants to make sure I'm safe. I appreciate it more than he'll ever know. "I'm trying to get a tan," I tell him.

"You're pretty tan already, baby." He draws his finger across my bared shoulder, sending a shiver through me. "You know what my favorite thing in the world right now is?"

I frown. Where is he going with this? "What?"

He leans in close, his mouth hovering just at my ear. "Your tan lines," he whispers. "And the fact that I'm the only one who gets to see them."

I'm blushing. That he can still do that with a few words, a mere look, blows my mind. "You're bad," I say when he pulls away from me.

A grin flashes. "You like it." He glances over his shoulder, checking out his teammates. "Look, you should go on home. It's too damn hot out here for you to sit around. I'll be done in a few hours, okay?"

I nod, sad he's kicking me out. But he's right.

Owen's around here somewhere, helping out with carrying the equipment, organizing stuff, handing out water and whatever else is needed. Drew got him the job, though it's more of a volunteer thing.

Owen doesn't care. He's thrilled to be hanging out with a bunch of cool football players. Plus, it's keeping him busy.

Keeping him out of trouble.

"I'll see you later?" Drew asks, grabbing my hand so he can pull me in for a kiss.

"Of course." I don't work today. My job at The District is still going strong. Colin is a pretty great boss. I think he has the serious hots for Jen and she's either blind or doesn't want to see it. That place is like a hotbed for juicy sexy scandal. Not that I play a part in any of it.

I'm riding the happily-ever-after wave with Drew, remember?

"I'm taking you out tonight. Don't forget, okay?" He smiles at me and I smile back. We haven't had much time to go out lately. Not that we really care. We prefer to stay home and watch movies. Make out a lot on the couch, as Owen likes to complain.

I did end up moving into that apartment with Owen . . . and Drew. After what happened with Adele in the parking lot, right in front of his old place, he wanted out of there. I was the one who offered for him to move in with me after a long discussion with Owen, making sure he was okay with it. Which he was.

Now we're like one big, happy family.

"Where are you taking me?"

"That's a surprise." His eyes darken, his expression turning ultra-serious. "I love you. You know that, right?"

I frown. "Yeah, I know. I love you, too. Lots."

"Lots?"

"Mega-lots."

"Sounds like a discount store." He grins and kisses me again as if he can't help himself.

"Come on, Callahan! Quit smooching on your girl and get over here!" one of his teammates yells, making us both laugh.

I watch him jog back to where they're all standing in the middle of the field, my gaze never leaving him. He's so gorgeous. He's endured so much, yet this is truly the happiest I've ever seen him.

I've gone with him to a few sessions with Dr. Harris and she pulled me aside at the last one, wanting to talk to me privately. She said she believes I heal him. That the reason he's been able to cope so well with the aftermath of Adele's suicide and the near mental breakdown of his father is the unconditional support I offer him so freely.

It's only right, considering what he does for me. My mom has mostly fallen off the face of the earth. I can deal for the most part, but her disappearance has been a struggle for Owen. He doesn't know how to handle it. Since Drew remembers what it's like to be an angry, screwed-up teenage boy, he spends a lot of time with my brother. To the point that one night, as we were drifting off to sleep, Drew confessed that if this football thing didn't work out for him, he was considering staying in school so he could become a counselor and help troubled teens.

I threw my arms around him and told him I thought that was a great idea.

He has the kindest, sweetest heart you could ever know. He's funny, he's smart, and he knows just what to say to make me smile. Though he does get grumpy when things don't go his way. Oh, and also when he's hungry. He's too much of a neat freak and I'm sort of a slob, so that's caused a few fights. I get hormonal and sort of bitchy during that time of the month, so he tends to steer clear. My job stresses me out, and I like to tell him he has no idea what I'm stressing over since he doesn't work a real job.

Oh, that really pisses him off. I only said it once. I learn from my mistakes.

Mostly.

We argue. But we always make up—and that means makeup sex, which is awesome. We finally did it doggy-style months ago and I'm a total fan. No nipple rings, though. He won't let me. Though we did get matching tattoos on the insides of our right wrists a few weeks ago.

Our initials entwined—D+F.

We laugh together a lot. We've also cried a few times. He's trying to heal his relationship with his dad. I'm trying to come to terms with the fact that my mom is never coming back.

Our relationship is not perfect. Drew Callahan isn't perfect either.

But I wouldn't have him any other way.

Drew

I'm nervous as fuck about tonight and wonder for about the eight millionth time if I'm doing the right thing. I try to ignore the doubt that lingers in my mind as I pace the living room, waiting for Fable to come out of the bathroom and finally announce she's ready to go.

Sometimes she takes too damn long getting herself all primped up, or whatever it is girls do. I've told her before that I love her just the way she is. Makeup, no makeup. Pretty dress, old raggedy shorts and T-shirt—whatever she's wearing, I'm all for it. She's gorgeous.

But then she'll blow my mind walking out of that bathroom after being in there for a solid hour and I forget all about my impatience. She's pretty good at that trick.

She's pretty good at a lot of tricks.

"You need to chill."

I turn to find Owen watching me, amusement lighting his green eyes. "What do you mean?" I ask.

"You're all anxious and crazy. Stop worrying. She's going to fucking love it." He slaps a hand over his mouth. "Don't tell her I said that."

"Don't worry about it." I shake my head. The kid has a foul mouth, but so do Fable and I. How can we give him grief when we can't lead by example?

"Seriously, dude. She's going to love your surprise. Love. It. You'll make her cry." Owen shakes his head. "You must be pretty far gone over my sister to want to do this already."

"I can't live without her." And that is no lie. "We belong together. Why not make it official?"

I sound confident, but I have a major case of nerves. I'm taking her out to dinner at The District because Colin—who I'm friends with now, unbelievable—offered up the private room for us to use. I jumped at it, because no way am I going to do this and make a spectacle of myself.

What if she says no?

She won't say no.

Her scent precedes her, light and floral, making me long for her. And then she appears, coming down the hall with a little smile on her face, wearing a pale pink sundress that makes her skin look even more golden. All I see is legs and arms, and the material of the dress is so thin . . .

I can practically see through it when the light hits her just right.

"Fable." I clear my throat. "You're not going out in that, are you?"

She twirls around, the flared skirt flying out, offering me a tantalizing glimpse of bare, slender thighs. "You don't like it?"

"I fucking love it." I glance around, thankful Owen's disappeared. I hear the click of his door closing. *Smart kid.* "I can see through it."

"You can?" She glances down with a frown. "But I don't want to change."

I slip my right hand into my pocket, fumbling around with the tiny box that's nestled within. I don't want her to change either. She looks amazing.

But I don't want anyone else seeing her in that dress.

"Where are we going?" she asks when I don't say anything.

"Uh, The District?"

Now she's frowning harder. *Uh-oh.* "You're kidding. I work there all the time. I want to get away from that place, not hang out there on my night off."

I'm messing this up. I can already feel it. Shuffling my feet, I study the carpet, my brain scrambling to come up with a different plan.

"Drew." I glance up to find her watching me, her gaze narrowed. "What's up with you? Are you okay?"

Fuck it. I'm doing this now before I totally lose my nerve and really screw up. I go to her without a word and take her hand, falling to my knee in front of her. "What are you doing?" she whispers, her eyes wide, her hand cold in my grip.

"Fable, I love you. I want you to be a permanent part of my life forever." I clear my throat, notice how her fingers are trembling. "We haven't been together very long, but when something feels so right and so good, you know you don't want to ever let it go."

"Ohmigod." Her voice is a breathy rasp as I reach inside my jeans pocket and pull out the little box that's been burning a hole in my mind ever since I bought the damn thing over a week ago. "What is that?"

"Let me show you." My fingers are shaky as I lift the lid, revealing the simple round solitaire engagement ring within. "I want you to marry me."

Her eyes widen as she studies the diamond, her mouth hanging open. She finally lifts her gaze to meet mine, tears sparkling in her eyes. "You're serious."

This girl is truly, truly going to drive me out of my mind. "I'm definitely serious. I love you."

"I love you, too. But marriage?" she squeaks as she reaches out and touches the diamond with the tip of her index finger.

"Marriage. I want to make this all about the forever." I drop her hand only for a moment, taking the ring out of the box so I can put it on her finger. She holds out her hand, her fingers quivering as I slip the ring on. It's a perfect fit.

The ring looks perfect on her finger. And this girl is perfect for me.

She brings her hand up to her face, admiring the ring close up. "Oh my God, Drew, it's so beautiful."

"*You're* beautiful," I say. "But I need an answer. Don't leave a man hanging."

"Yes." She grins as I stand and draw her into my arms. "Yes, yes, yes. I'll be your wife. Are you sure you're ready to take me on?"

Leaning in, I kiss her. "Hell yeah."

"I know I drive you crazy," she murmurs softly.

I press my forehead to hers and stare into her pretty green eyes, winding my arms around her slender waist. "You keep me sane," I whisper. "You make my life worth living. Because of you, I'm a better man. And with you by my side as my wife, we can take on the entire world, baby. Just you and me."

She sighs, pressing her lips to mine in a soft kiss. "You are so romantic. Is it wrong to admit I was sort of hoping for a poem?"

"Hell." I completely forgot. Pulling away from her, I dig in my other pocket, withdrawing a crumpled piece of paper. I labored over this one, hoping to get the words just right. I planned on giving it to her before I actually showed her the ring. "I wrote you one."

"You did not." She takes the paper from me and unfolds it.

"Did so," I say with a grin, waiting anxiously as she reads it.

Most of the time I'm thinking of you
All of the time I love you
Remembering the good times and the bad
So much has
Happened and
Maybe I'm moving too fast
All I know is I . . .
Love you. And want to
Live with you
Only you
Will you be my wife?

"Oh shit!" She's crying, tears flowing down her beautiful face, mascara streaking her cheeks with black. "My makeup's ruined, damn it."

I laugh. I can't help it. "Did you like it?"

"I love it." She bursts into full-on tears now and I pull her into my arms, hold her close. "I love you," she whispers against my neck.

"We're going to make this happen, Fable. You and me." I kiss her forehead. "Together."

"Together," she agrees.

Forever.

Acknowledgments

This is going to be quite the list, but I have to acknowledge everyone who made this possible. First and foremost to all the readers out there who have emailed me, messaged me on Facebook, Twitter, Goodreads, etc., letting me know your thoughts about my book. I seriously, *seriously* love you all. Your love for Drew + Fable knows no bounds and it blows my mind on a daily basis. Let's hear it for marshmallows.

To every reader who took a chance on *OWG*, who bought the book from a complete unknown author and liked it enough to want to read *SCB*. Writers are nothing without our readers, so thank you.

The support I received from *soooo* many readers and re-viewers on Goodreads was tremendous and meant so much to me. When you guys take the time to put together the reviews with the gifs and funny comments (and the marshmallow re-views! So amazing), I love it. So stinkin' much I can hardly stand it. Oh, and Amy Jennings—OMG you really jump-started the buzz for *OWG* there, so THANK YOU. And thank you for allowing me to join the Triple M'ers. To the Triple M ladies (and gent), I love all you dirty birdies! ;)

To the early reviewers who took me up on my offer of a free book: Christy at Tyhada Reads, Becky at Reality Bites

(Becky, you are one of my biggest advocates *tackle hugs*), Anna at Anna Reads Romance, Lyra at Defiantly Deviant, Momo at Books Over Boys, Carole at Life Over Fiction, Nereyda at Mostly YA Book Obsessed, Debbie at the Talk Supe blog, and Christine at Shh Moms Reading, thank you from the bottom of my heart. To Christine especially, for taking the time to organize my blog tour. You don't know how much that meant to me. I am floored by everyone's support.

A big shout-out to all the book bloggers who reviewed and/or had me on your site—thank you so much. I wish I could list everyone, but it would probably end up being half the length of the book—just know I appreciate you all. To Becca the Bibliophile for creating the *OWG* cover reveal book trailer—I feel like I didn't say enough how much I loved it. Because I really, really did.

To Sarah Hansen for creating the amazing covers for both *OWG* and *SCB*. And for tweaking them and making them even prettier for Bantam—I can't say enough about you and your design work.

To Lauren Blakely for being such a great friend—we have way too much in common and that's sorta scary. To Katy Evans for being the best critique partner a girl could ever, ever have. I'd be nothing without you. To Nyrae Dawn for the almost daily email exchanges—we've known each other a long time and I appreciate your support. To all the wonderfully talented self-published authors I've met—you guys rock and you put out such amazing books. I'm honored to be a part of such a wonderful and supportive community. To Kati R. for helping me so much with all sorts of stuff and for the squeeing feedback in regard to this book. I heart you and need you, so don't ever leave me.

A big thank-you to Kelly at Inkslinger PR—I know this is going to be a great matchup and I'm looking forward to working with you.

I might get weepy writing this, but I just . . . I can't get over the support I've received for this book. That Drew + Fable touched so many people, that I made you laugh and cry and shake your fist and want to throw your eReader/tablet/ phone when you read *OWG* . . . I can't explain how awesome this entire journey has been with you all. I hope like freaking crazy that you're satisfied with the story I told in *SCB*. That you believe Adele got what was coming to her (though I sorta felt sorry for her near the end—did anyone else? Or was that just me?). That you really believe Drew + Fable can be happy together.

Because I totally believe these two can be happy together. She gets him. And he gets her. Together they might be a bit of a fucked-up mess (who said that? I think it was Fable) but sometimes, in the mess, you can find something amazing. And I believe that's what happened for them.

It's so crazy, because they feel real to me. As though I have no control over them and they completely took over when I worked on their books. I was merely the instrument who told their story. And even though this book is finished and in my heart, their story is finished, Drew is still whispering in my head. And so is Fable. It's hard to let them go . . . and I don't know if I ever want to let them go.

So thank you. Thank you for reading my little story about a broken boy and a broken girl who only became whole when they found each other.

Get more of the characters you love!

Jen and Colin's story takes center
stage in Monica Murphy's latest
Three Broken Promises

Available soon from Bantam Books

Turn the page for a sneak peek!

PROLOGUE

I don't want to let her go.

She's going to leave me and I can't stand the thought. I've been coasting through life, confident with the fact that she's always there. Working with me, living with me, talking with me, laughing with me, and sometimes, in those rare moments we never discuss, late at night when we're all alone, crying with me.

Lying in my bed, wound around me like a vine wrapped around a trellis. Her hands in my hair and her breath on my neck, making me feel so alive I want to tell her how I feel. Tell her what she makes me feel.

But I've never had the courage to confess.

Now, she's leaving. Wants her freedom, she claims. As if I've been holding her down, holding her back. I'm offended when I know I shouldn't be. She's not ungrateful. She appreciates everything I've done for her. And I've done a lot—probably too much.

Guilt eats away at my insides. I started doing everything for her out of that sense of guilt. Truthfully, it's my fault she left her family. My fault she ended up all alone, on her own, struggling to make it until I swept back into her life like some sort of Prince Charming on my mighty steed, saving her from a world of shit.

As time went on, the guilt I felt slowly but surely morphed into something else.

Something real.

I have to be honest and tell her how I feel. I need her. Desperately. Losing her would be like losing a part of me. I can't risk it. I think . . . holy shit, I'm in love with her.

But I'm the last guy she should be with. I have this way of ruining those I'm closest to. No way could I do that to her.

No way can I let her leave me either.

CHAPTER 1

Jen

"So why a butterfly?"

I lean forward, my boobs smashed against the back of the chair. I've been sitting here for what feels like hours, a needle pressing relentlessly into the sensitive skin on the back of my neck. The needle's buzz fills my head, drowning out all the chaotic noise that usually occupies it.

I much prefer that incessant buzz. Easier to deal with compared to the endless stream of questions and worries that run through my brain.

"Yo, earth to Jen." Fable waves her hand in front of my face, then snaps her fingers twice. Brat! I wish I could smack her but I'm too busy gripping my knees, bare-knuckling them like a little wimp.

"What?" I grit out from between clenched teeth, wincing when the needle sketches over a particularly sensitive part.

Oh, who am I kidding? *All* the parts are sensitive. Time to face facts. I'm a complete weenie. I thought getting a tattoo would be a cinch. I've dealt with a lot of emotional pain in my life, but not too much physical. What's an hour or so sitting in a chair under a needle?

Apparently, it's pretty shitastic, considering how much it hurts, and how much I have to gird my loins to get through it all.

Gird my loins—something silly my mom used to say. Back when she was happy and carefree and our family was whole.

Now we're broken and distant. I don't talk to my father. Mom calls only when she's crying and drunk.

It sucks. That's why I had to get away from my family. I have other reasons for wanting to escape *this* place now.

"I want to know why you chose a butterfly for your tattoo. What's the meaning behind it?" Fable asks, sounding beyond irritated with me though she's smiling, so I know she's not. She came with me downtown to Tattoo Voodoo, the little shop she recommended for us to get our tattoos.

She got one too but she's already finished, considering it was only a line written in elegant, simple script. A surprise tattoo for her boyfriend, fiancé, or whatever you want to call him, though considering they can't keep their hands off each other for too long, I'm guessing he'll discover his "surprise" sooner rather than later. Drew Callahan is so madly in love with her, it's sort of disgusting.

But it's also cute. Super, super cute, especially since it's a line from one of the poems he wrote for her. How they make Fable swoon, and nothing makes that girl swoon. She's pretty hardcore. She's had to be, what with the things life has dealt her.

I could take a lesson or two from her. I'm too soft. I let people in.

And then they stomp all over me. Or worse, ignore me completely.

"Freedom," I finally tell her, exhaling loudly when the

buzzing stops and I feel the washcloth brush across my freshly tattooed skin. "I'm ready to break free of this stifling cocoon called my life and find my own way, instead of relying on someone else. A butterfly's a perfect representative of that, don't you think?"

I can practically taste it. Freedom. I've always relied too heavily on others. My friends. My family. My brother especially, not that I can anymore considering he's been gone for awhile now. I might have run away that one time and tried to make it on my own, but I failed.

Spectacularly.

Not this time around, though. I've thought things through. I've saved money. This time, I have a plan.

Sort of.

"You really believe leaving is the best thing for you?" Fable asks, her voice incredulous, her expression . . . sad. She's my closest friend, the first real friend I've made since I fled my old life. But even she doesn't know everything. She'd never look at me the same if she knew. "Do you want to leave because of what happened to you before?"

Nodding, I wince when the tattoo artist—Dave—wipes the washrag across my skin yet again. "Finished," he says matter-of-factly.

"Yeah, I can't deny that my past comes into play." I'd told Fable what happened for the most part when I worked at Gold Diggers, that sleazy strip club on the outskirts of town. My family doesn't know, and I swore Colin to secrecy. The public story is that I was a cocktail waitress. The private story is that I stripped.

The secret, no-one-else-can-know story is one I can hardly think about, let alone admit.

"We all have a past," Fable points out. She has a pretty bad one, not that anyone calls her on it. Drew won't allow it.

"I know. I just . . . I can't stay here forever. Even though you want me to," I murmur, sending a pleading look in Fable's direction. I don't want the lecture again, especially in front of our new friend Dave. I don't think I can stand it. I know she means well, but the words she says halfway convince me I need to stay every single time I hear them.

"I'm not the only one who wants you here," Fable points out, brows raised, a knowing look on her face.

Her statement doesn't need an answer. I know who she's referring to. He'd want me to stay indefinitely, but I haven't even told him I'm leaving yet. I'll let him know tonight.

Hopefully.

He provides the place I live, my job. He does it all with no strings attached, or so he claims. Really, I believe him. A deep, dark secret part of me wishes there *were* strings. Plenty of strings that tie me to him, bind us together until we're so connected that we'd become one long word. Not just Jen. Not just Colin.

JenandColin.

No way is that gonna happen.

So if I can't have him—and really, I shouldn't want him, or have allowed myself to become completely dependent on him for far too long—then I'm going to claim my freedom completely.

Stupid and risky and totally freakin' scary, but . . . I need to do it. Recent events have pushed me into doing it. My past has come calling in the form of a customer at The District just a few nights ago. He came into the bar and ordered a drink.

Thankfully, I was able to avoid him and he left without incident.

This could happen again, though. Having the man there was a reminder that I can never escape my past. I don't want Colin to know what I've done. He won't like me anymore. He'll look differently at me.

I don't think I could stand that.

Desperately needing to change the subject, I ask, "How does it look?"

Fable tilts her head, examining the tattoo on the back of my neck. "It's beautiful. But you'll never really see it."

"There's such a thing as mirrors, you know." I take the very one Dave is handing to me and I look into it, see my reflection bouncing off the mirror that lines the entire wall. My long hair is piled on top of my head in a sloppy bun, revealing my neck, the reddened skin, and the butterfly.

It's a delicate sketch in gentle shades of blue and black, looking as if it could somehow flutter its wings and fly right off my skin. If I like it this much now, imagine how awesome it'll look when the skin is healed!

"I love it," I breathe as I hand the mirror back to Dave, who sets it on the counter beside him.

"It's pretty," Fable agrees with a smile on her face. "I'm proud of you, Jen. I know you were scared to come here."

More like petrified, but now I'm proud, too. I did it. I got a tattoo and I didn't cry or run out of the shop before big, burly Dave got his needle on me, which I was afraid I might do. Kind of stupid, to be proud of something as simple as this. If my mom ever sees it, she'll flip out. My dad will think I'm a common gutter tramp—his words, not mine. Not that I plan on seeing them anytime soon. I don't want to go back, and they're not exactly welcoming me. I think they're almost glad to be rid of me. I was a burden.

I have a feeling Colin won't really like my tattoo either. But I didn't get it for anyone else. Just me.

Dave's now placing a bandage on my fresh tattoo, rattling off the care instructions in a monotone, as if he's said this before a million times, which he probably has. He hands me a sheet of paper with the instructions listed on it and I glance it over, not really seeing the words. My brain is too occupied with these people in my life who I wish I could please but rarely do.

They haunt me, hang out in my head like ghosts I can't get rid of. Even Colin makes an appearance there, which is dumb considering I live with the man.

Fable's cell rings, and from the smile that pops onto her face when she glances at her phone, I know it's Drew. I watch her step away to talk to him privately and jealousy clutches at my heart, making it hurt.

I want that, though I'd never admit it out loud, and certainly not to Fable. Unconditional love, a man who would do anything—and I mean anything—to ensure I'm happy. Safe. Secure. Loved.

If I'm being honest with myself, I'd like to have that with Colin.

He acts like he wants more, but then he always pulls back. I've shared more intimate moments with him than with anyone else in my entire life. I've slept in his bed. He's held me close. He's kissed me . . . but nothing beyond the sort of kiss a brother bestows on his sister's cheek or forehead.

Confirmation that's the only way he'll ever think of me. We grew up together, Colin and I. Well, Danny, Colin, and I. My brother and Colin were best friends. They were supposed to join the Marines together, but somehow Danny was the only one who ended up going into the service. Then he went to Iraq.

And never came back.

He's the ghost who hangs in my head the most, though he doesn't judge or make me feel bad. Not necessarily. It's more like my big brother reminds me that sometimes, the choices I make aren't always the best ones. If he knew everything, he never would have forgiven me.

Also, he makes me feel guilty for having certain . . . feelings for Colin. I always wonder if Danny would approve. Would he want me with Colin? Or would he have fought like hell to ensure Colin and I never happened?

It doesn't matter. Danny isn't around, and Colin and I are never going to happen. No matter how badly I want us to, he doesn't. Not really. He likes having me around. He likes counting on me being there as a sort of crutch for him when his emotions, his demons, get out of hand.

But he doesn't want me. Not in the way that matters most. Not in the way that I want him to.

So forget it. Forget us.

Tonight, I'm giving a month's notice to Colin. More than enough time for him to find a replacement waitress. That's also more than enough time for me to find a new apartment, a new job, and a new life in a new city. I know exactly where I'm going, so it's not like I'm flying by the seat of my pants and changing my life on a whim.

Well, sort of. I've always been an impulsive person. That's gotten me in trouble in the past. Hopefully it won't get me in trouble now.

Colin's going to be angry that I'm leaving, but maybe, just maybe, the tattoo will give me strength. Will remind me that what I'm doing is the right thing. I need to go. I need to really learn how to live my life on my own, not this childish running-away shit and living out of my car like I did last time. I'm older now. Smarter. Wiser.

I need to fly and be free.

Colin

The restaurant is hopping. It's late August and the students are back in earnest, which means The District is back in business. The bar is packed, my staff is hustling, and the kitchen is a steamy pit of never-ending appetizers, giant plates being taken out again and again, since it seems none of the customers want a full meal tonight.

They all want to get their drink on. Celebrating being back at school, or drowning their misery in alcohol because they're . . . back at school.

I don't care which it is. As long as they keep buying drinks and leaving hefty tips for the hardworking staff, I'm satisfied.

"Hey, you're the owner, right?"

Glancing up, I see a pretty girl standing in front of me, a hopeful smile on her face. She probably wants a job. I just hired a new hostess late last week, so at the moment I'm not looking, but I always give out applications. You never know when you're going to lose someone, and good help is hard to find. "I am," I answer, returning her smile, my gaze dropping to take her all in. Check her out.

She's attractive. Not makes-my-heart-feel-like-it's-seizing-in-my-chest gorgeous, but not put-a-paper-over-her-face-while-I-bang-her, either. I like the way she looks at me.

So I look at her back.

"I thought so." She takes a step closer, leaning her fore-arms against the hostess station counter, plumping up her breasts, which threaten to spill out of her skimpy top. She's stacked. I have a thing for big breasts but I keep my gaze fixed on her face for as long as I can, tomorrow's printed-out sched-ule clutched in my hand forgotten. It's already near eleven and the kitchen's just closed, which means I can get the hell out of here if I want to.

But I don't. Jen's scheduled till midnight, so I'll wait for her and give her a ride home. Like I always do. Anything to spend as much time with her as possible.

"Are you looking for a job? We don't have any positions available at the moment." Finally, I give in and let my gaze drop, blatantly studying her cleavage. It's been a while. Hell, I seriously can't remember the last time I got laid. And with where I work, with the endless stream of women that come in on a daily basis, I'm not being an asshole when I say I could get laid anytime I want.

Not being an arrogant prick, just stating fact.

She still hasn't answered me. "Let me grab you an applica-tion." Leaning down, I'm reaching for the stack of blank ap-plications on the shelf when the girl laughs and shakes her head.

"I'm not interested in a job. I'm interested in *you*," she says point-blank.

Blinking, I stand up straight, studying her. The smile curving her glossy peach-colored lips is coy, the look in her eyes hot. As in, she's definitely interested in what she sees.

Women rarely leave me at a loss for words, but lately I haven't been myself. Despite my hangups, despite my not wanting to disappoint the one woman who means the world to me, I like what I see standing in front of me, too.

I've fucked plenty of women, and this one looks ripe for the picking. She smells good, looks good, and the gleam in her eye tempts. Invites.

I'm no saint. Some might even call me a man whore, though that's more in my past. What can I say? I like women and they usually like me. I'm not stupid. This pretty face of mine has gotten me into trouble. Both the good and the bad kind.

Only one woman is off limits. I might be an asshole, but I at least have a small amount of scruples left within me. Besides, there has to be something untouchable and holy in my world, right? She's it. The sweet little girl I knew when we were kids. The pretty teenager who I tried my best not to look at for fear she'd know I was lusting after her.

The woman I deny myself from ever having. We're friends, and that's all it can be. I'm scared I'll ruin our relationship if I take it further. I need her friendship more than I want her body.

Well. Just barely.

Thinking of her makes my heart and libido sink, and my interest in this woman in front of me withers up and blows away like a dead, dried-up leaf.

That's all it takes. Think of Jen and I'm done for.

"Uh, I'm flattered, but . . ." I run a hand through my hair, wondering how I'm going to let her down easy. I've never had to do this before. When a woman's interested, I usually let it happen. I let her in. Not all the way, but just enough so we both get what we want.

I let no one in all the way. Jen's the only one who's ever gotten close. I still keep her at arm's length, though, for the most part. Except for those quiet, intimate moments in the dark, when the despair threatens to overwhelm me and she sneaks into my room to offer me comfort.

Those moments I keep to myself. We've never talked about them. They're like our dirty little secret.

"So I guess you have a girlfriend?" The woman laughs, cocking her head. She has dark blond hair, with perfect curls that tumble past her shoulders. Her makeup is subtle, her outfit tempting. A few months ago, she would have been my type. I would have had her naked and been buried deep inside her within an hour of this meeting, if not sooner.

But anonymous sex doesn't appeal to me anymore. And the woman I want, I can't really have. Correction: I don't let myself have her. So instead of having *her* naked and me buried deep inside her like I desperately want, I suffer. Like a true martyr.

Or try more like a true asshole.

Clearing my throat, I decide to be honest. "I—"

"He does." Jen appears beside me as if I conjured her up like a magical spell, made of smoke and mirrors and so much beauty it hurts to look at her. She curls a slender arm around mine, her fingers settling on my biceps, and my skin burns where she touches me. Nestling in close, that sexy lean body of hers is plastered to mine, making me sweat, making my skin tighten. She's wearing a mysterious smile and a defiant glare in her dark brown eyes that would deter even the most aggressive female on the planet.

The look clearly says, *Back the fuck off, he's mine.*

Hell, I wish.

"Sorry." The girl doesn't sound sorry at all as she pushes away from the counter and walks off, shaking her head. "Didn't mean to step on any toes."

"Keep walking. Nothing to see here," Jen calls after her as the girl disappears back into the bar. Then she releases her hold on me immediately, stepping away, and I feel the loss keenly. "God. Don't you ever get sick of that?"

"Sick of what? Women hitting on me?" I once lived for that shit every single night. Flirting, drinking, being surrounded by beautiful women—they all helped me forget what I'd done. How I disappointed an entire family. How I abandoned my best friend and he ended up dead. How I let this girl in front of me down most of all.

My fault. All of it.

"Yes." She sounds irritated, but she looks hot. The simple black dress she wears accentuates her curves, stops about mid-thigh, and showcases those endless legs of hers. Legs I'd like to have naked. I imagine gripping her slender thighs and wrapping them around my hips. "She's been circling you for the last twenty minutes like she's a shark and you're blood in the water."

I hadn't noticed. Am I a dick for liking that Jen had? This hint of a jealous streak is new. I wish I knew what spurred it on. "I would've taken care of her."

"By what? Inviting her back to the house?"

Glancing around, I'm thankful no one's left in the restaurant. The remaining customers have moved on into the bar. I don't need anyone witnessing this exchange, especially my employees. The rumor mill at The District is bad enough. Jen and I don't need to add fuel to the fire. They already talk about us. Wondering what the heck we're doing, if we're together, if we're not. The constant speculation is exhausting.

"I don't do that. Not when you're there," I finally say, my gaze meeting hers once more. "Since when do you care, anyway?"

Wrong thing to say. She looks ready to blow up—all over me. "So you would've brought her back to the house if I wasn't there? Is that what you're saying? God, you're such an ass," she mutters as she stalks off.

I follow her, my gaze zeroing in on the back of her head. Her long brown hair is down tonight, but when she tosses her head I see the edge of a white bandage peeking out between the thick, silky strands. "What happened to you?"

She glances over her shoulder with a withering stare. "What are you talking about?"

"The bandage." I grab hold of her arm and stop her in her tracks. She almost stumbles, what with the high heels she's wearing, and I grip her tighter to keep her upright. "Did you hurt yourself?"

She reaches for her neck with her free hand, rubbing the back of it self-consciously, a little frown wrinkling her brows. "I, uh . . . it's nothing."

Crossing my arms in front of my chest, I block her from

ditching me. I know that look. She's ready to run. Something she's real good at. "You're hiding something from me."

"I really don't want to do this here." She blows out a harsh breath, and I wonder what the hell she's talking about. "Can't we talk about this when we get home?"

"Talk about what?" I'm confused. Where is she going with this?

Jen yanks out of my hold and throws her arms up in the air, frustration written all over her beautiful face. "Fine. Let's do this. I need to give my notice, Colin. I'm quitting."

New York Times and *USA Today* bestselling author MONICA MURPHY is a native Californian who lives in the foothills below Yosemite. A wife and mother of three, she writes New Adult contemporary romance and is the author of *One Week Girlfriend* and *Second Chance Boyfriend*.

monicamurphyauthor.com
missmonicamurphy@gmail.com
www.facebook.com/MonicaMurphyAuthor
www.facebook.com/DrewAndFableOfficial
www.twitter.com/MsMonicaMurphy